LIMITS OF
THE LAND

By Curtis Harnack

LIMITS OF THE LAND

UNDER MY WINGS EVERYTHING PROSPERS

WE HAVE ALL GONE AWAY

PERSIAN LIONS, PERSIAN LAMBS

LOVE AND BE SILENT

THE WORK OF AN ANCIENT HAND

LIMITS OF
THE LAND

Curtis Harnack

DOUBLEDAY & COMPANY, INC.
GARDEN CITY, NEW YORK 1979

ISBN: 0-385-12502-x
Library of Congress Catalog Card Number 78–8191

CONTENTS

I

The Burden

Love and death are absolutes, this time of year, not merely tendencies. On March 14 the old hasn't quite ended nor has the new begun. Sows farrow and now and then eat a piglet who looks particularly delicious. The smarter ones know their mother is dangerous and pay attention to her moods. In the barnyard cattle mount each other, milch cows on top of milch cows, eyes rolled in mindless passion; and the bull prowls restively, the juice high in him.

The terrible force of all this creation began to weary me—perhaps I was getting too old for it. This year the groundhog had seen his shadow, and long ago I'd seen mine. My wife and child wished me many-happy-returns in the somewhat foolish way appropriate when you've reached forty-five. Nothing was to be made of the occasion because I didn't want it. The rebirth of the land each spring seemed to coincide with my own unfolding life.

With a flashlight I searched the basement north walls for the moisture level, to determine how fast the frost was going out and when I might begin spring plowing. The trees had lost their slim, nerve-end look, but leafing out was still a month away.

In the afternoon I was out along a fencerow hunting a break

in the windmill guideline, a rope-and-wire contraption stretching from a well in the hollow to within fifty rods of my barn. A car stopped on the road and the driver blared his horn at me. Salesmen did this sometimes without realizing how irritating it was. They hoped the farmer would walk across the field to them; but I never did.

The driver hurried out of the car, climbed the fence, and fell on his face. Then he picked himself up and ran toward me. It looked like my brother-in-law, E.J.—but I'd never seen him move so fast. Across that windy, open space of stubble field, I felt the man's wild urgency.

About ten yards from me, face flushed, eyes wild, he shouted: "Winnie's . . . Winnie's dead!" Then he turned back toward the road.

"Hey! Wait!" There was no stopping him. Cleared the fence, scrambled through the ditch and into his car.

Driving to town for help? Winnie must have gone crazy on him again, killed herself this time. She'd tried, often enough before. Every couple of years he hauled her off to Omaha for shock treatments. She'd come back docile, apologetic, wondering what'd happened.

When I reached my back porch, I was heaving for breath. As I pulled off my muddy boots, Maureen opened the kitchen door, and I had to say something. "Trouble with Winnie again . . . I don't know what. E.J. came to the field . . . told me." I couldn't risk the whole truth now because there wasn't time for hysterics. I reached for the car keys on the end table inside the door.

"Wait, August! I'm going with you."

"No, no, I don't—"

"I'm coming, I tell you!" A ratchet in her throat always meant she was in earnest. She loosened the apron knot, and the gingham fluttered to the porch floor like an undergarment.

Sheila stepped out and picked it up carefully. "Oh, Mom, you got it dirty."

"Out of my way, girl!" Quick in temper, magnificent in full flare that way. "I've got to help your Aunt Winnie."

"She sick again?"

"We won't be long," said Maureen.

"What's wrong with her?" Sheila was curiously fond of Winnie—had stayed a month with her and E.J. the previous summer.

"I don't know. Now get back inside or you'll catch cold!" She grabbed a black shawl from a porch hook. It flapped around her shoulders like bird wings. She pulled it tight under her elbows and wound it along her arms.

"Listen, Maureen, I'm going over there by myself—see what's wrong, first."

"But she's *my* sister!"

"Half sister," said Sheila, arms around her mother's waist. "You can't both leave me, anyhow. I'm sick." On her menstrual days she always stayed home.

"Such a baby! Thirteen years old . . ." Maureen said.

"Stay with her. I won't be long." I turned toward the Chevy at the yard gate. The dog became excited by the tone of our voices, barked at a flock of low-flying crows and almost ran into a tree. We looked at him racing around but none of us could even smile. "It's a bad day—back inside, both of you." I glanced at the bleary sun in the overcast sky. Every time Sheila had her period she got as queer as her Aunt Winnie. If only the girl didn't enjoy her oddness so much and the discomfort it caused us.

I barreled along the graded dirt road, fast as the queasy surface allowed. When the rear wheels began to spin, a lurch toward the ditch, I steered into the slide, exhilarated by my recklessness, and saved myself on the edge. *Winnie's dead.* I hated the thought of everything to come—because of this. And on my birthday!

We shouldn't have allowed Sheila to visit the Walczaks last July, but Maureen wouldn't recognize Winnie's mental troubles because it you didn't talk about something you wouldn't fix it as a fact or make it real. Sheila must have witnessed a few of Winnie's mad spells—shrieking gaiety followed by weeping jags. Or those deep depressions when E.J. had to keep scissors, knives, and pills locked away. Somehow, Sheila was fascinated by Winnie's "difference" rather than afraid of it. Our refusal to discuss Winnie's craziness gave Sheila a peculiar leverage on us. Although Winnie was only a half sister, madness in any family is catching, Maureen felt—and didn't want Sheila to get notions about herself or act anything out. "So impressionable, at that age." But both of us knew there was more to Sheila's attraction to Winnie than that. They recognized each other; there was something between them.

I drove along, flat dead acres on both sides of the road, some fields a rich chocolate brown, exposed soil from last fall's plowing, others a morass of used-up cornstalks, withered and broken like the dismembered legs of insects. The straggly grove of E.J.'s farm lay just ahead: random box elders, plum brush, sumac—trees and shrubs that hadn't been planted but simply allowed to grow wherever they'd sprung up, from seeds cast by the wind or carried in the stomachs of birds. The clapboard house, naked on its strip of sod, was enclosed by a chicken-wire fence strung between two rotting stumps, and a broken cement walk led to the rear porch and kitchen. I studied the place carefully as if I'd never seen it before—perhaps I really hadn't —knowing Winnie was dead in there, the way you try to get the facts right, at the very start.

On the first floor, two rooms in addition to the kitchen; a bedroom, and a parlor with a bay window and a never used door facing the road. Upstairs was a low-ceilinged chamber Winnie called "the guest room," though Sheila, so far as I knew, was the only guest they ever had. It was all fixed up, a peacock chenille bedspread; and two dolls won by E.J. at a carnival lounged against the pillows, eyes in a death stare of jollity, legs straight out as if they'd taken a terrible tumble. Sheila loved the isolation of the room, cozy under the eaves. Winnie had once hoped it would become the nursery, but luckily for everyone, no offspring developed. E.J. hinted to me there wasn't anything wrong with *his* equipment, and from his stud reputation, I'd no reason to suspect he was at fault. Ten years before, during the worst of the Depression, E. J. Walczak arrived from nobody knew where, looking for farm work, anything. He was the first Pole most people in the neighborhood

had ever met. No woman could resist his rugged blond good
looks, whether she was married or single, young or old, if he
really set out after her. "The Polack" showed an enormous capacity for liquor as well as snatch. A couple of towheaded kids
in the neighborhood who didn't match the rest of the family
were said to be his. Probably were.

Such talents usually attract friends, but oddly enough E.J.
wasn't very close to any man. Rather guarded, always choosing
his words before he said them. Didn't want anybody "to get
something on him," Maureen felt. I wondered if he could be
running from the law, but that was only a wild guess. Why'd he
come here, we all felt, when he could've gone anywhere?
Though E.J. and I were "family" of a shirttail sort, we never
achieved any kind of alliance. He kept his distance, and I made
no move to encourage friendship. The truth was, I never liked
him much.

Actually (though I didn't admit it at the time), E.J. and I
were alike in our peculiar isolation. My college education, such
as it was those years in Denver, and my many years of city life
away from the farm, put me a little at odds with the neighbors
who'd stayed put. They couldn't forget or forgive me for my
different history—or understand why, when I was out in the
great world making a living in a modern way, I chose to return
to Iowa and harness myself to the land, submit to the old burden of the seasons I'd been born to—that relentless cycle of
Nature which *they* couldn't get out of. Nor could I. When Father died I felt the old earth-pull to take up husbandry. This
farm of my grandfather's making seemed my destiny, and father's death was the sign. To the neighbors E.J. and I were
both outsiders because we'd lived away. We might look at them
and their doings with foreign eyes; make judgments about
them.

As I drove up, E.J. stood under the box elder that dominated
the yard, as if he were waiting there for me. "Where is she?" I
asked, stepping to the ground.

"August . . . we're in a jam here."

We? You mean *you*. "What happened, anyhow?"

"I . . . I don't really know." A blank, surprised stare. E.J. was a two-hundred-pounder with an expressionless Slav face and a certain careful gentleness about him.

"She in the house?

"On . . . the floor in the kitchen. That's where the fire started."

"Fire? I didn't hear a fire siren."

"I never phoned the fire department."

"Got it out by yourself?"

He nodded. "I was down in the barn milking, when I—"

At this hour—or when? I groped for my watch in the overalls bib but stopped when I saw E.J.'s panicky glance. He started talking quickly: how he'd smelled smoke, saw it seeping out of the house windows, black at the panes. The kitchen door was stuck tight from the heat and he had to smash a window to break in. The gap-toothed opening made the house look abandoned already. Inside, he found her under the kitchen table. "Gone—choked on the smoke."

I nodded as if I were the inspector and accompanied him to the back porch. I leaned hard to force the door but it gave at once, and I lurched into the oil-smelly room, catching my fall on the table edge. Right next to Winnie. A heap of charred rags, only her hair visible and most of that singed to the scalp. My heart pounded and my mouth went dry, but I somehow couldn't move from that kneeling position. I couldn't grasp the full impact of Winnie's death, even though I'd seen a lot of dead people in my time—a lot of death—what farmer hasn't? But Winnie's horribly blackened, old-wick look—and the agonized way in which she lay there—made her suffering still evident.

Something was demanded of me I couldn't give, and yet I couldn't turn away. Only E.J.'s rambling talk got me up off my knees. He realized a frame had to be put on all this in order to deal with it at all. "Found the kerosene can right there. I didn't touch it. She must've been lighting the stove with a soaked cob, or tipped over the can right into the flames. Then again maybe she thought the fire'd gone out and she poured straight in from the can. Fire flew right up—caught her hair and clothes. Guess that was it." He moved slowly around the slick-floored room. "Curtains gone, too. Everything got it, all in a flash."

I felt Winnie listening, or that he was talking for her benefit. That whole part of the kitchen where she lay seemed charged in a queer way. "How'd you snuff the fire out, then?"

"Extinguisher."

"Lucky you had one handy." A peculiar story. What would the sheriff make of it? "Phone work?"

"Haven't tried it—suppose so."

"We have to call *some*body. And pretty damn quick."

What had E.J. been doing with himself these many hours since the fire and her death? Kidding himself that he might be able to keep this mess from being known? Alone with death, as the two of them had been alone in life. Sometimes a farmer can't bear the thought of the coroner, undertaker, minister, and relatives trampling upon his solitude, and he buries the old lady himself under the apple tree rather than admit outsiders to the homestead. I've known several instances. When the body's discovered they wonder if it was murder. But it was only a matter of privacy. After all, why should death make things so different? It's mostly fake concern anyhow, and after the death certificate is signed and the undertaker presents his bill for several hundred dollars, and everybody's gone, you're left all by yourself again, the way things were when the old lady died. Only now it's official. And your privacy so trampled upon it'll take a long time to grow back your rightful sense of aloneness again.

"So . . . are you going to phone Doc Shepley, or you want me to?"

"The doctor? But she's . . ."

"He's county coroner, too." And an old family friend of Winnie and Maureen, through their father.

"Oh yeah, sure."

But would he? If he hadn't by now? "I'm going home to tell Maureen."

"But you'll come right back?"

"She'll be over, too." We stepped outside, into the eerie

stillness of the March day. Not a pig banged a feeder or a steer scratched himself on a loose barn door. The entire farm seemed to know about Winnie. Keeping quiet about it.

"I can guess what you're thinking," E.J. began.

"You should've phoned somebody before this." And why come to *me?* If I was his best friend it was news to me. He had no right to draw on family obligations—now when it came to a matter of death, since he'd done nothing before this.

"I didn't know . . . what to make of it."

"Oh . . . you *must've!*" I wouldn't let him get away with that —not with me. "All that kerosene sloshed around."

He opened his old suede jacket nervously, closed it, fumbled with the zipper. How hard it was for him to try to take me into his confidence and win me over. He'd not felt the need for a friend before, and I'd be damned if I'd be sucked into intimacy now. The suicide was aimed at *him,* of course. All Winnie's rage directed squarely at him; she hoped her final act would succeed in knocking him down. But nobody ever is, at least not for long. That's the advantage the living always have over the dead. E.J. was already recovering from his dazed shock and perhaps considering how pleasant it could be to live a new life somewhere without the trouble of Winnie.

I wasn't much better than him on this score. A little shaken by the heap-of-rags look of her there under the table, but I didn't feel anything else. Only love makes a person's grief real, and I'd never cared much about her one way or another. My emotions were all pretty crimped. I was about half dead, but only forty-five years old. I thought I'd felt and experienced all I was going to. But that day was a real birthday, a beginning.

E.J. was wary of me. "How's anybody going to figure out . . . what really happened? Could've been accidental—couldn't it? I just don't know . . . what the story's going to be."

"That why you've been fooling around here all day—without telling anybody? Let Shepley decide what happened. *He's* the coroner." I turned toward the car.

"Phone Maureen instead—don't go!" A desperate look.

"But *I've* got the car! She'll want to drive over right away— how'll she get here?" Anyhow, I'd certainly not tell her such news on a party-line telephone. I hated the idea of informing her, wondered what would be the best way. No matter how I told the tale, she'd flare up hysterically in her Irish way. Not that I minded all that much. I'd married her partly because of her emotional immediacy—she seemed so warm. Married to her, she'd keep me close to the pulsing springs—she'd keep me alive. But how quickly she had subsided into stolid parenthood, how rapidly religion took over and cooled her sensuousness. Maybe Winnie's mental troubles suggested to Maureen that the same fate could be hers someday. Anyhow, she'd just about succeeded in folding herself upon God's lap because she couldn't stand the full-blooded rush of herself. Things weren't better in our household as a result. I'd far rather have had the wild old Maureen instead of the would-be saint who'd taken her place, feet in bed as cold as a plaster statue's. Love and talk between us gone, all affection dissolved in prayer. It wasn't much of a life. No wonder another birthday got me so upset.

Driving out to the road, I felt opened by the level plains stretching away in all directions, the horizon a perfect circle. Here I was in the center, it seemed. Winnie now and then must have looked across the land and sensed this same enclosure. All bound in by the rectangular land tracts which had been sold to settlers by the railroad seventy-odd years before. Some people believed in the reality of possessing this piece of earth or that—until a day like today, when the old verities presented themselves.

Winnie was well out of it, released from the torture inside her head and life with a husband who no longer loved her (if he ever had) but certainly coveted the land she owned. Most likely E.J. married her only because of her property, using his charm and sexual experience to advance himself.

As I approached my own fields, I couldn't find pride or comfort in the thought of them. These acres had been staked out by Grandfather and were now solely mine, but someday . . . whose? The earth certainly didn't care, and I felt the chill of such elemental indifference. Isolated on vast farmland, you sometimes had to bear troubles no man or woman should ever have to face alone. The difficulty was, you didn't know it—

didn't realize what was the matter, thought it was *your* fault, somehow. When you make your living off life directly, as I did, you have a hard time seeing your own. You start to wonder what your limits might be, and when you'll be forced to know them.

I pondered the best way to break the news to Maureen. Uneasily, my knowledge gave me a momentary teasing power over her, but I hate the lip-lifting pleasure of I-know-something-you-don't. And yet, every little ripple has an enlivening effect in a marital relationship. Something new like this would change the whole, too set way we had of dealing with one another. To be thinking such thoughts when the fact of death should have been uppermost puzzled and saddened me even further. I'd accepted Winnie's death under the kitchen table as calmly as I might coming upon an old and not much valued milch cow, legs stretched stiff.

When I opened the kitchen door, Maureen was standing at the ironing board doing the sheets. "There was a flash fire—over there."

"A *what?*"

"Winnie's clothes caught. She suffocated in the smoke—before E.J. could get to her. He couldn't revive her. She's gone."

"Gone!" She staggered under the assault of my sentences, caught the rim of the padded board and slumped to the chair.

I'd been too brutally direct—she looked slugged. A fire? When? She hadn't heard the siren.

And so the dialogue I'd put off began after all, with all the repetitions necessary until the news could sink in. What did I think happened? I couldn't say. I looked out the window and noted that the wind had changed, the trees were thrashing, perhaps a storm approached. I didn't know what to think of my emptiness and lack of feeling.

"August?"

I watched the agitated trees and fast-moving white clouds behind them. It was hard to figure out what connection I had with those trees, clouds, and sky—and yet a farmer was supposed to know, all the time. That was his business.

"August—why do you turn away?"

Sheila crept into the kitchen, asked about Winnie, and Maureen, weeping, told her what I'd said. She accepted her aunt's death matter-of-factly, but I detected a little flush of excitement in her voice. Although she'd been fond of Winnie, she possessed a child's typical indifference to such matters; she knew, herself, that she'd never die.

Maureen collapsed the ironing board and asked me to drive her to the Walczak farm at once. "See what has to be done . . . what else can we do? Next to E.J., I'm next of kin. Might have to make funeral arrangements, even."

"I'll come, too," Sheila said.

"Absolutely not!" I replied. She'd like nothing better than to bend over the blackened body—get herself unsettled—fly right out of her wits. She kept trying to achieve these shocks. But I knew the jolt might throw her into a prolonged state of "nerves," such as happened the previous spring when she strayed too near the barns at butchering time and got scared by the white, eviscerated hogs hanging on meat hooks from the hayloader shaft. She'd insisted upon sleeping in our bed for a whole week after that. Right between us. Sheila was much too big a girl for such bed nonsense, and it worried me.

"I don't want to be left alone here. We should stick together, like the Allies against Hitler."

"Maureen, I tell you she shouldn't come!"

"It's not *right* to leave me behind—at a time like this!" Tears falling.

"Oh, child, child!" Maureen said, from the depths of her tiredness. She'd still not quite recovered from her hysterectomy of last fall.

"Stop bawling, Sheila—you hear?" I shook her arm, pulling her away from Maureen. She submitted so limply to my roughness I stopped at once, remember her menstrual flow. The passivity of her young body, half falling against my thigh, suddenly had a sexual overtone, as if she blamed *me* for her monthly wound. "Maureen, let's go."

"I won't be here when you two get back. I'll run away."

"Maureen, *say* something to her. How you've spoiled her!"

"I have?"

"All right, *we* have."

"What're you trying to do, drive me crazy? You come with the news Winnie's dead—died horribly—and you spill it out like a monster without a bit of pity. And now *I've* spoiled the girl. Who're *you* to deal out the gifts of the devil?"

"I'm sorry."

"I'll get my coat," said Sheila, knowing I could say nothing against her move now. A look of triumph. She enjoyed coming between us, just as she loved separating us in bed. Probably sensed we no longer had a sex life together and she preferred it that way. How she loved to apply the pressure! Knew just where we were vulnerable, where we'd give in.

"Uncle Eege needs us. Let's go."

"Smart aleck!" I drew back my hand threateningly.

"August, if you slap her, I swear I'll—oh, Lord God!" She sank upon a chair and threw her arms forward across the table as if a whiplash had struck her shoulder blades. Faint convulsive heaves of the body—while we watched. She was going through the motions of sobbing, not really doing it. Trying to win my sympathy, make me feel awful. She'd done it a hundred times before, and the posture had worn itself out.

I gazed at the quivering trees out there as if to join their mindless tremble of existence. When placed into a situation of this kind I often removed myself mentally from the unpleasantness at hand, searching the wind for another kind of reality. And though I never found it, by the time I returned to myself, things had changed.

"Mommy, please don't cry." A play-acting, sweet voice.

Maureen's face looked so ravaged for a woman only forty-six—and I felt responsible. She'd given me her best years out of her own free will, and I'd taken them. I and the farm had taken them. Her periods ended just as Sheila's began. I looked at my two women with a male bereftness, knowing they'd always manage to shut me out.

"What would I ever do without my little girl?"

Their locked fingers waved in the air like a single frond. I left the kitchen, slamming the door in comment—exactly the sort of brutal thrust they expected from me. They shouted they were coming.

I felt the balm of the March afternoon, trees alive in the breeze, fixed in their relationships—ash to oak and birch to maple, and each to earth and air. In the barns recurring generations of livestock were aswoon in the rhythms of nature, for my economic advancement. Where was the beat for my own life? The cats meowed at my feet, yearning for milk or at least a pat on the head—skimming, surface desires of no real consequence. The animal world thrived calmly and the vegetable growth was beginning to stir with spring—both realms unaware of the mayhem on the human level. And the earth itself made the most silent comment of all. So silent I couldn't hear it.

Maureen, wrapped in her fluttery, raven's wing shawl, emerged from the house and headed for the car, leaning into each step. Sheila came behind her in a too small blue coat, her womanly legs looking large in winter stockings. She'd be taller than Maureen in a couple of years.

We said nothing the whole ride. E.J. emerged from the machine shed as we drove up; the women climbed out. When Maureen asked what'd happened, he put his arm around Sheila and shook his head solemnly. They walked to the house to look over Winnie, E.J. speaking slowly—but I didn't follow them. Had he called the coroner yet?

Not even a dog on this farm to keep an eye on the regularity of things, sound the alarm if something was amiss. Chickens banished, too—Winnie hated the smell of them. Would E.J. stay on here, working this heavily mortgaged farm, try to make a go of it alone? Or pull out and begin life all over again somewhere else? Whatever equity he had on this place would make a stake for some new venture. Strange, how every pruning gives a spurt to an organism—it hurts but it's good for you.

I sat there in the car, heavy and dead—unable to move. Winnie had loathed her rough life in a "hired man's house" (as she termed it), on land inherited from her first husband, a banker in the county-seat town. This farm was one of the few things left after the crash wiped him out and the bank went into receivership. Only because he'd placed this property in her name did

she have it, afterwards. Quite a comedown for Winnie from the
fourteen-room house in town and a daily cleaning girl—but
someplace to live after her husband got himself drowned (acci-
dentally or on purpose, nobody knew for sure). How Winnie
was acquainted with E.J., none of us found out, but he stepped
in quickly to "take care of her," look after her interests. He
raised the money which he and Winnie badly needed by
mortgaging the land. Their marriage occurred so soon after her
widowhood began most people assumed they'd been having an
affair for some time—and speculated plenty on what'd driven
the husband over the side of the fishing boat in Mille Lac,
Minnesota.

The nearness of this farm to us was the important thing to
Winnie, for she and Maureen had no other relatives in the re-
gion, and in these hard times you had to fall back on blood
connections; all else failed. We did precious little for them, just
kept up cordial connections, a few phone calls, visits now and
then. E.J. was very standoffish, didn't seem to want us around
much. But having us close by bolstered Winnie in her solitary
life. They didn't entertain, never attended church, one scarcely
ever saw them in town, even on Saturday nights—and that was
because Winnie knew she was "queer," that people stared and
tried to find her queerness visible in her face or obvious in her
dress. So, she mostly stayed home, while E.J. whored around
the neighborhood just like always. Maybe he once found sexual
excitement in her frenzied mental condition; after all kinds of
women, this was a new wrinkle. Perhaps his lovemaking drove
her to the very brink of insanity, and that would surely please
his ego. Sometimes Winnie fell over the edge. Ecstatic screaming could easily change into shrewish yelling, and shock treatments became part of his armor to be used against her whenever he needed to reaffirm his control. He possessed her farm,
her body, her life, and he meant to keep it all. But she got away
from him in the end.

Maureen had always refused to listen to my theories about
what went on in privacy here. "Gossiping—bad as everyone
else!" Or, "Not in front of the girl, August." And yet she'd allowed Sheila to live in the bedroom right over E.J. and Win-

nie's. A bad idea, I'd thought from the beginning. Maureen believed if you felt something *should* be all right, you could make it that way by your attitude. One step away from religion —or the very move leading her to God. I never quite figured that out.

E.J. came back to the car to tell me that Maureen and Sheila were busy cleaning up a little in there. He still spoke in a dazed manner and wouldn't look at me. "Maureen's thinking about the wake already, what to do about the mess in the kitchen. People coming and all. It's got to be scrubbed. But I said, 'Don't worry about the rest of the house—it's clean as a whistle, the way she always kept it.'"

"Yeah." Phony chatter. Wanted me to fall into a country cadence with him.

"Always ready for unexpected company—she was."

He meant: She countered the smell of the barnyard and the mess of mud tracked into the house by becoming fanatic on the subject of cleanliness. Washed clothes every day, spent hours polishing and dusting, bathed each night—twice a day in summer—and insisted E.J. do the same. But she received no company and was afraid to speak to the Watkins salesman or the Rawleigh man, if one of them drove into the yard, fearing they'd talk to the neighbors, say wicked things about her.

"The whole house, just *so*. And now it turns out . . . ready for *this*."

"Where you going now?" I climbed out of the Chevy to follow him.

"Come on."

"Is Doc Shepley on the way—or what?"

"Should be here any minute." E.J. paused in front of the machine shed and threw back the roller door. Several sparrows roosting on the railing, protected from the chill wind, flew out, feathers floating down as if they'd been pinched. His machinist's bench was professional-looking, every tool neatly arrayed, screws in proper cubicles. The power lathe and drill had cost him a great deal. I'd heard the neighbors try to guess how much. They'd bring over a broken part for him to fix now and then, pay him a dollar or two for the trouble, knowing E.J.

didn't do favors out of friendship. He'd been working in a foundry at the time of his marriage to Winnie, and though he went into farming, kept a corner of his life furnished true to his interests, as if he needed this to remind himself who he was: not just "a dumb farmer."

"Intake section on my water tank is shot." He flicked on the dangling light bulb and inspected a short pipe held in the vise as if by its throat. "That's how come I was away from the house—all that time. Have to get water for the stock!"

Tell it to the jury, mister.

E.J. dusted his fingers across the pipe, blew the last of the filings away, then threw the switch and lowered the power drill. The bore cut cleanly, throwing small slivers into the air. I flinched and drew away.

A few minutes later Shepley drove up and quickly entered the house. I didn't notify E.J., bent over the lathe, figuring the doctor would like an impartial view of the situation first, before getting into alibis. The noise of the drill made talk impossible.

When Shepley reappeared I went up to the yard to speak with him. The white-haired doctor, a fierce hussar in his ratty beaver hat, heavy coat, asked, "Where's the husband? What's he doing?"

"Fixing something—there, in the machine shed."

"Maureen shouldn't have touched anything."

"I know."

"Till I got here. Now you tell Winnie's husband I want him!" Under tufted white brows, his eyes flashed angrily—like a trapped winter weasel's.

I had to touch E.J.'s shoulder to get his attention, and even then he seemed reluctant to lay down his goggles. "Shepley? Made good time considering the roads."

So cool!

When we approached, Shepley stared hard at him, taking measure. "A fine state of affairs . . . what the hell happened, anyhow?"

E.J. plodded through his tale once more: the kerosene can, the smoke at the windows, the suffocation.

"Dead since nine—ten—this morning. How come you didn't phone somebody before this?"

He mumbled his way out.

"Never saw so much kerosene in one kitchen in my life! To light a stove! Tell me another. You don't light a stove by dousing the walls and floors, dipping the curtains in kerosene. *Yes,* you heard me! Curtains soaked in kerosene! And my guess is, it took more'n five gallons to do it. I'll have to phone the sheriff —you know that!"

Maureen heard the last of Shepley's outburst. "No, no, now wait a minute. Let E.J. explain. It's like I said."

"Maureen—it was either accident, self-inflicted, or homicide. I have to sign her death certificate, and I want E.J. to tell me what I should put down."

Homicide! Hadn't thought of *that,* nor had Maureen, who'd been so intent upon having the death registered as accident, not suicide.

Shepley listened to E.J.'s careful account, frowning in disbelief. "No, no, it'll never do. Won't stand up—sorry. Winnie was physically strong, weak though she was in the head. Not sickly in the least. Yet you tell me she was asphyxiated— couldn't get out the kitchen door—or smash a window for air? If you can't breathe you get a shot of adrenaline, superhuman strength. Winnie could've lifted this house if she had to."

"If she *wanted* to . . ." Maureen added. "But she didn't. She's been in a bad way lately."

Nonsense! We hadn't seen her in three or four weeks. Not a phone call, no communication.

"Yeah," E.J. chimed in, "she was awfully depressed."

How quickly he seized upon Maureen's help. Something rather suspicious about his alacrity, I thought. "Depressed over ill health" was the phrase every newspaper used in reporting a suicide, or "depressed by financial worries." A polite, public way of explaining the outrage, the act of violence against all the living; and a convenient way to end an obituary, which relatives would clip for the family album or Bible.

Sheila slipped furtively from the kitchen, startling us. We'd forgotten her entirely. Suspected for a moment that the dead might be walking. "What's the girl been doing in there alone?" Shepley asked.

"Sheila, go sit in the car," said Maureen.

"Can I read *Batman?*"

"Just this once. Your father'll get it out for you."

We kept a copy locked in the glove compartment for times of emergency, to soothe her. Normally she was forbidden to read comic books because they excited her imagination too much. She had nightmares over "Alice the Goon" and "Mr. Coffeenerves." When I handed her a *Batman* she complained of having seen it twice already. "Well, read it a third time."

"Haven't you anything else in there?"

"Oh, shut up and crawl into the back seat—under the robe. You'll catch cold otherwise, the condition you're in."

She gave me a funny, grown-up look, almost a wink, alive with sexual knowledge. "You shouldn't have come along, Sheila, if you're too sick for school today."

"I'm not exactly sick."

"I know, I know."

"But I wanted to see Aunt Winnie . . . while I could. It wasn't as bad as I thought."

"All right, Sheila, that's enough!"

"When'll she get to heaven?"

"She's there by now."

"No, she's all covered up near the kitchen sink"—in her little-girl-innocent voice.

"But her soul's gone. You remember your Sunday-school lessons?" The monkey, she knew I didn't believe in religion, so she always asked *me* these questions, not Maureen, who could rattle off the church's answers.

"She'll rise again on Resurrection Day, but I won't want to see her then. She hasn't any hair left."

"God'll take care of that."

"How?"

"I don't know. I wonder, too. Now, here's your *Batman,*" and I slammed the door.

The two men had moved close to the porch, Doc Shepley still

angrily firing questions; Maureen had disappeared into the house. "You mean to say . . . you didn't even turn her over? Didn't try knocking the smoke out of her lungs? Didn't *touch* her?"

"She was gone—what was the use?"

"How'd you know?"

"I could tell." E.J. fingered the zipper of his jacket nervously, making dry runs up and down, looking like a somewhat stupid hired man. Shepley kept after him, and I watched E.J. squirm, but he stuck to his story.

"Coffee's ready," Maureen called. "Come in out of the cold."

The room still stank, but most of the oil slime was gone from the floor, and the chairs were clean enough to sit on. We avoided looking at the blanket-covered body along the wall near the sink. We took up our coffee cups seriously—for the moment this potation came ahead of everything. Shepley stirred in two teaspoonfuls of sugar and simultaneously began to crank up the conversation. "Now listen, E.J., this here wasn't an accident, it simply wasn't! If you won't tell exactly what really happened, then I'll have to—"

"Of course it was accidental!" Maureen said.

How she'd hate to read an account of Winnie's suicide in the newspapers! People would stare musingly at her with that glint of curious pleasure so horrible to see, once they got something on you. She'd sense their gossipy conversations hanging in the air like bags of wind or huge balloons, a thousand times bigger than the speech clouds in comic books. They'd pin a donkey's tail of insanity to the whole family—which could have a devastating effect upon Sheila. And what difference would it make to Shepley how the story was set down, what he put on the death certificate? Why tell the whole truth, Maureen would argue, when evasion caused nobody harm and might prevent a lot of pain?

She started talking like this but Shepley cut her off, as if she were a waitress he could easily squelch.

"Now, E.J., tell me, what *was* that conversation you and Winnie had . . . before you left the house this morning?"

E.J. studied a spot on the plaid oilcloth, set his cup down and lifted it to his lips again carefully.

"Come *on*, before the undertaker gets here. I suppose I'll have to perform an autopsy if you won't—"

"We—we quarreled. Pretty bad."

"I thought so! About what?"

"Well . . ." He stared soddenly at a plaid square.

Maureen could barely contain her suspense—fearful that his next words might undo her accident theory.

"Out with it! What'd you quarrel about?" When there was still no answer, Shepley quietly added, "Of course, you've your legal rights. Don't have to say *any*thing without asking counsel first. Nothing that might incriminate you. And I could start an official inquest."

E.J. came alive at last. "You can guess . . . what it was." An uncomfortable glance at Maureen, as if she knew, too.

"How she always threatened to. The times before. *You* were the one recommended treatments in Omaha, the other times."

"Go on."

"She's tried . . . before . . . you know that. Only this morning she swore she'd do it good and proper."

"Why?"

"That was the kind thing she's always saying. Threats, you know."

"What was the quarrel about?"

Silence. "Could we go outside, once?"

Shepley rose and accompanied E.J. to the porch. In silhouette they stood there talking, all the dirt coming out, a regular confession—like to a priest.

"So the men can't speak of such things in front of a lady!"

"Now keep out of it, Maureen."

"As if the whole countryside doesn't know what that nasty man's been up to!"

"You'll get your way with Shepley, don't worry. He'll hush it up. And if E.J. was fucking his neighbor's wife, *that'll* convince Doc . . . about what made Winnie do it."

"You talk that way here? Right in this very room?" She glanced at the body with a sickened expression. She'd always objected to four-letter words—it was mostly that—but I was a bit surprised she got to the nub of the matter so quickly, by herself. I wondered what Winnie had written to Maureen in those letters she used to mark *personal* and *private,* which I hadn't the interest to try to read anyhow.

"I want Winnie buried with decency . . . respect . . . you hear? Not under a cloud of scandal."

"Oh, what difference could it make to Winnie?" I turned to the body against the wall. It seemed longer than a corpse could be, as if it were growing and would soon fill the room.

Maureen squinted, looking through the window at the men talking there. "How long does it take to tell, anyhow?"

"Maybe he fucks a lot."

"August, do you have to—" She was as upset as if I'd reached down and opened my fly. It was a bit perverse of me to keep at it, but somehow I had to rub her nose in it, perhaps because she continued to turn a cold back to me when we lay in bed together.

"Well?" she asked Shepley, as he opened the door, alone. "Satisfied with his smutty secrets?"

"Now, Maureen, don't—"

"Can we have a decent, respectable burial? Or are you going to let some disgusting story spread across the countryside—to blacken Winnie's memory? So what if he's got a neighbor girl pregnant? He's done it before."

I hadn't expected her to be so blunt with him.

"You and Father were such . . . such close friends. For *his* sake, please!"

"Oh, Maureen, I—"

"What a thing . . . if you put this down as suicide, we can't have a church funeral for her."

"Maureen, I have to do my job. It *was* suicide—obviously!"

"What possible difference could it make, how you list it on the death certificate? Do you suppose it'd be the first time it's only half the story?"

"No, not the first time." He looked old and full of compromises. Not for him would it be unusual. He'd been coroner now for eight years. Nobody ran against him because the younger

doctors were overworked, didn't have time for it. Shepley had
only a meager practice left, ever since he aroused the anger of
farmers during the worst of the Depression by snapping up
their land cheap in bankruptcy sales. They swore they'd get
even someday. They'd use any other doctor. "Why're you buying land?" I asked him point-blank once. "You going to be a
farmer instead of a doctor?" He gave me a sideways look. "A
fella knows he's got something, with land. It's better'n gold." I
don't know why that matter-of-fact hardness in him surprised
me—just because he was so compassionate at your bedside,
would do anything to save your life. Since he professed to have
a loftier purpose in his life than the rest of us, I was saddened
to find him like anybody else—only worse. He took advantage
of farmers down on their luck. He couldn't resist the tempta-
tion. Lately he'd been drinking a lot and no longer performed
surgery at all. The heavy Chinese incense in his office bothered the few patients who showed up, for they missed the
sharp alcoholic odors they were used to encountering along
with their pains and worries.

"It'd be awful not to have a church funeral for Winnie," said
Maureen.

"Was she Catholic? I didn't know."

"Certainly not!"

"But then, I don't—"

"She didn't belong to any church, that's why. She was in
Unity for a while, then Universalism. She was religious but
hadn't settled down yet to one particular brand. So, I want her
buried from *our* church, and Reverend Kallsen will do it if he
thinks this is just a regular, accidental death . . . if that's what
the newspapers say. Otherwise—I know him very well. I've
heard him on the subject. That old Mr. Wiener who gassed
himself in the garage with the vacuum-cleaner hose—they tried
to have him buried from our church but since he wasn't a
member, his folks just had to have it in the funeral home instead. I couldn't stand it, if that happened to Winnie. I couldn't
bear to think . . . that she . . ." Tears began dropping, large
spots down the front of her housedress.

Then, footsteps on the porch. The undertaker and his son

entered, removed their hats, woodenly offered Maureen sympathy and shook her hand, then came to me.

"Are you going to—are you coming to town with us, Doc?" the older man asked.

"No, no, proceed in the usual way. I'm through with the investigation. Suffocation. I'll sign it."

They shifted the body onto a stretcher and carried it ceremoniously out of the house.

"Thank you," Maureen said after they'd left, touching Shepley's arm. "Thank you, and God bless you."

"Don't thank me . . . I've—I've done nothing out of the way."

Sheila pushed into the kitchen. "Can we go home now?" She closed the latch behind her and wriggled her nose. "It's over, isn't it? Phooey, what a stink in here!"

We looked at her but none of us could think of anything to say.

"You often told me, Mommy, never pour kerosene on a corncob fire. You should've told Aunt Winnie!" That awful little-girl voice, saying the lines expected. She knew more than she let on—she knew everything.

"Oh, she just forgot," Maureen said. "It could happen to anyone."

When I entered the kitchen after finishing chores, expecting to sit down to supper, I found Maureen in the half-dark, staring at the sunset over the top of the polka-dot café curtains. Dusk is the hour that corresponds to memory. I knew she really didn't see the woodshed and old hollyhock stalks out there, nor even the dark thicket of the grove, crosshatched against the glowing west. Everything was turned inside and she was mulling over those long-ago struggles with her half brothers and half sisters (favored children of her father's second wife), Winnie the only ally among them, and now *she* was gone.

Maureen didn't notice me, and in that dim light she looked as beautiful as she had fifteen years earlier, at the start of our courtship. When I returned to Kaleburg to work my inherited farm, after a decade in Denver, I'd found her locked into a du-

tiful-daughter situation, caring for her invalid father—and
that's how she happened to be still single at the age of thirty-
one. To me she poured out the story of her underprivilegement,
and I felt like the protector she'd needed all along. Perhaps I
loved her purity of spirit because there was nothing pure in my
life. I was a sour, lonely bachelor—making do in the usual
fashion. Occasional binges in the company of Orvall Beams,
the trucker, who knew the waitresses in the Stockyards Café.
Our foursome would end up at the Railroad Hotel, sometimes
in the same room, too drunk to know whose girl was whose—
and in the morning waking like a family on a camping trip. The
farm when I returned to it never seemed lonelier, each thunk of
the pig feeder like a nail driven into my life.

Maureen's love gave me back my self-respect. From the start
she was more infatuated with me than I with her, which was
just the way I wanted it. I'd been burned a few times. I wanted
to be in control of my emotional life, make the right moves to
protect myself, and so I pursued her ardently, made her my
wife, and hoped to settle in with children quickly. Otherwise, I
feared I might lose the track entirely, for the "regular way" of
life prevented a person from the possibility of those other ways.
No one talked much about them but a few I knew had lost
themselves on strange routes, and I could be one of them. So, I
chose to be normal—like anybody else—but I ended up not
being able to stand it. I'd stare into a sunset—just as Maureen
was doing—go right out to the edge of the grove and watch the
last light of day spill across the fields and rosy the barns and
gild the trees of my neighbors' farms. Those homesteads, sur-
rounded by sentinel groves, had a strange, medieval look in
such a light. I'd stand there without moving, as if in a trance.
But if you look too long at a sunset you're in danger of dropping into it. Something existed on the rim of ordinary life that
fascinated me, and yet I knew it must not be explored for fear
of paying more dearly than I cared to imagine. I didn't know
what that "something else" might be but felt intrigued by it.

Sheila came downstairs and into the dark kitchen. "What's
the matter, Mom? When're we going to eat?"

Maureen jumped, flicked on the light switch, and hurried to the cupboard without even asking me when I'd come in. "Go play with that jigsaw puzzle while I fix supper."

"I hate puzzles."

"Or, get your dollies out."

"They're too young for me."

"I don't care *what* you do, but clear out! I have to peel potatoes."

"You haven't—yet?" I asked.

"Now don't *you* start in on me."

"Aren't we going . . . somewhere tonight?" Sheila asked.

"No—why?" Maureen said.

"I thought we'd be over to Uncle Eege's and sit around with a lot of people, the way we did once—last year. Who *was* that who died? Us kids went upstairs and played with toys."

"None of that now. Plenty to do . . . just notifying the relatives. Your father's going to town right after supper to send telegrams."

Sheila asked the identity of these persons I'd be wiring, wondered how she was connected to them. A canny expression in her eyes as she listened, no "little girl" act now. She didn't want to miss out on anything having to do with the funeral. Perhaps it was a good sign. She'd behave maturely, not seek attention just because we were so preoccupied with other things. Winnie's two brothers ("My half uncles—they'd be?") had long since left Iowa, disappeared into the new world of California and Oregon. They mailed yearly Christmas cards with printed signatures, the lettering as it might someday look on their tombstones. Such a ghoulish attempt to fulfill family loyalty and yet remain impersonal never bothered Maureen or Winnie, for they were happy even to receive this bit of remembrance. Winnie's sister had not written at all since the death of the father: angry because she hadn't been granted as much as Maureen and Winnie in the will. She swore she'd never have anything to do with either of them again. "Typical family stuff," I said to Sheila. "Nothing out of the ordinary, believe me."

"August, you won't forget Uncle Jasper? But he's so old I can't imagine he'd want to make the trip. Still . . . he's Father's only brother. He ought to realize he belongs to us."

I laughed. "Why, you haven't seen Jasper in thirty years, have you?"

Sheila wanted information about *him,* but we knew little except that Jasper lived in North Dakota, kept taking up different occupations, married late and fathered one daughter. Nothing much else. Not everybody—Jasper included—felt the way Maureen did about the duties of relatives.

"And there's Elsie and Marie."

"I know. I was trying to forget 'em."

"They'd be awfully offended if they read about Winnie in the papers—and hadn't heard from you."

"But they're *my* cousins, not Winnie's." Family obligations overlay one another like a wild and unending game of patty-cake-patty-cake-baker's-man.

"Or, put it the other way. Elsie and Marie are the only family *you've* got. Besides us."

I realized she hoped to fill up that first pew in the church, the day of the funeral. We'd make a pitifully small bench of mourners, even with Elsie and Marie. For most funerals a family nearly filled the entire church.

"I suppose E.J. has folks *he* should wire," she said.

"His friends—if he's got any—will hear about it like anybody else."

She looked at me and smiled. Whatever contempt I could heap upon E.J. would gratify her. Sheila watched us, caught our fleeting closeness. "What about supper? When're we going to eat?"

"Forget the potatoes, Maureen. Scramble some eggs."

"Sheila, isn't it time for your radio program?"

"Oh! I forgot."

When she left the room an odd, new intimacy developed between us. For once Maureen had maneuvered Sheila out of our life, instead of always giving the girl first place. After today's dreadful business on the Walczak farm, Maureen and I were put in the same corner, closely allied, able to move in unison to

face the world. The emergency enlivened and refreshed her—
she looked years younger. One night soon we might even become lovers again, I thought, provided I hadn't forgotten entirely how.

"Don't just stand there, August. Take off your coat and sit
down. I won't be a minute with these eggs."

She hadn't called me by name quietly that way in so long!
Perhaps she sensed the happiness we could share if we were
just able to be close again—in bed, as well as here in the
kitchen. Alas, Maureen believed the Lord meant lovemaking
only for procreation, and these last few years when I groped for
her in the blackness of the bedroom and forced myself upon
her, she submitted like a slain animal. She preferred to think
her sexual life was over and damn near succeeded in ending
mine, for nature sees to it you get what you deserve, and I was
half dead already in that department, just by the celibacy imposed.

"I *can't* seem to get that oil smell off my hands," she said,
going to the sink. "Did Doc Shepley ever light into me for
cleaning before he got there!"

"You shouldn't have." I scarcely cared what she talked about
—what fueled our new intimacy.

"Sheila 'n' me got right down on our hands and knees to
scrub the floor."

"I know."

"Somebody *had* to mop. And I . . . I noticed an odd thing.
Thought sure Doc Shepley would spot it, too, but every time he
looked there he'd something else on his mind."

"What're you saying?"

She leaned close so that Sheila in the next room couldn't
hear. "Fresh marks on the floor." I felt her breath on my
cheek. "Scratches—or grooves—right where she was."

"Under the table?"

Maureen nodded, face flushed. "Like scraping"—her hand a
claw—"the floor gouged there. Could *she*'ve done it, you
think?"

"You mean Winnie might've been tied down—couldn't get
up?"

"She had a grip like a vise."

"But if she could dig into that floor with her fingernails—which doesn't seem possible—couldn't she've lifted the table—gotten out of the house?"

"Unless, like you say, he tied her there, or something. I wouldn't put it past him. She was in the way—he wanted to get rid of her. And Winnie sure had the goods on him!"

I felt myself falling away from her. "Shouldn't you be telling this to Doc Shepley?"

"But if they start an investigation, you *know* how it'll end. They'll never snare E.J. He's too smart. It'll be 'suicide' or 'self-inflicted'—however they call it—and I don't want all that in the papers."

"Surely Reverend Kallsen couldn't object to burying a person murdered by her husband."

"I never should've said anything to you."

"But if you're suspicious—"

"You know, nobody's ever going to find out what *really* happened. Time and again, that's the case. And I don't want you starting anything, August, you hear? I'd just like everything over and done with—decently. How you live with what you'll never know about for sure—*that's* what counts. We all have to, now and then. Keep on, never knowing the facts."

"Not even trying?" Every penny-for-your-thoughts turned out to be counterfeit.

Sheila came in and asked if she should set the table.

"I'm starting the omelette. We'll eat in a minute."

I sat there heavily while Sheila laid out forks, knives, plates. Was Maureen being cowardly—didn't want the challenge of where a proper inquiry might lead? Instead, I'd have expected her to be so angry and suspicious she'd want the law to hound E.J. until he paid in full for his misdeeds. Or did high regard in the community count so heavily she'd trade her soul in exchange for a public good name? Perhaps the notion of murder happening just down the road to one's half sister was too awful to contemplate. I really couldn't imagine E.J. deliberately tying Winnie to the table legs after having given her some knockout medicine, then sloshing kerosene around the kitchen and throwing a match on it. Nobody in his right mind solved his marital problems that way. It only made sense to believe she'd killed herself to cause him a hell of a lot of trouble—to get even.

Maureen served and Sheila said grace, our heads bowed. We looked up and fell to, all of us betraying a fresh appetite for food, life. There'd been a lot of dull days recently but this hadn't been one of them.

The evening *Flyer* from Chicago had already come and gone by the time I reached the depot to send telegrams. Luckily, the station agent was still sorting bills of lading in his mesh cubicle. I penciled the messages in strong block letters, as if these very pieces of yellow paper would be rolled up and shot along the telegraph wires.

"How'd it happen, anyhow?" the agent asked. "A thing like that!"

I told about the fire in E.J.'s very words, and the agent clucked sympathetically as he tapped the machine. He knew I was giving a "public" story already, that I'd never tell my secret views. The nervous electronic sounds punctuated my spiel, giving it a configuration, the way a piece of music looks on the scroll of a player piano.

"Ah, it's terrible, terrible. Poor woman."

"Yeah . . . what can you do?"

Something. Not for her perhaps, but we could be doing *some*thing. The agent began shutting off lights, locking up. I called good night and stepped outside, pausing with a foot on the running board of my car. From the depot one had a fresh perspective of Kaleburg, for the train station was already half on the way to elsewhere, part of the outer world. Overhead the Milky Way seemed to spatter across the entire sky, brighter than usual, the way the heavens often were in spring. Beyond the darkness where I stood, the streetlamps of Main Street illuminated a nearly empty town, false-front stores reflecting light on painted wooden surfaces, the rear sections dark and sham-

bly as if each edifice were putting only its best face forward.
The Catholic church towered over the town, a moonlike clock
in the steeple.

I'd come back here willingly, joining my past to my future as
if it would make me a whole man, my life all of a piece. Uni-
versity of Denver student days and my job in the livestock
commission company, in charge of accounts, all seemed remote, hardly real, for I never saw any friends from that world
anymore. In 1917 I'd enlisted in the Army so that I could experience a fresh sense of destiny. Not many farm kids did that,
unless they also wanted to escape the family occupation. And
then after the Armistice, I took up the government's offer to
provide the doughboys with cheap irrigated Colorado land if
they wished it—only to reject the proposition when I saw the
desert out there. Not my notion of land! So it was the city of
Denver instead. Away from Kaleburg those ten years, I could
always view this town as if from the outside—and that perspective helped.

Maureen possessed no such double vision. She was caught
completely in the atmosphere of this place. When I married
her, I hoped to lift her into my own more enlightened (so I
thought) wider view of life. I figured she'd drop her stern
religious convictions and loosen up a bit sexually, but of course
nothing of the sort happened. She'd had a difficult life and my
sentimental regard for her wouldn't soften it. As a child of
seven she'd seen her suffering mother writhe soundlessly on the
sickbed, clutching her stomach, tears on her face. The doctor
said stones were inside her, and the bottles of colored medicine
were supposed to melt them, unlikely as that seemed, for stones
persisted like the earth. And so Maureen wasn't surprised when
death finally dissolved her mother, not the stones. The minister
saw his chance to claim a young soul and told Maureen how
blissful it was that her mother enjoyed heaven now, whereas
the rest of us had so many miserable years to wait for the
blessed reward. And then he smiled. In her grief she wanted to
scream or leap out the window—anything to get away—but the
preacher ordered her to pray to God, and she did. An inky,
narcotic calm settled upon her—but no hope. God the Father

Who Taketh Away. She knuckled under to Him, broken in an instant, the old Adam crushed. And she'd walked a narrow, nervous way since then, with the Lord at bay, just out there in the dark, up among the stars, ready to smite her down if He felt like it. A stepmother came next, new babies, and a busy father who had little of the old special time for her—until he became ill and old—then he fell upon her neck, asked her to hold up his life.

The hour bonged in the Catholic church tower: nine o'clock and the night was God's. I didn't feel like going home just yet. The events of today made me restless, on the prowl in some undefined way—perhaps a premonition of the radical change about to take place in my life. Or, my restive condition actually precipitated the change. One never knows. And what you can't know—for sure—how you live with *that* determines what becomes of you.

Instead of phoning cousins Elsie and Marie on the party-line farm phone, I decided to use the telephone office, where I'd get a private wire. The small brick building just off Main Street had so many telephone lines threading its roof they seemed to hold up the place. The night operator took down the number and began to put in the call. He was a timid, soft-spoken bachelor who lived with his mother and did needlework for a hobby. Encountered in daylight, he seemed terrified and on the run, but over the phone he sounded crisp and businesslike—people became disembodied voices and he could deal with them fearlessly.

Elsie and Marie took turns speaking to me; all the repetitions consumed ten minutes on the staticy connection. Both of them wanted to drive up from the city and help out in any way they could. They were determined to have this funeral count for a little diversion—I knew they would—and in order to stave them off I finally had to hang up. Just how matters stood between us I wasn't sure. No doubt they'd be on the phone to Maureen in five minutes. They were full of an awesome sympathy for her, and I knew they'd end up making a nuisance of themselves somehow.

My mouth was nervous-dry and I felt like a beer. I chose the

saloon next door to the Kaleburg Hotel, rather than Meecher's
Tap, because I'd be less likely to run into acquaintances, who,
like the station agent, would shove me into the spotlight with
my heavy news about Winnie. The bar was almost empty and I
nodded greetings to the proprietor, Buzzy Burns, who never
talked much, was known to be discreet—had to be, with the
kind of trade he allowed upstairs, especially on dance nights in
the Cornflower Ballroom. Girls would drive up stag from the
city, just to meet somebody—like me—and spend an hour in
one of those upstairs rooms. It sure beat the back seat of a car
or a stand-up job in the alley behind the ballroom.

Buzzy dried beer glasses slowly, careful not to look directly
at me—but ready to speak if I made the slightest move of
friendliness. I sipped my schooner and stared absently at the
Blatz cardboard display: two sweethearts trying to drink out of
the same stein. When I set the glass down Buzzy finally looked
at me. "You—you wanted to see E.J.?"

"No—no, why?" The town's sensitivity to our family trouble
was unnerving!

"He's upstairs."

"He *is?*"

"Checked in 'bout an hour ago."

What the hell did it mean? Was he planning to meet his girl
friend here, talk over what'd happened?

"Had his supper across the street."

"The place—at home—is quite a mess, still." Or maybe he
hated the thought of spending a night alone out there. Sheila'd
been right after all—to think of a wake. But Maureen loathed
him so, she hadn't thought of asking him to stay with us. For
once the conventions had been put aside because of her personal feelings. The town gossips would note this—unless, with
Buzzy Burns the only witness, it would go no further.

A bus arrived and Buzzy strolled out to the hotel desk to
take care of matters, leaving me alone in the bar. I should have
paid up and left, but my curiosity over E.J. wouldn't let me.
When Buzzy returned I asked, "E.J.'s alone up there?"

"Yeah." A swallowed look. He knew what I'd been thinking.

"What room?"

"Nine. End of the hall."

"I might just go up, see how he is."

Buzzy said nothing, and for a full five minutes I didn't stir. Then I plunked down my fifteen cents, called good night, and walked up the stairs to number nine. "E.J.?" I knocked.

He opened the door a crack, eyes dark, suspicious. "Oh—*you*. Come in." Still fully dressed in pants and blue chambray work shirt, he'd been propped against the pillows under the bed light, shoes off, reading *Detective* magazine.

"You all right?"

"Ain't any bugs in the mattress, if that's what you mean."

"Off night—it'll be quiet here, I guess."

He returned to bed and looked up at me, puzzled.

"I—I was wondering—about your chores tomorrow morning. Like me to help?"

"If you want to."

No bereaved family in this community ever had to go through the hard farm routines after a death, taking the blank stares of cows and pigs—livestock glances which suggested nothing at all had happened which made any difference to the universe.

"I was sending telegrams . . . and heard you were up here."

"Uh-huh." He looked at me shrewdly, seemed to be sizing me up.

By seeking him out, I'd put myself at some kind of disadvantage. Explaining myself to him—when it should be E.J. doing the talking. This was a mistake on my part, a kind of weakness. Until now I'd maintained a pose of indifference, hadn't allowed E.J. to get cozy with me; but now I was leaving myself wide open, asking to be used. E.J. was a man who'd figure out the best way. "So . . . I better get on home."

"Sure . . . good night."

Downstairs I drank another beer. Buzzy plugged in the juke-box to make a little noise, but when the song ended it was quieter than ever. I went home.

I awoke next morning when Sheila pulled the blankets off me, shouting, "Lazybones! Lazybones!"

I fought for a piece of sheet to cover my aroused state. But she noticed me there, and a secretive look erased the teasing, little-girl expression.

"Okay, okay, I'm awake," I said quickly. "You must be feeling better this morning." I regretted the remark at once. No need to emphasize the importance of her menses. Believing I'd shriveled more quickly than drunken Lot discovered by his daughters, I leapt out of bed and strode in my pajamas across the room, right in front of her, so that if she thought she'd seen something, she'd figure she was mistaken. Alas, I wasn't as far gone as I imagined, and she looked at me silently in a queer way, then scurried from the room.

What a way to begin a day! I hurriedly pulled on overalls and walked out to the kitchen, where the breakfast dishes looked settled, as if they'd been on the table a long time. A fat cellophane bag of Quaker Puffed Wheat lay like a bolster across one end. "Why didn't you wake me?" I asked Maureen, who stood, back to me, at the stove.

"It's not so late."

Early morning was a special time of privacy for her, and so she encouraged the rest of the family to linger in bed. If I stepped into the kitchen too soon after her, I always felt I was smashing something.

"By the time I finish *my* chores, it'll be too late to help E.J. with his."

"Oh, were you going to? Careful, the coffee's hot."

"That's what I told him. Neighbors usually do."

"Why were you so long last night?"

"Got to talking."

"You smelled of beer."

"Didn't think you heard me when I came in. You never said a word."

"*I* heard him—thought it was Uncle Eege, coming to sleep at *our* house."

"Oh, I never even thought to ask him!"

Sheila had an uncanny way of picking one's brains, seemed to know everything going on before it was spoken of. I didn't reveal I'd seen E.J. at the hotel last night. Why the secrecy, I couldn't say. Maureen ladled pancake batter onto the skillet; tips of flame under the stove lids flickered. A corncob fire—fast and hot. Nobody should pour kerosene on a corncob fire. Maureen always started the range in the morning by using one kerosene-soaked cob—no more.

"You got the telegrams off, August?"

"And phoned the girls. No doubt you'll be hearing from 'em."

"Did some phoning myself. Getting organized. I'm having everybody deliver the food they're bringing for the funeral to the church basement—not try to drive to E.J.'s or come here with it. The roads like they are."

"All this eating before and after a funeral! Who's hungry at a time like this?"

"Everybody—usually."

The original idea must have been to fortify mourners who'd come by carriage from a great distance, but now with restaurants everywhere, the custom seemed archaic.

"Chance for visiting," she added, "you know."

I did indeed. A clan could become reacquainted, catch up on the news, observe how the children had grown. All country people craved the chance to be sociable and made the most of a wedding or a death—they were geared to the primal turnings.

"I'm not going to school today."

"Why not?"

"Because . . . what happened to Aunt Winnie."

"*Tomorrow's* the funeral. You'll stay home then."

"I won't be missing anything—at school."

True, she was even ahead of the teacher in her grasp of mathematics, but we didn't tell Sheila that. In a one-room schoolhouse a teacher has so many subjects to master, there's never time to do any of them justice. "You've plenty to learn yet, Snicklefritz." We always stood up for the teacher.

"It's not *right* I should go today."

"What'd you do if you stayed home?"

"August, leave her alone."

"No, Maureen, I want to know. How'd you help out here at home?"

"Other kids'll think it funny if I show up. And—and they'll ask too many questions. About it." She gave me a rifle-shot look that nearly felled me. She must have heard us talking about Winnie tied under the table.

"Sheila can stay home these two days. Let's not fight about it."

"I'm not fighting, Maureen, I just want to know what Picklepuss here is planning."

"Don't call me that!"

"You should see yourself in the mirror."

"You can hardly expect the girl to smile, picking on her that way."

"I'll go fill the cob basket. That's something I can do."

In grisly memory of the fire, no doubt. I watched her head for the back porch.

"Not now, Sheila, sit down and eat these pancakes I've made."

"And then I'll do the upstairs, dust the hall. *That* should be enough."

"Plenty, plenty."

"You two've got it all figured out, I see."

"Why shouldn't we?" Sheila smiled in triumph. "We've been up for hours!"

I pushed back from the table.

"Finished already? You only had one plateful. What'll I do with all this batter?"

"Feed the cats." I walked to the porch window, where Snowball, a scrawny white cat with scabby ears and very pink scalp, sat on the ledge. Every time Snowball noticed someone watching her, she let out a yell, mouth agape. I tapped the pane directly in front of her nose, and she reared back.

"Haven't you anything better to do than tease the cats?" asked Maureen.

"I've *other* things, but maybe nothing better." I pulled on my blue denim jacket from a hook and my red plaid visored cap. Upon opening the door, I was greeted by a meowing chorus. The cats followed me all the way to the cow barn, crying, in spite of the encouraging sight of me going about my morning chores at last.

By the time I reached E.J.'s yard it was after nine-thirty. My apology for being late because I'd overslept seemed a poor way to begin our meeting, but I could think of nothing else. E.J., at his workbench in the machine shed, merely shrugged. The chores were finished an hour ago.

"Not much to 'em, only feed a few hogs . . . and the milking. I sold the chickens last fall, they bothered her."

"I know."

"Kept her up nights crowing. Crowing at all hours. Didn't know what the hell was the matter—those were new hybrid chickens. Supposed to be resistant to coccidiosis and cannibalism, bred to be healthy. But can science breed out sickness altogether? I doubt it."

"They get control over one thing, only to have another pop up." I hated the helpless way I sank amiably into this conversation, like two farmers talking over a back fence.

"They told me down at the Extension Office I should leave the hen-house lights burning all night. Keep the hens laying round the clock—they're worn out in two years. Then you sell 'em for a dime apiece. So . . . it was the lights on all the time, made 'em restless. When I told the county agent about the crowing—how it bothered us nights—he laughed and asked what the hell did I have roosters for? Why'd I want fertile eggs, since they don't keep as good as sterile ones? So there you have it, August. A cock ain't needed no more. How about that?" He laughed and rolled the door shut.

Certainly *his* cock had gotten him into a hell of a lot of trouble. How could he laugh like this—crack jokes—and expect me to join in? But I did.

"What're you going to do now?" I asked quickly, meaning what immediate task, this morning. What needed to be done?

"I'm clearing out."

"Huh?"

"Leaving. Soon's everything blows over."

"I see."

"I've had enough of farming." He looked at me defiantly, certain he could get away—no questions asked. We'd put him in the clear yesterday, and here I was, hanging around, ready to help even further if need be.

"Where'll you go?"

"California."

"Been there—ever?" I'd tuck away anything he might say until such time as this information might be important, when everything that happened here yesterday would be properly gone into.

"No, but I'm thinking of L.A. or maybe Long Beach. Lots of factory jobs out there now, with the war and all. Defense industries. And those wages!"

"Should think you'd want to check it out first."

"Hell, what's keeping me here?" His pale green eyes glanced at me steadily, then at the house.

"But—this farm."

"Just what I wanted to ask you about. I been thinking. Wouldn't *you* like to buy me out?"

"Buy you out! Whatever gave you that idea?"

"We'll work out a good deal."

"Oh, don't count on me." I couldn't think what cat-and-mouse game he was having with me.

"I mean it. The bank will let you take over the mortgage at the same interest rate. I know they will. They don't want this farm on their hands—they've still got so many! So, all you've got to do is pay me what equity I have in it. And that's not much."

"I'll have to . . . think about it." The idea glowed attractively. But he was moving too fast for me. How would this compromise me or make it possible for him to escape safely?

"Hard to find good land like this. I know a dozen farmers who'd jump at the chance."

"The bank will surely have something to say about that mortgage—it's not just up to you."

"Listen, I'll work it out with Wolbers, don't worry. You've always said how you need more land to farm, all that machinery you've got."

"I have?"

"This farm's so near—it's ideal."

Pigs banged the feeder lids and I turned toward the barn. "Don't see how I could keep livestock here, with the water system not reliable."

"Well, don't, then. I'm having Orvall Beams ship out my hogs tomorrow night. I didn't imagine you'd be interested in anything but the land. Never *did* have a proper feeder setup here. So . . . what do you say?"

"How much equity you got in this place?"

"I'm asking fifteen thousand."

"I don't have that kind of money, and I won't mortgage my farm to get it."

"Oh, you've got it all right. Don't kid me, August."

I probably did. Here and there, with life insurance policies and savings accounts, Maureen's, too.

"So, shall we drive to town, see Wolbers at the bank?"

"Can't I have a minute—to catch my thoughts?"

"I haven't got that much time."

I knew my expression betrayed mounting dismay.

"Well, how can I live here after what's happened? And I don't go for the Kaleburg Hotel much. Never did."

"It'll take a while, to wind up your affairs."

"Not so long. I told the secondhand dealer to come by and cart away all the stuff in the house. I won't have trouble getting rid of my machinery—the lathe and tools. If I don't get every penny coming to me, I don't mind."

Not if you get away with what you've done.

"I . . . I just don't know, E.J."

"Won't have trouble finding a taker. Thought I'd give you first crack at it."

"I'm tempted all right, but I'm—I'm not sure it's the thing I should do."

"Come to town, have a talk with Wolbers. He might even extend the mortgage if you need more cash. Drop a hint you'll try that new seed corn of his. Anybody doing business with the bank becomes a customer of Wolbers' corn."

"I might've guessed."

"Wolbers ain't so bad, once you get used to the windy side."

I couldn't stop myself from leaping ahead as if the deal had already gone through. The new four-bottom plow and the International Harvester picker I'd bought at a sale last fall would be fully utilized, and my tractor was only two years old. "You've got about a hundred fifty workable acres?"

"More like one-forty, because of that slough. Two acres here, with the buildings. If you add it to your one-sixty, August, you're really getting up there. You'll want to pick up a lot shipment of Texas feeders, fatten them on your own corn—make your money there. Without land a farmer's got too small a base. You need this farm—you know you do."

How could E.J. talk this way, so soon after his wife's death? I studied the thick face for some sign of tension but saw nothing but his usual placid self. And so, it was easy to dispel all suspicions of foul play—as if I were a boy playing sleuth who pulls off his disguise the minute he hears the dinner bell ring. "Let me have a look around, once, will you? I never really noticed your layout. Anyhow, I'm not about to talk to Wolbers yet."

E.J. pointed out where he had trouble in spring with gummy spots, demonstrated the peculiarities of the windmill gears, and suggested how I might fix the pump if it failed to function. I was shown what fences needed attention and where the insulation was dangerously worn on the electric wiring. He knew the longer the idea of my farming this place was discussed as if it were a reality, the easier it'd be for me to accept the scheme.

And thereby end all hope of bringing about an inquiry into how Winnie died. Maureen was right: you have to live with what you can't know about for sure. There are many ways to do this. I was now sliding away from my responsibility in this mystery of Winnie's death. I wasn't likely to be the good citizen I should be. I'd never live up to the best intentions that first flashed within me. And I'd probably soon be justifying this course as if it were the only sensible way.

When we parted at close to noon, E.J. said, "Talk to Maureen about it—she's levelheaded."

He meant: she's already capitulated and she'll bring you down, too. The devil had led me to the mountaintop and shown me his kingdom, promising me all of it. Of course I'd accept the offer—who wouldn't? "Yeah . . . Maureen's got good judgment."

The dog announced my arrival home and Maureen ran out to meet me, coat flung around her shoulders. "Where've you *been* all morning?"

"You know."

"I rang and rang over there. Is the phone out of order?"

"We weren't anywhere near the house."

"Uncle Jasper's coming—he called from North Dakota. That means we have to delay the funeral one day, to Thursday. He can't make connections to get here sooner. Course, I'll have to check with E.J. to see if it's okay."

"He won't like it. He wants to clear out fast."

"He's leaving? Just like that?" Her voice deepened. "Where's he going?"

"California."

"But what's the hurry?"

"Soon as he disposes of everything."

"I see." She bit her lip and looked away.

"Looks kind of bad to me, Maureen. Don't you think we ought to speak to the sheriff?"

"Not so loud! Sheila's right at the window. And she's got funny ideas already."

"Don't we all? Shepley could still perform an autopsy—have a good look."

"Oh, why make trouble just when everything's set—and the story coming out in today's paper."

"But with Uncle Jasper—this delay—we've got time."

"No, no, they've already—prepared her—you know that, August. It's too late. I'm sure Doc Shepley would change the certificate to 'self-inflicted'—gladly. But then we'd be in a mess with Reverend Kallsen over the funeral, so what's the point?"

"That's *not* what I mean and you know it. If he did something to her . . . he shouldn't get away with it."

"Oh, don't get the wind up. Who can really believe such a thing?"

"*You* did, yesterday. Those grooves in the floor . . ."

"I wish I'd never said anything. Every thought that enters a person's head doesn't have to be accounted for, does it?"

"I wish I knew what to do—and you're no help."

Maureen quickly changed the subject to describe the arrangements she'd made. The wake would now be held two nights in a row. Should any family members show up in response to the telegrams, they'd simply have to stay over. "I figure, if Uncle

Jasper's going to travel all that way, it'd be terrible if he didn't get to see Winnie."

See her? She was dead, wasn't she?

"So, he's arriving on the noon train, Thursday. I told him to come right to the church basement for dinner, before the services. I wonder . . . if I'll recognize him after all these years. Suppose I will." Her uncle moved ahead of her in time, his physical deterioration a sign of what would happen to her in due course; what he suffered, she'd come to suffer.

The noon siren from Kaleburg interrupted us as completely as if Gabriel's horn had sounded. She returned to the kitchen to finish preparing the meal, and I walked out to the road to pick up the mail, which I'd forgotten when I drove in. I opened the newspaper to the obituaries and found a small notice—for this was the city paper (the county biweekly would do up the story properly): "accidental death . . . suffocated in smoke from a flash fire in the kitchen." Shepley had held true; as soon as Maureen saw this, no further argument could be advanced to change the reading of the event. Now it was surely too late to do anything, she'd say. Newsprint established the facts, and that was that.

I slipped out of the house after eating in order to avoid talking to Maureen about the obituary, which of course she, too, quickly read. She didn't explain to Sheila why she was suddenly so news-hungry, when normally she didn't settle down with the paper until the midday dishes had been washed. Sheila glanced shrewdly at her mother, quietly picked up the newspaper, and read the notice herself.

All afternoon I chopped wood in the grove, fuel for the furnace to be used instead of coal these between-season days and nights. I tried to review everything as I worked, but no aspect became clearer. My reverie was broken by Maureen calling from the back door. "Aowgie! Aowgie! Aowgie!" The only time she used my boyhood name was when she tried to project her voice to a distant part of the farm. I figured she enjoyed howling like that once in a while and didn't respond quickly. "Aowgiee! Aowgieee!" again and again she called, the singsong rhythm of it almost a tune. Whenever I heard her voice riding the wind with my name, I felt curiously touched. (Some deep memory of Mother calling me home?) To think that a woman would do this: proclaim her connection to me for the world to hear!

When I answered she ceased at once, knowing by the direction of my response that I was in the grove and would soon be hauling wood to the rear of the house, where the cellar window was propped open. She waited for me there. Shutting off the tractor, I asked, "What's the matter? E.J. won't postpone the funeral?"

"No, *that's* okay—he doesn't care—but Elsie and Marie are driving down to stay the night here."

"Tonight?"

"They asked if they could."

"What for—anyhow?"

"I told 'em the funeral's not till the day after tomorrow, but they'd already gone to their boss. Now they're gettin' the extra day besides."

"Sort of a vacation, huh?"

"I *knew* you wouldn't want 'em here, but what could I say?"

"They should drive up from the city on Thursday. The weather'll be okay."

"E.J. asked if you'd stay the night with *him*. So he won't have to go to the hotel again."

"I'm supposed to *sleep* over there? What the hell for?" My stomach turned over and surely my eyes betrayed my uneasiness.

"I said you would."

"But what does he want with me?"

"Why didn't you tell me . . . you'd seen him at the hotel last night?"

"I guess I forgot."

She looked at me in open disbelief. Such was our separation, I knew she wouldn't pursue the matter. You can't get confidential by dogging a person. But how had we become so devious with each other—and why? She had tricks up her sleeve, too, that I knew nothing about. And Sheila was no doubt peeking at us from behind the bedroom curtain. If only we could find some common ground where we could all meet again and be together. The only thing likely would be the project of buying E.J.'s farm. A challenge for us. Something to join our efforts, make us forget this past we seemed mired in. I'd even use the subject against E.J. tonight, if he tried to put pressure on me because he figured I was the only person likely to blab to the police about what I suspected. I'd talk of nothing but his farm and how pleased I was to become the new owner. The land would save me—would save us all.

Since Maureen had too much on her mind now to bear the freight of this land-purchase news, I decided it'd better wait until another time. The right moment—to be used like a trump card.

At supper, Sheila began acting up. "Without Daddy here, who'll protect us?"

"From what?"

"Elsie and Marie are driving up, dear. We haven't had over-night company in a long time." Her manner was false, cajoling; she was afraid of her own daughter's tantrums. "It'll be so interesting for you."

"We'll keep lights on all night."

"Certainly not," I said.

"Can I sleep in *your* bed tonight, if Dad's not here?"

That bed business again—always a bad sign. She longed to be a helpless infant, clinging to her mother.

"You're much too big a girl," said Maureen calmly.

"Uncle Eege wants Dad to sleep with *him,* so what's the difference?"

"Oh, stop it!" said Maureen.

"Uncle Eege must be afraid of *some*thing, and I bet I know what."

In a second I felt she'd blurt out precisely what we refused to say. I almost hoped she would.

"I'll keep my eyes open all night, watching."

"Watching for what?" Maureen asked, relieved by the play-acting voice, a role of Sheila's she could handle.

"You know . . ."

"I don't."

"Yes, you do. And *that's* why Dad's going over to Uncle Eege's—to watch there."

"What kind of nonsense . . . watch for *what?*"

"Aunt Winnie's ghost."

"Oh! Why, you wicked—" Maureen slapped Sheila's face. She shrieked and ran crying from the kitchen.

"Now you've done it, Maureen."

"I don't care. It's about time she thinks of other people's feelings—about *my* feelings, for a change." As if it were a surprise even to herself, tears ran down her cheeks. She rubbed her eyes and buried her head in her arms, pushing aside the plate.

Animal-quiet, glancing fearfully at me, Sheila crept back, face pale. "I—I was just—teasing."

"A terrible thing to do to your mother."

"I didn't expect she'd cry."

"These two days have been awfully hard on her. You ought to realize—it's been a terrible time."

"I don't think it's so terrible."

"You don't?"

"Not as bad as some days. I mean, yesterday was bad, but today—what was so awful about today?"

"You heartless child—what can I say to you?" I left the room. Thank God, I could always escape. There was the great outdoors—ten feet away—seldom farther. It worked every time.

With darkness the temperature fell below freezing and the dirt road to the Walczak farm was firm under my wheels. As I swung the Chevy into E.J.'s lane, my lights flashed on him standing in the yard under the box elder, as if awaiting my arrival before venturing into the house alone. He took the blaze full force without lowering his eyes or blinking, the way farm dogs look blindly into the headlamps of strange cars. I shut off the motor at the chicken-wire fence but didn't immediately douse the lights. "Haven't you got a yard light?" I called out the window.

"Yeah—switch is in the house."

What was he afraid of in there?

"I talked to Wolbers about you this afternoon and he was tickled to hear it."

"He was?" I flicked off the head beams and climbed out.

"Course, you'll have to go over it with him yourself, but you're like money in the bank, far as they're concerned. No risk at all."

"I'm not, huh?"

"He figured I'd probably pull out, when he heard . . . about yesterday. But he never thought I'd get a buyer so fast."

"Haven't said yes yet, have I?"

"Stop the kidding. How can you refuse?"

"Fifteen thousand. A lot of money to scrape up in a hurry."

"Not for you. What'd Maureen say?"

"I—I haven't told her. She's got enough on her mind." But I'd need her five thousand inheritance, built up over the years in her savings account. I couldn't swing it alone.

"Had supper yet? Come on."

E.J. snapped on the porch light and we entered the kitchen with elaborate casualness. I noticed the broken window had been blocked up with a wedge of cardboard from a Northern Tissue carton. "They've been bringing food out here all day. Look at it!"

The table was laden with bowls of potato salad, ham, sausages, three loaves of bread, coffeecake, and a tureen of raspberry Jell-O, the lurid color of a child's sucker, with blobs of torn marshmallows in a scum on top. I looked at the names on adhesive tape stuck on each bowl—mostly the neighbors. E.J. lit a fire under the coffeepot, and I cut off several wheels of summer-sausage, tasting one. "Pretty good, but a little too fresh." We discussed various methods of making sausage and which wood smoke produced the finest flavor until the topic wore thin. Then we fell into a guarded silence.

"That curtain in the doorway—always there?"

"No, she liked to put it up for company, that's all." He glanced at the kitchen clock. "Say, it's time for Fibber McGee. Let's go in and listen."

We carried our plates of food, cups and saucers, and settled into the green sculptured-plush easy chairs. The amber dial on the radio shaped like a tombstone glowed and the loosely woven cloth over the speaker trembled as the voices burst forth. Fibber was on his way to begin spring gardening, and Molly told him to be sure to wear his cap because it was damp out there. He went to the hall closet.

E.J. gripped the arms of his chair and smiled in anticipation. Then the crash came—the whole closetful tumbled out. "There it goes! Every week. You'd think he'd learn."

"Or that we'd stop laughing at it." Still, it was a relief to drop into the midst of the McGees and their neighbors every Tuesday, be invisible among them. I scarcely listened to the goings-on; instead, I kept wondering if Winnie had indeed been tied to the table in the kitchen. Perhaps I could find marks from her struggle on the varnish of the legs, near the grooves in the floor.

"Gildersleeve! Listen to him!"

He sounded like a bass drum laughing.

What should be done with this house, if I owned the land? Demolish it? A building like this left empty would soon be vandalized. Perhaps this place could serve as a storage bin or another corncrib.

"My God, is it nine already?" said E.J. "Here's Bob Hope. Do you like him?"

"I'll say." The breezy, collegiate voice came at us fast and the laughs from the studio audience were like machine-gun fire. Actually, I preferred the family comedies like Fibber McGee and Charlie McCarthy, but in E.J.'s presence I couldn't seem to tell the truth about anything. "You wonder how he thinks up those gags."

"He's got plenty of help, they all do."

In the kitchen the phone rang and E.J. leapt up as if he'd been shot. "I'll get it!" Nearly slipped as he rushed past the silk drape in the doorway.

Who was he expecting a call from—his worried girl friend?

"It's Maureen," he said sheepishly.

"Lord, what now?"

She shouted on the other end of the line as if she still didn't quite believe in the invention. Elsie and Marie had arrived, but when they learned I was spending the night with E.J. at the scene of the tragedy, they insisted on coming over for a visit. They were on the way right now.

I couldn't scold her for being unable to handle my cousins, for I'd never had the slightest sway over them either. They did whatever they wished—just like their mother, Aunt Gertrude. She'd fallen in love with a music instructor at the Normal School, eloped, and spent a miserable existence in the city until her husband ran off with another woman. Then Aunt Gertrude and her two girl-babies "came crawling" to Grandfather, asking forgiveness. He agreed to support her and the girls on a small stipend (which Dad continued after Grandfather's death), provided they remain in the city and not press to come home and live on the family farm. Gertrude was now dead and the two girls, who'd never married, lived in a brick apartment building within walking distance of the largest department store in town, where both worked, Elsie as a salesclerk and Marie in the bookkeeping department.

Head lamps soon flashed in the yard, and although E.J. was puzzled by the impending visit of these two ladies whom he scarcely knew, he turned on the yard light and stepped outside with me to greet them. In silhouette they came up the walk, calling hello in false voices. Marie was large and carefully picked her way as if stepping on ice floes. Elsie behind her was "the nervous one," a fluttery, jerky gait; she was like a napkin drawn through a ring. They shook hands with each of us and said, "My sympathy," then entered the kitchen, glancing around like inspectors. They accepted E.J.'s offer of coffeecake but said they never drank coffee at this hour. Marie, who was also the driver, chatted about the miserable trip down from the city, thirty-odd miles away, and what a hard time they had finding my farm—my name on the mailbox nearly washed away by the rains. But while she talked she looked closely about the room, her words merely a screen to allow her time for scrutiny.

Elsie was always transparent, rather naïve; she could never dissemble. "Tell us, how'd this happen, anyhow?"

While E.J. told Elsie his story, Marie moved about the room, peered under the table, studied the charred windowsill. She was a formidable examiner and kept firing questions over her shoulder: "What time did you say?" and "How long did it take to put out the flames?"

I remembered the last time Maureen, Sheila, and I had visited "the girls" in the city—and the cake we'd eaten, which was one year old. A dear friend had died on her birthday the previous year without having had a piece of her cake, and so it'd been placed in the freezer, to be thawed out and eaten on each anniversary, as a reminder. Appropriately enough, it was angel food cake—and it tasted pretty good.

E.J. by now had gone through everything twice.

"How strange . . ." Marie said ominously. "That she couldn't manage to get out the door or break a window. Don't you think—it's very odd?"

Elsie nodded vigorously. "Who ever heard of such a thing!"

E.J. herded them into the parlor and served them glasses of grape juice made from Welch's concentrate. The radio in the background provided the party noise we needed, since conversation was heavy-going. And yet, for the first time in years, their company eased me. I could sink back and do nothing, think my own thoughts, watch E.J. squirm. When they left I'd be on my own again.

How'd I ever manage to fall asleep tonight? I'd be on guard every second, leave quickly at dawn.

At last "the girls" moved toward their coats, E.J., the gentleman, right behind to help. "Well, now we know, don't we, Elsie?"

"We know—yes, we know a little bit better."

"—how it was here."

Perhaps they hadn't been so bent on catching E.J. in a lie as eager to imagine the tragedy to its fullest extent—feel the presence of death in the room. One of the kicks to be gotten out of life.

After they'd gone, E.J. sighed heavily. "How about a shot of whiskey? Seems we could use it."

My eccentric cousins had thrown the two of us into a closer camaraderie, for men could always get together laughing at women. *"Now* you keep whiskey in the house, I see." But I was sorry I said it. There'd been a time when E.J. hid his liquor in the garage, for Winnie drank heavily when upset. But that phase passed and she became a fanatical prohibitionist. I certainly didn't wish to congratulate him on his present, easier life.

We lifted glasses in a silent toast to whatever and tossed it down. "Ah, *that* goes the right place." He rubbed his ample stomach. "You know I gave up smoking because of her? 'Nasty, filthy habit,' she'd say. 'Never see an animal with such a dirty habit.' And she was right, of course. Shitty taste in your mouth, cuts down on your breath. I wasn't able to stop entirely. But if I had a smoke outside somewhere, she always smelled it in my clothes." He unplugged the bottle. "Let's have another. You want water, I can get you a glass."

"No, I like it straight."

He smiled. The arm of this brotherhood circled closer around me. "Yeah, August, this tastes pretty good, all right."

Altogether too cozy—but how could I break it?

"People always do this, night of the wake, don't they? Sit around 'n' drink, tell stories."

I yawned, faking it at first, but then a real one erupted. "Think I'll turn in. The booze made me sleepy."

"Good idea. Better make a trip outside first. You know I ain't got a toilet in here. Another thing Winnie hated about this house. Had to use the outhouse even in the dead of winter. For baths, the wooden tub in the kitchen was sort of fun at first, if you know what I mean."

We groped our way off the porch, a little to the rear of the house. E.J. made a Boy Scout occasion of it and aimed his stream toward the very spot I let go at, as if we were pissing out a fire. We splashed the frozen ground, noisy as horses, E.J. winning the contest, for he was to the last to let up.

Back inside, he extinguished the radio lamp and turned on the hall light outside the bedroom door—which was also at the bottom of a steep little stairs leading to the upper room. "Well . . . good night, then." I started up, feeling suddenly rather drunk from those two hefty shots.

"Hey, where you goin'? We're sleeping in here."

"You've a bed up there—where Sheila slept?"

"Christ, that's a kid's room. You couldn't even stand up. You 'n' me'll sleep together down here, if you don't mind doubling up."

I did mind, but I couldn't very well make an issue of it. When he snapped on the bedroom light I saw the two depressions in the double-bed mattress, like the sunken ground in a pair of new graves. Night before last, Winnie lay there—on the inside—for that hollow was smaller. Would the mold she'd made in the mattress just about fit me?

E.J. calmly undressed, flinging his trousers and flannel shirt on a chair. In white winter underwear he looked enormous, particularly his upper arms and shoulders. I undressed to my long johns, which I planned to sleep in, but E.J. stripped completely. His porky body was nearly hairless, and his genitals hanging down under his belly looked as if part of his insides were half falling out.

Lights off, we lay in silence for some time, but I couldn't relax. The quietness didn't seem prelude to slumber—it just got heavier. A faucet in the kitchen dripped with annoying regularity, and though I tried to pay no attention to it, I couldn't stop anticipating each successive drip. I felt much too warm in my underwear. The springs were so beaten into a body shape I grew anxious about how deep I was sunk. We were under flannelette sheet-blankets, not cotton sheets, and I was too hot. Sweat moistened my brow and I felt clammy. But E.J. was breathing regularly—he seemed asleep. Carefully, I slipped out of my underwear and slid it down, pushing it away with my feet. I turned over to face the shaded window, from which a faint light came, around the edges. I was almost out when suddenly I jerked to in a muscle spasm. Wide awake again.

I listened to E.J.'s nasal wheezing for what seemed an hour and felt terribly thirsty from the whiskey. The dripping water in the kitchen became a two-way torture. Very carefully, each spring of the bed announcing my escape, I rolled out. The cold air on my naked flesh made me shiver, so I found the wadded underwear and pulled it on before moving out of the room. I could make out the dark shapes of dresser and chair, the parallelogram of the half-open bedroom door. As I pushed aside the piano-drape hanging and entered the kitchen, the cool silk caressed my feverish face. I groped for the light switch, the sudden flash blinding.

But where was the dripping faucet? The sink had no spigot, only a hand pump, and the spout was dry. Far away I heard a steady drop-drop—from the eaves, probably ice thawing, near the exhaust pipe leading from the hot-water heater. I began pumping for a drink of water; it came in a rhythmic, pulsing flow, like ichor from a beating heart. I put my head under and let it gush into my open mouth and wash my hot face. Then I turned to the table, dropped to my knees to examine the floor, just as Marie had done, and found the yellowish raw streaks Maureen had mentioned. Couldn't possibly be fingernail scratches, though. I clawed the surface. Impenetrable. No abrasive marks from rope or wire on the bulbous legs.

The drape rustled—E.J.! I saw his bare feet and ankles beneath his maroon bathrobe. I jumped out from under the table so quickly I hit my head, the blow a bad crack, and for a moment I couldn't rise, just as if E.J. had bludgeoned me.

"What the hell you doin' under there?"

"I—I don't know." I rubbed my aching head. "Marie got me wondering, that's all. I mean, I was thirsty—that's what kept me awake—and that drip."

"What drip?"

"Listen."

Neither of us moved but there was complete silence. "I don't hear a thing."

"Now it seems gone."

"Let's go back to bed, huh? I thought if I had company I could sleep better, but *Christ,* August!"

"How can you expect me to sleep? When I still don't know what the hell happened here."

"I told you all—"

"Nobody believes you. You ought to know. Only, we can't figure out exactly what *did* happen."

"Do I have to—"

"You keep saying the fire started—after she threw kerosene

around. But that wasn't the way—was it? The house would be gone. *You* must've set the fire yourself—and kept it under control."

A look of relief on his face—and sudden vulnerability. "So *that's* what you're after."

"I can't stand these lies. I can't keep it all straight in my head."

"I been debating whether or not to tell you."

"I knew there was *some* reason you wanted me over tonight." My words gave me power and cleared the air miraculously. Asking the right questions at last. "So what happened—shoot."

"I didn't . . . didn't *do* anything deliberately. It was an accident."

"What was?"

"She came at me with a butcher knife, lunged for me—right here." He cupped his famous lower parts. "Damn near put me out of commission for good."

"What started her off?"

"She'd heard about . . . about a girl I've been seeing."

"That part you told Shepley, huh?"

"Came after me with a knife, she was so mad. I ran round the other side of the table, she after me. I caught her arm and slammed her hard against the table edge—knocked her right out. Sometimes I don't know my own strength. I let her lay there, thinking she'd come to. But after a bit, when she didn't move, I gave her a shake. Then I realized . . . her head rolled funny . . . she wasn't breathing. I'd broken her neck. Or maybe it was the concussion killed her—there was blood in her hair. Anyhow, she was gone. And I got real scared—when I realized the fix I was in." He sounded scared even now.

"Should've called me *then.*"

"I knew I was in for it. Nobody'd believe me—saying it was self-defense—even with the butcher knife laying right there. Big guy like me—and a little thing like her."

"You'd've been better off, making a clean breast of it. Everybody knew she had crazy spells."

"I wouldn't be on my way to California now, though—would

I? There'd be a long investigation. I'd have to stand trial. Good chance I'd go to jail."

"You say that—'cause you've been there before?"

"August, you know me right down to the ground."

"You never talked about where you were born—"

"Chicago."

"—where you came from. So I figured you must have a record, somewhere."

"It wasn't much. Me 'n' a buddy robbed a filling station with cap pistols. Got caught. Spent two years in Joliet."

"I see."

"They'd look up my record and I wouldn't stand a chance, if it ever came out—how this thing really happened. When I realized I'd killed her I had to figure some way out—for me. It ain't right for a normal man to be dragged down by an insane person, is it? I mean, I didn't feel I'd done anything I should have to *pay* for—since she was the one started it, chasing me with a knife. If she'd stabbed me, August, you know what would've happened to her? They'd lock her away in the booby hatch for a while, that's all. But since it was *me* who done it, they'd send me up for a long time. So, I had to figure a way out of this mess. She was dead and what difference would it make."

"But kerosene? That was risky—hard to control a fire like that."

"I wanted it to look like I'd tried to save her. I was lucky—able to put it out. Everybody knew she'd tried suicide before. This time it seemed I hadn't gotten to her in time to save her. Fortunately, Maureen got to working over Shepley, so he didn't even perform an autopsy."

"A break for you, all right."

"You can say what you want, but wouldn't you've done the same—in my shoes?"

"I'm not you—I can't compare."

"Now you know everything, August—so, what're you going to do about it?"

"You wouldn't've said anything if you thought I'd go to the sheriff."

"The important thing is, I didn't do it deliberately. It was an accident."

"Could happen to anyone, yeah." But my heart was too heavy for irony.

"Glad we had it out, August. I *had* to talk to somebody."

"I couldn't've taken over this farm, without knowing the full story of what happened. I'd've always wondered, you know? It would bother me." I felt freer now. I'd been yearning for greater honesty between myself and others, and here I'd hit open ground at last. We stood face to face; but my relief began to cloud over. I had the first inkling of the responsibility this new confidence imposed upon me. "Those marks on the floor there." I pointed, almost angrily. "Did Winnie make them?"

He shook his head. "She moved the kitchen cabinet last week —that's what did it."

"Maureen wondered. She's got suspicions about you."

"I know, but she wants the funeral to go off without a hitch, so I guess we don't have to worry."

"'*We*'?" I felt a sudden flush of rage at this big bull of a Polack who'd pulled me into his troubles. "You shouldn't— shouldn't involve people this way. You've no right to! Now what am *I* supposed to do about all this?"

"Let's go to bed, huh? There's time tomorrow—to talk."

"I feel worse than I did before. I wish you'd never told me anything."

"*You* kept asking."

"But why call me over here tonight?"

"You kept after me. The hotel last night, here for chores this morning. You sure wanted in on everything."

"Now what?"

"Just ask yourself, August, what you'd've done in *my* place."

"What makes you think that'd work? I'm not you—I'm not anything like you. I keep to myself and have my own problems —I don't need yours. You've always been in some scrape or other. If it ain't the booze, it's some woman. I don't live like that. I never have."

"Sure, you're a better man than me, who's denying it?" He pulled the sash of his robe tighter and walked to the light switch. "Let's go to bed, huh? I feel I've been through the wringer."

"I'm not sleepy. Maybe I should go home."

"The dog'll bark and you'll wake everybody up over there."

"Is it that late?" I saw by the clock it was 2 A.M.

E.J. shut off the light and we froze in the dark, waiting for our eyes to adjust to the blackness. Then with careful footsteps, almost heel to toe, we returned to the bedroom, E.J. leading the way. He flung his robe aside and threw himself heavily into bed. I knew I'd be awake until dawn. I sat on the edge of the mattress for a while, then lay back, extending my legs full length.

E.J. was already asleep. How could the murderer sleep when I couldn't? The weight of conscience had been shifted so that he was free and now I had the burden of it all. How'd this sleight of hand been accomplished? What a heavy brother this was beside me, wheezing softly; what a mound of flesh! It was a mystery how any woman could find him appealing, how he'd managed so many seductions—with such an ordinary, insignificant button of a prick, too. I knew so much less each day that passed. Winnie had discovered he'd been screwing somebody and rushed to cut him with a butcher knife—but who'd told her? How had she found out? She lived in such seclusion here.

The silence circled out and held. E.J.'s regular breathing sounded peaceful, innocent. Finally, I slept.

At daylight I slipped from bed without waking him and arrived home to find Maureen plumping biscuit dough in the aluminum pan. The range roared like the north wind. Having spent the night by herself in bed, she seemed refreshed; at least our meeting this morning had a new, intimate quality. She'd been able last night to probe the far icy corners of the bed with her toes, deliciously stretching the muscles of her lower back. It'd been years since we'd been separated overnight. But of course, she would not reveal any of her feelings to me. We'd fall into an easy give-and-take, as solid and predictable as the thump of overshoes dropping on the back porch.

"You back so early?"

"I didn't sleep much."

"Neither did I."

Could she be about to admit she'd been unsettled, not having my body next to hers?

"Elsie and Marie were so restless—kept talking about Winnie's passing, going over it again and again. Getting Sheila worked up."

"You should've sent her to bed."

"I tried, but she wouldn't go. And with you not here, she knew she could get away with anything. Marie and Elsie took *her* side. They all sat together in the living room and looked at photos in the album. Found some of their mother, and *that* set them crying."

"Oh, those two!"

"And the after-midnight running around upstairs! Marie's bladder is pretty bad."

"I didn't know."

"Back and forth to the bathroom all night—keeping Sheila awake. She must've been curious to see what was going on, so she opened her door a crack. You know, Marie lets out her bun at night, hair all the way down her back—well, when she went flying down the hall, Sheila let out a yell that curdled my blood. I figured somebody was getting murdered up there. I ran upstairs to Sheila, but by this time Elsie was trying to comfort her—though *she* looked a fright . . . cream all over her face, a chin strap—and her fingers in bandages for arthritis. To quiet 'em down I made cocoa, but by that time it was nearly two."

"I was still awake then myself."

"Sheila begged to crawl into bed with me, but I kept her out. I remembered what you said—she mustn't be allowed to sleep with us again, so I wouldn't let her. Upstairs, Elsie and Marie kept talking and muttering. Sounded like they were crying half the time, sort of long-drawn-out squealing. Dreadful business. And turning on those wheezy springs—turning and turning—you could hear it all over the house."

"That bed's terrible."

"Even the dog got to barking. *That* made 'em think we had chicken thieves. They turned on lights and shouted down to me, asking what I thought was wrong—why the dog was barking. 'He hears *you* two,' I said. 'Now go to sleep.'"

"I should never've gone over to E.J.'s—and left you."

"Well, it's over. Unless he wants you to spend tonight with him, too—did he say?"

"No. We talked a lot about what's to become of his farm. He'll let me have it for fifteen thousand, taking over his mortgage. What do you think?"

"Fifteen thousand! Where'd we get that kind of money?"

"I'd need your savings account to do it."

"Of course." She knew nothing about business and always let me manage. "You think it's a wise move?"

While I talked, she drew up a chair and began to peel and section grapefruit. Whenever I worked on my accounts in the ledger at the kitchen desk (and I kept careful track of everything, right down to the nails from the hardware store), she always hushed Sheila and tiptoed around the kitchen so as not to disturb my concentration. It was flattering to think she figured I held the family's destiny in my hands. She'd no idea how much money I had in the bank—how much we were worth. Only her little island of family inheritance in that savings account gave her a tiny bit of economic independence. And now I would possess that, too.

When I sold a load of cattle or hogs and the check came from the commission company, she never asked how much it was. Even though I listened to the livestock report almost every noon, the special lingo of the stockyards—barrows, feeders, gilts—remained a mystery to her; she never tried to understand any of it.

"I could sure use the extra acres—all this machinery I got. Spread the cost. I'll take down the fences over there and let the rows run, like in those big wheat ranches in Kansas. So you don't have to turn around in the end rows all the time."

How easy to talk about *this,* instead of what'd happened to Winnie. I used the farm purchase in the offing as a perfect deflector. I could almost hide in this news, too, instead of brooding about the other. Maureen noticed the rounded dish towel on top of the biscuit dough—it'd already risen. She said her double-action Fleischmann's was so much quicker than the old single-action yeast—almost as if she had to show me that a special area of knowledge belonged to her, too, about which I knew nothing.

Farm prices were rising, I said. Always, in wartime.

"Sounds like our big chance, August. Is there much risk—with that mortgage?"

"The farm'll pay for itself and then some. We'll have extra, too—maybe buy a new car."

"And clothes, something nice." She'd no longer have to thumb through the Sears, Roebuck catalogue, comparing every item with its counterpart in Montgomery Ward's, trying to envision how a dress pictured there might really look when she found the package hanging from the mailbox flag. Instead, she'd shop in the smart city stores and buy a good coat with a fur collar as fluffy and expensive as the one the banker's wife wore. "How many acres, then, all together—will it make for us?" Scarcely contained pride in her question.

"Three-twenty. His one-sixty and mine."

"Half a section!" Only a few rich farmers around Kaleburg had that much land.

"We'll have our work cut out." I knew she loved the idea.

"I'll order another hundred laying hens—and let's buy more baby chicks this year. Put Sheila to work, with chores. I think it'd be good for her, August."

Together this family would labor with only one goal in mind, and all unnecessary expenses would be cut until the profits began coming in—till we were in the clear. She said she'd no longer save out half a pint of cream for household use each day, but sell every ounce. She'd plant a larger garden this spring so that next winter we wouldn't have to buy canned goods. "Sheila can help me garden. She's old enough to take responsibility there."

"A wonderful opportunity. Thanks to E.J."

Remembrance of Winnie's death clouded her eyes and she turned away, embarrassed by her excessive greediness.

"I mean, it was lucky he offered *me* the chance first—good land's so hard to get."

But nothing I could say diminished her shame in having slipped into unseemly avarice. The Lord was always watching, and He'd caught her licking her lips over the possibility of making money.

"I'll start the milking. What're your plans for Elsie and Marie?"

Her voice sounded shrouded. "They can help me buy groceries for tomorrow's church dinner. And pick up sympathy-answer cards from the printer. Then, over to the funeral home to see how the flowers've been arranged. They did real well with Winnie, wait'll you see."

"Should be a closed coffin, I think."

"But they put folds and nets across her head and you don't notice about the hair. She's like a nun laying there. Everyone thought she looked real nice."

Hearing noises upstairs, I made my escape. The cries of cats washed against me like surf as I left the house. Clouds diffused the sunrise and a pastel glow lingered on the tree trunks; I could feel all creation's excitement in the new day.

In my case, it was almost a new life. I'd wrestled like Jacob all night, but whether to free myself or to become more deeply involved, I was still not sure. But in some way I now carried E.J.'s burden—that heavy guilt over what he'd done, strapped like a bag to his back. How cleverly he'd let me come close enough to sense the trouble, smell the mystery, and now suddenly I'd helped him shoulder it. Between the two of us we'd keep the great, heavy bag of trouble from bursting and spoiling everything.

The Holsteins in the cow barn moaned from the pressure in their udders, but I paused at the boot scraper, unwilling to squelch by haste whatever morning wisdom might well up. I was waiting for an insight to come. With the inner, turbulent voice of myself stilled, I felt at peace, waiting for the oracle to speak out of the void. This conscious quieting of myself was the closest I ever came to prayer. I tried to dissolve my consciousness, let the stream of eternity take over. But nothing happened. I was left standing there, an empty vessel and alone. I knew I couldn't accomplish much by sober thinking about my problems, for I never seemed to learn much by considered reflection, except that eventually I'd come round to where I'd begun and glimpse the backside of an idea hurrying to complete the circle.

I'd be getting E.J.'s farm in exchange for helping him carry his burden. A fair deal. He needed me, and I should be compensated for taking risks. Almost an accessory to the crime.

E.J.'s life from now on would be utterly different, and I envied him that change. How often myself I'd half hoped for a spasm of some sort, even a violent act of nature, to whip me away and settle me into some new situation. Not that I wished anything terrible to happen to my family—but I hoped to be tested, made to feel new again, forced to act in the face of fresh circumstances. It was as if I'd been stumbling along through time, season after season, accumulating a burden. How heavy my life was getting to be! I couldn't imagine how to dispose of this weight, but it'd been easy to join E.J.'s struggle and take on his, too. Now everything seemed different and therefore somewhat better.

Snowball shinnied up my pants leg—I'd been standing there like a tree! I cuffed her away and resumed my trip to the cow barn.

Later, I hauled manure. The stuff was getting so high my steers were beginning to look out the windows. I deliberately took on this dirtiest of all jobs, just to remove myself from everyone. Shit was real and had to be dealt with—not like those other things bothering me.

I never carried a watch but nevertheless knew the hour pretty well. Some farmers tell time by gauging the shadows under the eaves of a barn; however, those angles change throughout the year, so I look at the sun itself. I knew within a few minutes when it was noon, before the siren in Kaleburg blew. Such mastery always gave me a certain pleasure.

When I reached the house, I left boots and outer clothes, rank with odors, on the back porch and changed to a fresh pair of overalls in the washroom. Sheila opened the door just as I stepped into clean clothes. At the sight of me in my underwear, she was about to slam the door, but I called, "Sheila! Come on in. How's my girl?" The invitation to intimacy didn't work. She closed the door anyhow.

In the kitchen I found Maureen making gravy from the drippings of the pork roast. The nutty smell of roast pork and bay leaves filled the house. "I'll be a few minutes yet, August. Go talk to the girls."

"What happened to Sheila?"

"She always runs off when I'm about to ask her to set the table."

Marie and Elsie were deep in easy chairs in the front room. Puffy-eyed, sallow, they looked fagged out from last night's binge and could scarcely muster smiles of greeting. Fit candidates to sit around the coffin at the wake tonight, I thought.

"I'm glad we have a chance to speak with you—" Marie began.

"Alone," Elsie added.

"Is Sheila—?" Marie glanced into the dining room.

"She ran off," I said. "What's the matter?"

"Something must be done. About what happened to Winnie."

"It's not right, August," said Elsie. "You know it's not right."

"What isn't?"

"She didn't die the way E.J. says."

"She didn't, we're sure of it," Elsie echoed.

"Why'd she lay there under the table and let herself choke to death? Have you asked somebody to look into it, or should we—"

"Call the sheriff . . . the district attorney," Elsie said.

"You girls, now listen, we thought of all the angles on Monday. When Doc Shepley—he's the coroner—was out to investigate."

"Oh . . ." said Elsie, "then there *was* an investigation?"

"If it was okay with Doc Shepley, why're *you* two getting fussed?"

"I feel much better about it, I must say."

"Don't be a fool, Elsie! What sort of inquiry was it? Did the sheriff come out?"

"Now, Marie, the coroner's the medical officer. Shepley asked E.J. all sorts of questions how it happened. And *he* was satisfied."

"I'd like to have heard some of those answers."

"We don't trust E.J." Elsie lowered her voice and glanced toward the other rooms. "We think maybe he wanted to get rid of her."

"Aw, come on!"

"What does anybody know about the man? Where'd he come from—who is he?"

"There's no reason, just because—"

"I saw it in his eyes—he looked guilty," said Marie. "Shifty, sneaky eyes. And he pretended he remembered us!"

"Well, I told him you were coming."

"Don't think we met him but twice before—yet there he was, trying to be agreeable, cover up if he could."

"Marie's going to phone the sheriff."

"Now just a minute. Making accusations is a pretty serious business. You better have something to go on."

"Suspicions," said Marie, "not accusations."

"You'll make fools of yourselves."

"Have the sheriff set our minds at ease," said Elsie.

"No wonder you two were eager to have a private talk with me. Maureen'll hit the ceiling when she hears what you girls are up to."

"We don't plan to tell her anything—"

"Unless there's something to report," said Marie. "If it turns out we're right—and there's something funny about the way Winnie died."

"You'd only be hurting Maureen, don't you see? She doesn't want to admit to anybody how it *really* happened."

"Oh, then you *know?*" asked Marie.

"Of course we know! It wasn't—wasn't like it says in the papers. But what difference does it make? So long as Winnie gets a decent burial—not have the thing called suicide. That's what Maureen wants. I don't know if you realize what Winnie was like. Shock treatments down in Omaha—crazy spells. Nobody could handle her. And those times she went off to the sanitarium to get straightened out—I thought you girls understood that. You think Maureen likes to have that madness in the family always brought up? It's best—especially in front of

Sheila—to stick with the story, the way E.J. tells it. Don't go speculating."

They sat there like two owls on a stick. "Oh, I see," first Marie, then Elsie: "I see."

"Winnie had one of her mad fits and did away with herself. It's perfectly obvious."

They shook their heads and clicked their tongues.

"Maureen wants a church funeral of course, and she knows Reverend Kallsen won't bury anybody who's done a thing like that. We talked the whole matter over with Shepley. There's nothing wrong."

"You think people'll believe—the newspaper story?"

"There'll be talk, of course."

"Dinner! Dinner!" Maureen called.

"So, you girls hush up now, won't you? Don't make Maureen feel bad."

"What're you three gabbin' about? Come *on,* dinner's on the table." She was always in a frenzy until her family settled into their chairs and had taken their first bites. *Then* if they dawdled and let the food become cold it was their responsibility. "Now where's Sheila gone? Sheila! Sheila!"

I heard a faint creak of floorboards overhead and glanced up. In the bedroom, Sheila'd been listening through the air register.

In late afternoon when dark, heavy clouds piled together in the west, I stopped pitching manure and walked to the house because I'd lost track of the time. Maureen was astonished to learn I hadn't started my chores yet. "And now E.J. wants you to do *his,* too." One of Winnie's nephews, a senior at Iowa State, had arrived at the Kaleburg bus depot and E.J. planned to have supper with him in town. To complicate matters, Marie was afraid to drive to the wake because the roads were so bad. I suggested Maureen take our car, after dropping me off at E.J.'s.

"But how'll you get to town—when you're through with his chores?"

"E.J. could drive out for me."

"That's not such a hot idea."

"The wake'll go on till midnight, won't it? Plenty of time for me to get there."

"Suit yourself!"

Rain spattered the windowpanes and thunder rumbled with the sharp authority it always possessed in spring during the first storms. With the arrival of the shower, we broke away abruptly, the way the yard clears of chickens when the first drops fall. Rain came down suddenly in whitish sheets, lashing the sides of the house. Lightning snicked in the telephone and a spark leapt from the mouthpiece. The voice of the Lord! Thunder beat loud overhead and Sheila let out a yell. Maureen flipped the light switch but nothing happened. "Gone."

"Power plant maybe shut it off." I drew on my black rubber rain hat shaped like a coal scuttle. "Better get on down to milk my cows."

"You're surely not going—with lightning cracking like that!"

I winked. *"He* might get this sinner, huh?"

She gasped. How dare I tease her about God?

I found my rubber raincoat on a porch peg. The cats squealed when they saw me emerge. Fur bedraggled, they looked pitifully skinny and made the most of it. Only the hungriest ran with me through the cloudburst to the barn.

In the cobwebbed, dim milking section, warm with the steamy breath of animals, I heard rain whip the windows and felt the shock waves of thunder through my feet. But by the time I returned to the house, frothy milk in two pails, the rain had stopped, not in the spangled flash of a sunset through crystal-clear air, but quietly, with dark clouds still stacked in layers across the western sky and great thunderheads majestically adrift in the east, riding like galleons.

When I entered the kitchen after separating the cream in the back shed, the women were all at supper. Pinkish-gray cold cuts on platters in front of them, like human flesh cut and sliced. Slabs of gummy processed cheese. Marie and Elsie had powdered their dramatic faces to give themselves appropriate mourners' looks. Ghastly. White, as if the flour barrel had exploded in their faces. Their lips were cracked, eyes red-rimmed,

watery, and both wore dark lace veils over their heads. They
were dressed in black crepe satin, the kind everybody's mother
wore for best, fifty years ago. Sheila beside them looked like an
overly large child in her blue jumper and white blouse. Although Maureen was in her housedress, she'd soon put on the
navy eyelet, rhinestone buttons down the front, which she usually wore to church.

The power off, we ate by kerosene light. The familiar nos-
tril-itching odor of the oil brought memories of childhood,
when it'd been my chore to keep the chimneys washed, wicks
trimmed, and fuel in the lamps. Our family used to sit around
the dining table in the evenings, the lamp in the center. The
yellow glow fell upon the pages of my schoolbooks and softly
shadowed Mother's face, so that she looked surprisingly young
as she darned socks, mended my overalls, or did fancywork
(she almost never read). Just the three of us, those long quiet
evenings. Father's steel-rimmed spectacles, which he wore only
when reading the newspaper by lamplight, were always far
down his nose, giving him a scholarly look. The light was our
hearth, holding us together, and the heat on my face was the
feeling of happiness itself. But I only knew this years later.
Now, whenever a storm cut the electricity, I'd be quick to haul
out the kerosene lamp, with a feeling of elation.

Following supper, while Maureen dressed, I packed the
Gladstone bag with clothes for the wake. I'd change at E.J.'s
after finishing his chores. I folded my best suit on top of my
town shoes, then shirt, tie, and socks. Soon we were all set to
leave. Since Maureen would be driving the whole distance, she
took the wheel and I sat beside her to help navigate. Sheila was
wedged between the two ladies in the back seat. Each lurch of
the Chevy reminded us how easily we could land in the ditch. I
kept my hands tight on my kneecaps, trying not to look nervous. All of us leaned forward, staring at the road, and on a particularly bad rear slide, Elsie said, "Oh, dear!"

Maureen turned on the high lights. "That's better," said
Marie, honey-voiced.

As we descended a slight hill, a left slide began, and
Maureen steered into it; but the wheels kept spinning. She

slammed on the brakes, choking the motor. "Oh, good!" said Sheila. "That time we almost did it."

"If we fell in the ditch, *then* we'd be in for it!" said Marie.

"Daddy'd have to haul us out with the tractor."

"You'd like that, I suppose," I said sourly.

"It's awfully dark, isn't it?" said Elsie.

"The days don't seem to get longer—like they should," her sister added, as if she doubted the sun would do its business this year. We might be entering the last phase, the end of the world, as the Jehovah's Witnesses were always predicting.

"Don't turn into the road gate, Maureen. You'd have trouble getting back out. I'll walk in from here."

We looked at the black, rain-wet house in silence. Death had happened there—and it looked it. I leapt from the running board to the matted edge of the road. "Somebody'll pick you up, then . . . in an hour or so," Maureen called.

I watched the square rear of the Chevy until it disappeared over the hill. By the motor's more cheerful sound, I knew she'd safely reached the graveled arterial highway.

No light in the house or barns here—power gone, all over the area. The coil of chicken wire strung across the yard, enclosing a barren patch in front of the house, seemed like the twisted barbed wire of a battlefield. Why had Winnie allowed such an eyesore? What wrangle between them did it represent? The house looked abandoned, the sort of place high school boys would take over for their beer parties, screwing girl friends in the empty upstairs room, condoms out the window afterward. With E.J. off to California and the land to be farmed but the house not lived in, this would surely be the future here.

Near the barn I noted the deep, fresh ruts made by Orvall Beams's truck as he'd backed up to the chute to load E.J.'s pigs —perhaps an hour ago. The two Holsteins reluctantly allowed me, a stranger, to force them into the stanchions and, after holding back a bit, submitted to my unfamiliar hands on their teats. Later, I managed to run the milk through the separator in the dark shed attached to the barn. Then I heard the telephone ringing in the house. E.J.'s call was one long ring on the party line. Over and over again the switchboard operator gave one long ring. I thought it must be Maureen, for the wild bell had the particular quality of alarm she injected into her voice in emergencies.

I grabbed the receiver and said "E. J. Walczak" into the mouthpiece. When you answered someone else's phone you always said the owner's name.

"E.J.?" A strange woman's voice. "I'm at Buzzy Burns's hotel. Just drove down. I've *got* to see you. Is the coast clear— or is somebody there?"

"No—no . . ."

"Good. I'll be out."

Now I was locked into the deception. "The roads—"

"You know me. I'll be out." She hung up.

The blackness and silence of the room enclosed me. I stood motionless in front of the dead telephone as if in a confessional —and had just been told of a crime. *She* was the person who'd caused Winnie's death. A young, devil-may-care woman. She'd do *anything.* "Let her come," I said out loud, but my voice in the empty kitchen scared me. "Got to get some light."

I found a box of matches in the cupboard and lit one after another as I searched the pantry, cabinet, and parlor for a kerosene lamp or candle. Upstairs I finally found an oil lamp but the wick was rotten and I couldn't lift it out of the slot. I was still burning match after match in the kitchen, trying to get the thing going, when headlights flashed in the yard. I stood there immobilized, unable to think what to do, how to trap her —force her to explain who she was. I pushed aside the silk drape to see the yard through the front-room windows. She stopped the car under the box elder, leaving the parking lights on. Slammed the door. She carried a lighted cigarette as she walked toward the kitchen door. She knew the way. The burr of fire zigzagged around her left side like a firefly. "Jack?" she called softly, voice low-pitched, musical. She stepped onto the back porch, opened the door. "You in the house?"

"Mmm."

"Whyn'tcha turn on some lights?"

My mouth went dry and I felt a pull in my groin, a rapist's urge. Any moment she might discover the fraud and try to run away. I imagined myself grabbing her, hauling her to the floor.

"What're you doin' in the dark? Lights knocked out?"

"Uh-huh." She'd come for only one thing, now that the obstacles were gone. Must want it bad. I was so aroused I could hardly stand up straight.

"You sound funny. What's the matter?"

I stepped back, farther into the corner of the room. If she threw a flashlight beam on me now she'd think me a sex fiend ready to pounce—and she'd be right. I tried to cool myself by remembering what had happened here, how Winnie'd lunged at E.J. with a butcher knife.

"I'm scared, Jack. Why didn't you call me? Christ! I wish—I wish we'd been more careful. Where *are* you?"

I heard her rooting in her purse. "Here's my lighter." Suddenly the room was lit.

"Yaiiiiiiiiiiiii!" She gagged on a shriek that couldn't break through—and then her screams began. She wasn't looking at me—but past me. And I felt a weird sense of someone directly behind me at the silk curtain—a presence as sharp as an electric current. Then she threw the lighter at me. I pushed against the table and knocked over the kerosene lamp. She fell, and I heard a thunk of bone, but didn't stop. I rushed out of the kitchen as if propelled—and down the path toward the car. I jumped in, spun the wheels and ground the gears as I roared out of the yard. The spook in there had driven me wild.

Then I felt a piercing pain under my left nipple. An iron clamp squeezing my heart. I fell upon the steering wheel so heavily I pressed the horn, and the *aaaaaauuugah!* brought me to—only a second before the front wheels teetered on the brink of the ditch.

Sharp pains came in successive waves. I was surely having a heart attack and must get to the hospital before I lost consciousness. I reached the graveled road and sped off toward town.

But I wasn't driving my own car—it was the girl's! Not a '38 Chevy but a '37, and the seatcovers were blue plaid not tan. Maureen had our car. I slowed and wondered if I should turn back. My chest pains weren't quite so severe, but if I didn't make the emergency room, I might be dead. Let the girl in that dark house deal with Winnie's ghost as best she could. Surely she'd seen something. I'd felt a strange, unearthly tugging, some presence. Or was it just my imagination, brought on by Sheila's suggestion?

I stopped the car and tried to breathe slowly, ease the panic, still not certain if my heart was conking out or if it was all hallucination. An automobile drew up behind, slowly passed, the passengers twisting their heads to see who was stopping and *why*. The driver braked. He was going to be a Good Samaritan, damn it. I threw in the clutch and started forward. The vehicle ahead of me speeded up, disappeared.

When I lifted my arm to the top of the steering wheel, I felt the pain. Again I stopped the car. In a rush the past days came to me: my dark premonitions on my birthday, the despondency; I must've sensed I'd soon be leaving this life. Disasters, all misfortunes came in threes. Winnie's end on Monday had just been the beginning of this sackful of bad luck hanging over our heads. One feels the burden most fully in the moment of release from it.

But to my surprise I continued to number among the living. I drove slowly. Operating the car was one way to manifest my presence upon the earth, even though I'd no destination, nowhere to go in the borrowed car except back to E.J.'s farm, where that blonde waited for me—no doubt furious—me running off with her car. I planned to turn around in the next road gate.

All in good time. I felt drained of energy. The ghost of Winnie had sucked me dry. Upon reaching a hill crest, I saw glittering Kaleburg lying in the center of gentle slopes, windows winking like stars. The light on top of the water tank was just as big as the North Star behind it, and the Big Dipper seemed to be pouring into the tank. The Catholic steeple with its luminous clock was a dignified shaft, a reassuring sight. I felt like a medieval pilgrim returning after a long journey and setting eyes once again on civilization, friends, and the old faith. My limbs seemed so heavy, now that the pain was gone, I wanted to fall upon the seat and try to sleep. In the light of the dashboard I read the vehicle registration clamped to the steering wheel: "Betty Kinwald, 288 Ohio Street, Missouriville, Iowa."

Betty Kinwald and E. J. Walczak. When Winnie found out about their affair, she'd grabbed a butcher knife. Now I knew everything essential. Turning around, I noticed a bonfire glow on the horizon behind me—a farm fire!

She'd thrown her lighter at me and I'd knocked over the kerosene lamp when I fled. This time the house was *really* on fire—and burning fast. Had she been able to get out in time—even though I'd practically trampled over her in my haste to leave?

What should I do? I couldn't be an able-bodied man at the fire, even if I wanted to turn back. Only a hospital examination could determine what was the matter with me. Since I felt no discomfort in some positions and only suffered pain when I lifted my arm, I might have pulled a muscle in my rib cage—when I shoved the table aside.

How long had I been gone from the house? Ten minutes? Half an hour? I couldn't tell in the least. I sat there with the motor running, headlights on, wondering what to do—and excusing the fact that I was doing nothing. Each time I agonizingly turned to look, the glow of the fire seemed brighter.

At last the siren in Kaleburg began a whooping crescendo, followed by the smaller, sharper siren of the fire truck, clearing traffic from its way. I leaned forward to throw the car in gear, but the excruciating pain came back. I had to remain absolutely still. And yet, in a few minutes, the truck and cars of the volunteer firemen would storm down this very road. See me sitting here. Somebody would stop to ask what was the matter. How'd I explain Betty Kinwald's car?

Maureen, E.J.—everybody at the wake knew I'd been doing chores on the farm.

I let out the clutch and faced the traffic, and the siren baying like a hound after prey. Nobody would recognize me behind my headlight blaze. Horns blared, admonishing me when I didn't dim the lights, but soon the fire truck and the dozen cars were gone. I reached the paved highway. The hospital was still ten miles away. I felt much better. Hardly any pain, just a weariness. Was it still necessary to turn myself in at the emergency room?

I wanted to extricate myself from this mess as fast as possible. First of all, I had to dispose of the hot car. Leave it in front of 288 Ohio Street, keys tucked under the visor. It'd give me a little time to think out a story. No explanations could be demanded if I wasn't around at the scene of the fire. Everybody'd be so busy asking Betty Kinwald questions they wouldn't think about me—except Maureen, E.J., and the others. They'd be thoroughly mystified, perhaps alarmed. Sheila might blurt out something. The little snipe would love to get something on me! How she'd work me over, later, with her pert, seemingly innocent questions. But E.J. might be the most dangerous. Furious with me for scaring Betty and running off, leaving the house to burn. The guilty often turn upon an innocent bystander—implicating him if possible. Now the whole farm deal might fall through.

Surely the pain in my chest was reason enough to explain everything. A convenient malady of course, but none the less real to me. But what I couldn't account for was that peculiar sensation of Winnie's presence. Only Betty Kinwald could verify that —we'd shared an experience—though she'd probably say nothing about it to E.J.

I refused to let myself brood on the possibility that Betty Kinwald had died in the fire because of my panic. Instead, I pictured Maureen and the others at the funeral home the moment they heard about the fire. I imagined them rushing out to their cars and driving to E.J.'s farm, leaving Winnie alone at her own wake, the lace over her brow making her seem misty and distant, so quiet. Whereas actually she'd been right in that farmhouse. I'd felt her unmistakably. I'd swear to it in the face of every doubter. And yet, I'd never believed in ghosts before —and didn't now. Just in Winnie, and in her power to come back if she wanted to.

As I neared the city, I wondered if Maureen might return home before I'd a chance to get there and set her mind at ease about my safety. Like any crook fleeing the scene, I wasn't thinking well. I should never have driven the car all the way to Missouriville. I should've gone back, run toward the burning house like everyone else, hiding myself in the natural behavior of all my excited neighbors. Now, once I'd ditched the car, how'd I manage to get home?

Streetlamps lit up Betty's vehicle, exposing me. I drove directly to the business area, which was filled with traffic, for the movie houses were just letting out, and parked in front of the department store where Elsie and Marie worked.

"I'm scared, Jack"—about what? And, "I wish we'd been more careful." Pregnant . . . worried now that E.J. might leave her, even though she'd forced the issue by letting Winnie know. Probably as a last resort. The only way she could make E.J. take responsibility for the coming child. Work it through Winnie, never realizing the woman's mind could snap in such a crisis. And scared, now, because the consequences of her move resulted in death for Winnie. E.J. might turn against her for the trouble she'd caused. Worried because he hadn't tried to phone. Knew he'd probably be off to California soon—perhaps without her.

None of these speculations helped my present circumstances. Too many people knew I'd been on E.J.'s farm doing chores almost within the hour of the fire. Where'd I gone—and why? Even more practically, how was I to get home? Luckily, I never left without my wallet. Could buy a ticket—except there'd be no trains this late. Maybe a bus. But dare I show up at Buzzy Burns's in Kaleburg, step off a bus, and have people ask: You been on a trip somewhere?

Lord, what a fix! I started the motor and drove to Ohio Street, parked, and left the car as planned. Then I walked the six blocks to the Railroad Hotel, scene of my early, desperate debauches. First of all, I must phone Maureen. The lobby phone booth provided some privacy. Nobody answered at home. The Kaleburg operator wondered if I'd care to leave my name and number. The guy was snooping, perhaps recognized my voice. Everybody's gone to a fire on a nearby farm, he said. The Missouriville long-distance girl, voice heavy with sarcasm, having to deal with a bumpkin operator, asked if I'd heard that? Instead of replying, I hung up.

That nosy operator was fishing all right, otherwise he wouldn't have mentioned the fire. I wiped sweat from my brow and emerged from the booth. The desk clerk eyed me uneasily. They scrutinized strangers pretty carefully on account of the goings-on with the girls upstairs, sales of liquor by the drink next door in the hotel bar—all of these illegal activities squared with the local cops—but there was the danger, always, some snooper from the state attorney general's office might turn up. I glanced down at my overalls, Red Ball overshoes halfway to my knees, manure on them; I looked the farmer I was. As if I'd come to town with my trucker, accompanying a load of hogs to market.

Exactly! I'd go to the stockyards right now and bum a ride home with someone. Might even find Orvall Beams whiling away the time in the Stockyards Café, where truckers gathered before making the trip home. Since Orvall had taken E.J.'s hogs to market earlier this evening, he'd be on his second round by now. And with Orvall there'd be no need to explain anything. He loved company on the monotonous trips to and from the stockyards; he'd welcome me without asking questions.

I hurried along a street, took a stairs leading to the ground level, and crossed a no-man's-land of intersecting tracks, past a yardman's switch house, painted signal blades like weather vanes. The meat-packing houses were giant silhouetted building blocks set against the inflamed clouds hovering low, and the sickening, sweet smell of butchered flesh was strong.

I ran the risk of finding another Kaleburg farmer in the Stockyards Café. If so, I'd blab about Elsie and Marie, who'd wanted to attend the funeral. Talk about Uncle Jasper coming down from North Dakota.

I reminded myself I'd done nothing wrong except borrow Betty Kinwald's car without her permission, because I felt desperately ill and needed to get to the hospital. The pain in my chest returned at once, as if in confirmation, when I lifted my arm a certain way. I paused, dropped to one knee, and rested like a runner. If she suffered Winnie's fate and succumbed in the burning house, E.J. and I were bonded, shared a burden of private guilt. Brothers now, not just brothers-in-law. *Outside* the law, in fact.

The windows of the Stockyards Café were bearded with
steam from the vats of boiling fat and the coffee maker, but I
could see inside well enough to determine nobody was there I
knew. Even the waitress wasn't the usual Faye, a hearty bottle-
blonde, who talked like the saltiest thresherman in the country.
Nothing shocked her, and she could give back randy remarks in
full measure, so long as a man smiled while he talked dirty.
You could say any smutty thing you had a mind to. Many a
church elder and family man emerged from the café after a
running bout with Faye looking as refreshed as if he'd risen
from her bed.

As I walked in and sat down on a counter stool, I caught my
image in the mirror behind the custard pies: eyes bloodshot,
cheeks feverish pink. The shy farm-girl waitress slid me a glass
of water. "Yeah, what'll it be?"

"Coffee, regular."

Ten o'clock. Orvall ought to arrive soon, stomping in, shouting greetings to everybody, strangers and friends alike, ready
with a fresh off-color yarn. Tales came out of him like an endless tapeworm.

The minutes ticked away. Twice the girl filled my cup, and at
last I ordered apple pie, just to keep sitting there.

The door opened. Orvall at last! I waved him over to me.

"What the hell're *you* doin' here? Don't tell me you got yourself another trucker, you son of a bitch!"

"No . . . no, I figure you bruise my pigs bad enough in that
crate of yours . . . without having somebody else bang 'em up
worse."

"Whaddya mean? I'm so careful you'd think I was haulin' a
load of eggs."

We joshed back and forth, and I slipped in the fact that I
needed a ride home. Orvall said, "Sure, come along," then
pounced upon the new girl and tried to tell her an off-color
story to make her blush, but she turned away. "August, did you
hear the one about the man and woman in Pullman upper
berths? Talking love, back and forth across the aisle, wondering how they could manage to get together without one of 'em
having to climb down, over, and up. The guy was an ironing-

board salesman, see, and he happened to have a sample right in the berth with him. 'I've got something long and hard you could crawl over on,' he tells her. Then the fellow in the lower berth, who heard all this, pipes up: 'But how in the hell will she get back?' "

I laughed with him as we rose to leave, climbed into his truck. Orvall soon began another story. I had to be a genial companion and so I tried to listen, but I couldn't follow the yarn and feared I might miss the punch line. Then I remembered Orvall roared at his own jokes before anybody else had a chance to. This tale was more complicated than his usual ones —something about a lazy fornicator who had a device in the barn whereby his woman in a hay sling was lowered upon him by means of a block and tackle, with a team of horses doing the work. "Whoa! Giddyap! Whoa! Giddyap! Whoa! Giddyap! And *her* in the hay sling, up and down on top of him—under the block and tickle!"

An eruption of laughter. In the dashboard light, Orvall's face looked engorged, brown-berry eyes glinting behind oval lenses. He rocked left and right with each "Whoa! Giddyap!" until he nearly veered into the oncoming traffic.

"Where do you hear them stories, anyhow?" Thinking: You stupid ass, I could tell you something that'd make you sit tight on your prick the rest of your days. "I'm scared, Jack," Betty Kinwald had said. "I wish we'd been more careful." Winnie dead . . . and maybe Betty Kinwald, too.

Orvall urged me to tell a joke, but I said I couldn't think of any as good as his. "Let's hear 'em, anyhow!" High on the seat behind the flat steering wheel, he was like a mad child in a kiddy car. But I couldn't remember a single story. He began one, though I fell into a morose silence, which finally dampened his ardor. He apologized. "I forgot about—about the sorrow in your family. I mean, I didn't—"

"Don't worry. Helped take my mind off things."

He dropped me off at my road gate and I made my way down the lane toward the dark house. The weather was very unsettled, a slowly heaving wind and low-flying marbled clouds. It seemed the world was veering toward the outer reaches, and I was on the rim, watching. I longed to stay out in the wild night just a little longer, away from the pulls of domestic circumstances—family, work, property—these things consuming my life. How easy it'd be to let go and never return to any of this again—never come back. Why did I have to "face the music" and lie my way out? Many a man disappeared and found a totally new life elsewhere under a different name. E.J. would soon enjoy that rebirth. He was "Jack" to Betty Kinwald, though I'd never heard anybody else call him that. He'd be "Elmer" (his first name) to some girl in California.

The dog's vicious barking surprised me. "Shep! Shep! Don't you know me?" Weren't animals supposed to recognize their masters by scent? Unless, like Rip Van Winkle, I'd been on some long sleep of years. Shep finally leapt upon me, snorting with pleasure, relieved to be out of his watchdog responsibilities.

Why hadn't Maureen left a lamp burning in the dining room, which she usually did when she went to bed before I returned home? Could the electricity *still* be off? To my astonishment, the kitchen door was locked. Surely everyone was home by now—the door hadn't been locked this evening when we left together. I walked round to the front door but found it locked, too. Our car was in the garage—and Marie's was parked at the gate. They were all in bed.

Whatever possessed Maureen to lock up tight this way? I felt like rapping on the door and shouting, "Open up!" but knew I could quietly enter the house through the cellar window, where I'd been tossing wood. I kicked the frame open with my toe, for it hung loose from the top hinges. Then I eased myself through the casement and dropped onto the woodpile. Utterly black in the cellar, except for a faint red eye from the furnace door. Gradually my pupils adjusted, and I found the stairs leading up to our bedroom. Step by step, hands out in front in the strangler's position, I made my way. I moved as surely as a blind man in his own house. The hinges creaked as I opened the bedroom door.

For the second time that night a woman screamed in my face. "Aaaaaaaaaaaai!" Maureen wailed. "Help! Help! Oh, my god!"

"It's *me!* You locked me out."

"Oh, oh, oh . . ." She fell back upon the pillows, her body moving convulsively. I found the bed-light chain and pulled. She looked at me as if she'd never laid eyes on me. "Where've you been? Why're you sneaking up on me like that?"

"Mummy!" Sheila rushed into the room, in her flannel night suit. "What's the matter?"

"Nothing, dear. Father's home."

Elsie and Marie called from upstairs.

"The doors are all locked. I had to come up through the basement," I said to Sheila.

"Oh?" She looked at me measuringly . . . very interested.

Marie and Elsie hovered at the doorsill as if they weren't allowed in the marital bedroom, the way Shep was trained not to enter the kitchen from the porch, even if the door was open. They kept asking questions, and to quiet them Maureen offered to fix a pot of cocoa. As we moved toward the kitchen, Sheila told me about the fire. "The roof fell in just as we got there."

"A total loss," said Marie.

"The fire department hoses . . . sucked the well dry," said Sheila.

"We were so worried—where *were* you?" asked Elsie.

"We told everybody you must be around somewhere," said Sheila.

"I made you shut up," said Maureen. "We didn't tell *any-thing*." She glanced at me, angrily. Her uncombed black hair standing out from her head gave her a look of astonishment.

"I went along with Orvall Beams to Missouriville. He shipped out E.J.'s hogs tonight."

"But that wasn't the plan," said Maureen.

"I figured there'd be enough people at the wake—without me, too." Since they'd said nothing about anyone having been caught in the fire, I felt relieved.

"A second fire! It *does* seem suspicious," said Marie.

"If this doesn't bring out the sheriff, he ought to be impeached," said Elsie.

"And E.J.—was he there?"

"He certainly was," Maureen said.

"With his nephew . . . and cousin."

"A cousin?"

"Some woman the boy brought, I suppose," said Maureen.

I felt a great burden lift, like an angel going to heaven. "Well, E.J.'s probably more eager than ever now. To go off to California."

"Why didn't you tell us, Daddy, you were riding with Orvall Beams to the stockyards?"

"I didn't know then. It just happened."

"You were supposed to be picked up later—by Mummy, or E.J."

"What happened to the suitcase?"

"Got burned up, I suppose."

"No," said Maureen, "they found it on a hook in the cow barn."

"Oh, yeah, I forgot. That's where I slung it, first thing."

"Still there," said Maureen.

All of them looked at me queerly.

"No need to wear a suit to the stockyards, is there? I *did* try to phone you, Maureen, but nobody answered."

"At the funeral home?"

"No . . . here."

"Why'd anybody be here? You knew the wake was on." Maureen drew her robe closer. "Everybody finished? Let's go back to bed."

After closing the bedroom door, Maureen crawled under the covers. "Well, tell me now."

"There's . . . not an awful lot to tell." I kept my back to her as I undressed.

"I never let on to anybody, how worried I was. I pretended you'd made plans to go somewhere, would be back soon. But why did you put me through that? *How'd* you happen to set fire to the house? And then to run away like a . . ."

"I was lighting the kerosene lamp—and it broke somehow. The fire flamed up and it scared me so . . . so much, I shoved the table away. Then I had a terrible pain in my chest."

"You what?"

"Like a heart attack, I thought." Now with hand over my left breast it was cross-my-heart-and-hope-to-die.

"But you're okay now?"

"It comes back, now and then. Must be a pulled muscle in my chest wall. But I thought it was my ticker. I had to get to a hospital and grabbed the first ride I could."

"With Orvall? Just like that?"

"I'm tired, Maureen."

"The doctor looked at you—or what?"

"No, I never got there. But I'm all right now. Except, I'm exhausted!"

"I don't understand what's going on. But I know *some*thing is."

"I've *got* to lie down—I'm really done in. I'll sleep on the couch."

"Wait, August!"

"I—I can't talk anymore tonight, I tell you." I snatched the comforter from the foot of the bed and started to leave.

"Don't go out there to the living room! What'll Elsie and Marie think—if they find you there?"

"That's the important thing, huh?" I left.

I didn't want to lie close beside her because what was in my head might spill into hers. We'd often think the same thought at the exact moment and almost speak aloud in unison—those times we were close. Now I only wanted to be by myself to brood upon this business.

Stretched out on the couch, I tried to relax and think of nothing, but memory of the strange sensation of feeling Winnie at my back kept me awake. Easier to explain the phenomenon of a meteor landing in the back pasture.

I slept a little, and as it began to get light I rose, body aching, and went to the window. Another wintry day, though a few bars of rose and blue on the horizon suggested spring pastels. I moved into the kitchen to make coffee and experienced that delicious sense of early-morning privacy Maureen enjoyed each day. The cats on the porch heard me, leapt upon the windowsill, and I feared their cries might wake the household. I cut a wedge of coffeecake and drank the scalding coffee. I planned to stay far away all morning until I could get my thoughts in order. The farm would take me over; every stretch of my mus-

cles in chores this morning—even if my chest pained me—
would seem welcome exercise; the bushel of corn on my back a
pleasurable burden. I'd reached the limits of my mental endur-
ance, but the earth was here ready to have me on its own terms
of thoughtless labor.

By late morning I'd become increasingly uneasy at the
thought of not encountering E.J. until the funeral today. Whatever he had to say, I preferred to hear it in private. But when I
drove to his farm, nobody was around, the car gone.

The ruined house lay in a charred, smelly heap, one beam
slightly thrust in the air, like the mast of a sinking ship. The
house had been small, but its absence now loomed large; the
scraggly grove seemed more pathetic than ever. The yard had
been badly chewed up by heavy traffic. The barns were silent—
all the livestock gone, even the milch cows. An immense quiet
everywhere, now that death and destruction had ended. A
robin sang in the spindly grove. From now on everything would
be different here. I wondered if all the old had been eradicated,
or was there a rotten streak still in me waiting to be ripped
apart by further disasters? The sun was a warm mantle on my
shoulders. It was time for me to come once again into my own,
and this land would help me. I felt hopeful, almost exhilarated
—for the first time in years, terribly alive.

11

The Promise

T his town's changed a lot since 1914!" Uncle Jasper said, smiling, as the train chugged away from the station.

"So've you!" I picked up his suitcase and suggested we go up to the church for the noon meal, before the funeral.

"Cup of coffee first—have we time?" Eyes magnified behind thick glasses.

"Okay by me." I didn't like to hurry an eighty-year-old prodigal son the moment he returned home. He looked neat but poor, most of the nap gone from his suit and overcoat. He'd cut his chin, probably while shaving in the wobbly train lavatory, and a bit of toilet paper still clung to the scab. An old smell about him—musty from having lived alone in his own atmosphere in a closed winter room—but his step was lively enough.

I held open the café door and we found stools inside along the counter. He told me in 1914 there'd been no paved streets and on a day like this buggies and wagons filled Main Street. "You couldn't hardly move."

I remembered the scene well enough from boyhood but let him flatter me by suggesting I was too young to know anything about early times.

"Store roofs came right out over the boardwalks, and you'd tie your team to the railing. Mud everywhere . . . not this clean pavement. Hogs laying round in puddles or running loose among the wagons, chickens pecking kernels out of horse manure . . . what a sight! You should've seen Kaleburg then!"

Jasper asked about Winnie in a dutiful, uninterested fashion, then quickly changed the subject. "See that waitress? She's my girl Arlene—to a *T* . . . when she was that age."

"Where's she at now?"

"Married. Grown up, you know."

"How should I know? We don't hear from you—ever."

He grinned. "Arlene got married when she was only eighteen. Travelin' round the country with her man, ever since. Exhibit they show at fairs and carnivals—a miniature farm—works mechanically, underneath. Her husband made it. Nice fella. Born in the Old Country."

"I'd like to see it sometime."

"People pay money to look it over."

"Carnival comes here every summer."

"I'll tell 'em. Maybe they'll head your way."

"Have to keep an eye on the time. They're serving up at the church right now."

"Oh, sure, we'll get there." Jasper winked at the waitress, a shy farm girl, hair tied back with a green candy-box ribbon. She blushed but didn't dare smile back. "Good to be in the old home town, I say! Yet . . . when I married I wanted to run as far away from this burg as I could. Even before getting hitched, I was always slipping away . . . playing my fiddle for dances, earning a dollar here 'n' there. Haylofts . . . lots of barn dances back then. Nothing like dried bluegrass to make a smooth dance floor. Me 'n' my buddies played Mankato, Faribault, Sioux Falls, you name it. The Smilin' Six. Oh, what times we had! Wonder whatever happened to those guys. Smilin' Larsen—he was a real devil—always up to some mischief. Remember once in Minnesota we got an Indian girl drunk—a saloon girl, you know the kind I mean. They took turns on top of her, but I wouldn't. They couldn't get me to. I was so stubborn it made 'em mad and sobered 'em up. Course,

then they were ashamed of themselves and kind of hated *me*
for showing 'em up. When people are being animals, they've
got to *all* be animals. There was an awful lot about them early
days I never told anybody. Ordinary landladies wouldn't rent
us rooms. Had to find quarters with the scum of the town.
Treated like Gypsies . . . and the lice and bedbugs! Half our
crew had the clap—oh, it was something! Our drummer finally
quit 'cause his belly went bad, so he couldn't eat nothing but
milk and custard. Smilin' Larsen finally broke up the band . . .
in Mankato. Ever been there? A good railroad town. Larsen
sent for his wife and kids, opened a restaurant. I cooked and
helped out—met Agnes. Got married."

"More coffee?" asked the girl, pot high in front of us.

"No," I said, "we're goin'. Here's your dime."

"Agnes and me didn't have a church wedding, either. Just us
two alone in the world, *that's* how I wanted it. Right at the core
of things. Whatever we used for money, I can't say. Agnes had
saved a little from pulling beer. Anyhow, we put our money
down on a ranch in North Dakota because neither of us had
ever been there and it sounded like something to try. Poor land
—marginal land, I'd call it. Should've seen the little shack we
lived in. If the water in our well'd been much harder you
could've walked on it. Barnacles formed on the side of Agnes's
washtub, like on the prow of a ship. I thought we'd laugh and
get through, but just when *her* feet began to drag I'll never
know. After Arlene was born she got run down and depressed.
Delivered the baby myself in the middle of a blizzard. No experience with anything like that, except once I had to yank a calf
out, breech birth. It's all the same when you come down to it.
But Agnes didn't have no milk in her. Couldn't nurse the baby
—and she never got over it. I finally had to put her away. Kept
trying to kill herself. So, me 'n' the girl had to manage by ourselves. And we did."

Just then Bill Wolbers strolled in, letting the door slam dra-
matically behind him—as always—so that everyone would look
up and he could call, "Hi, Sam," " 'Lo, Pete," or "What do you
say, Joe?" Then he'd invite himself to sit down next to the most
important man for him to see at the moment, whether to sell

seed corn, talk about an investment, or hustle a new account. He quickly swung onto the stool next to me, pulled off his red-and-black lumberman's cap, which had polished his bald dome to a gloss, and loosened his jacket. I introduced him to Jasper.

"Bet you know where *I* been. Out to E.J.'s. Slept right through the fire last night."

"A fire?" asked Jasper.

"I was dead tired from a trip to Omaha—my old lady didn't want to wake me. How'd it happen, August?"

"Beats me. I was down to the city with a load of hogs."

Jasper wanted to know all about it, and I told him my lies without having to look at Wolbers. "What a blow for Winnie's husband—it must be," he said, shaking his head. "On top of everything else!"

"Hell, he don't care," Wolbers replied. "Even though he didn't carry a penny of insurance on it."

"That much less to get rid of now," I said.

"You weren't going to use the house, anyhow, were you, August?"

"Only for storage—a corncrib or something."

"So I guess E.J.'ll want to leave for California all the sooner —quick as we can get the papers in order and signed."

Uncle Jasper scrutinized us suspiciously, as if we were horse traders. I rose from the stool. "Maureen'll be wondering what happened to us . . . she must've heard the train come in."

"You're going to take over that farm—is that it?" Jasper asked as we drove away.

"The deal's not through yet, so don't say anything."

"Oh, I won't. But this is a break for you, I take it."

"Well, sort of."

"Poor Winnie!"

Cars were so thick I had to park two blocks from the church. In order to ensure a sizable crowd for the feast and funeral, Maureen phoned neighbors, church friends—anybody she could think of. The hum of talk in the basement sounded like a swarm of bees. We descended the stairs, following our noses toward the coffee just brewed. About sixty adults and a dozen children stood silently behind folding chairs because the min-

ister was about to invoke the blessing. Two trestle tables ran
the length of the basement, with a roll of white crepe paper
down the center for a tablecloth. I spotted E.J. and his tow-
haired nephew at the far end, but he hadn't seen me yet. We
found our places at once. The Ladies' Aid Sympathy Committee trooped out from the kitchen, each in a ruffly apron
adorned with needlework, and we all bowed our heads as Reverend Kallsen mournfully intoned grace. Since half the people
were Catholics he tried to insert the whole Protestant message
into his prayer—the blood of Jesus Christ and salvation
through faith not deeds. At last he uttered "Amen" and let us
sit down.

I was so nervous about what E.J. would do or say, first
chance he had, I failed to make things easier for Uncle Jasper
at the table. After a few halfhearted remarks about the weather,
nobody sitting near knew what to say to the stranger from
North Dakota. His presence caused them to half choke on their
food. Made them fidget just to extend themselves into the position of an outsider and guess what he might think of Kaleburg,
of them. Such a stretch of imagination could give a fellow indi-
gestion. If you could get out of yourself *that* much, you got out
of Kaleburg.

"Jasper used to live here, you know. Before any of you guys
existed!"

Relieved smiles, guffaws, handshakes, and a gaggle of talk.

I caught E.J.'s glance—not the fury I expected, almost a hu-
morous scrutiny, speculative. Waitresses kept passing bowls of
cold macaroni and cheese, platters of sliced ham and chicken,
rolls, pickles, fruit Jell-O, and then a series of homemade pies,
to which you helped yourself without looking at the adhesive
labels telling whose they were. We ate like threshers. We ate
and ate to stay alive—because this was a funeral.

Maureen next to Reverend at the head of the table had a
rapt, almost holy look on her face, as if the pastor were Jesus
and she one of the disciples at the Last Supper. She played her
religious part triumphantly, lifted up by ritual into the security
of final rewards coming. Here and hereafter were one and the
same right now. For the moment she'd forgotten Sheila, who'd

left the table with the other children and gone outside to play on the church lawn. Maureen looked radiant—and remote from me. She was really serious about God.

The men separated from the women and drifted upstairs to smoke and discuss in private the peculiar fires, the suspicious circumstances of Winnie's death. I wasn't to hear any of it, though. Whenever Jasper and I came near they talked about livestock prices, a subject Jasper couldn't be bothered with—for he carried around inside him the immense news of his arrival in Kaleburg after twenty-nine years away. Wasn't that *something?* Yes, everyone agreed, it certainly was. But just what?

His quest to nail down meaning to his return made people uneasy. Only the minister should be raising questions about fate, time, and eternity—subjects which in an ordinary man's mouth sounded embarrassing. At funerals you were forced to accept passings of every sort—but here was Jasper, chirpy and spry, still going around as if he didn't realize his own grave was about two feet from his toes.

"This Uncle Jasper?" E.J. asked, extending his hand. And to me, a peculiar look. "Well, August, how are you?"

"All right. Where's your nephew?" I glanced around. "And the blond woman?"

"Oh, she's back home now. Found you'd parked her car right in front of her house."

"Who's that?" Jasper asked, eyes blinking as if he expected ordinary answers.

"Nobody you know," I said. "Nor me, either."

"But you *will.*" A slow smile, as if the joke was on *me.*

"I don't see how."

"The house—that was terrible, having your house burn down," Jasper said. "Nothing saved?"

"No lives lost. That's a thing to be thankful for—right, August?"

"People tell me lightning did it, but I don't believe it," said Jasper.

"August here set fire to it."

"Don't you believe *him,* either. He's just joshing."

"The hell I am."

"You two've got business to transact, so I'll leave you," said Jasper.

"No—stay here!"

"I told Wolbers to make it snappy. Hope to leave for California tomorrow."

"I'm off to North Dakota. Everybody's off to somewhere."

"And she's not going with you. That why she came out last night to find you?"

"You'll hear the whole story from her."

"Who's this?" Jasper asked.

"Oh, a mutual acquaintance," I answered.

"She's damned sore about the way you treated her last night. She might not've gotten out!"

"I know—I was sick—I had to—oh, never mind."

"Wolbers says he's just about got the papers ready—will have, by ten tomorrow morning. Be at the bank. No need for a title search since it was done just ten years ago."

"You're selling out, I hear," said Jasper.

"Yeah, August is buying my farm. We made a deal."

"You get to be my age, you don't care who owns what. Makes no difference."

Maureen came up to tell us we should now proceed to the undertaker's, where we were to sit with Winnie until time for the funeral. "Folks who haven't seen her yet like to come over before the service and sign the book."

Then the undertaker instructed us as to the exact order of lineup behind the hearse. "But where's Sheila gone to?" I asked Maureen.

"In the car already." The dark voice I knew so well.

Turning, I saw Sheila in the back seat of Marie's car. She'd fled the company of the other children for some reason and now sat alone in her coach like a crazy princess who forces her servants on and on to harder tasks. Maureen looked as if a cold, wet dishcloth had hit her. *This* was how she'd remain tied to the world despite her knowledge of achieving salvation: she *had* to go and take care of Sheila. The girl sat there knowing her mother would come: her father, too. There might've been some consolation for Maureen in the thought that in the next world Sheila, our mad child, would become a sane angel, but for now the heavenly life was merely a promise. Maureen was still *of* the world, trapped in domestic circumstances. She could no more extricate herself than a corn plant could pull up roots and walk.

When we arrived at the funeral parlor (leaving Sheila to her back-seat sanctuary), a record of organ music was playing wheezily behind drapes somewhere; curtains darkened the windows. Candelabras with electric lights made the room like a church. We lined up in front of the casket, Jasper stepping close for a good look. For me, one glance was enough: Winnie had become the usual embalmed funeral-parlor doll.

"How pleased she'd be to know Uncle Jasper came," Maureen whispered to me.

Elsie and Marie sniffled in their handkerchiefs. Casual church acquaintances crowded into the room. Suddenly Marie pushed against them in order to get out the front door. "Where's she off to?" I asked Elsie.

"To get the Brownie."

"Heavens!" Maureen frowned. "You'd think she could've thought of *that* before."

A few minutes later Marie returned, flash camera in hand, and screwed in a bulb. Everybody stepped to one side while Marie aimed at the coffin. It took a long time for her to focus. She kept squinting through the sighter, changing her position, adjusting the lens. "Turn it the other way," said Elsie in a voice loud enough to wake the dead. "You've got the fool thing upside down! Horizontal. Make it horizontal!"

At last Marie was ready to shoot. The brutal flash made us jump even though we anticipated it. "Wait a minute—another! Elsie, run get me another bulb."

"Now, girls," Maureen said, "Reverend's here. We have to get on with the service."

"Oh, one more," Elsie begged. "Just to be sure."

Another flash, and then Marie subsided. The minister took over and read a few passages from the Book of John. He also talked directly to Winnie, complimenting her on a fine life . . . "Good wife, sister, loving and cherished friend."

Then we all left for the church in stately, formal order: E.J.'s car after the hearse, then ours, then Marie's. The pallbearers, who were elders of the church, carried the casket down the aisle and all of us followed. The pews were full of standing people scrutinizing our faces, taking a ghoulish interest in our grief—or lack of it. Uncle Jasper must have shocked them, for he couldn't keep a grin from his lips as he gazed upon the scene: neighborhood people, practically a kinship, standing there to greet him. He nodded left and right and many smiled back at him.

The long sermon was remarkably impersonal, since the minister didn't know Winnie. He dwelt mostly on trying to convert the Catholics present, and when it was over we filed past the open coffin, family last. The undertaker slipped Winnie's engagement diamond and wedding ring off her finger and handed them to E.J., then closed the coffin lid.

For the cortege to the cemetery most families could muster enough shirttail relatives to cause the traffic on the highway to be stopped by the town marshal. But not us. Just a half dozen cars. Under the pine trees of the cemetery we stood around the open grave on paper grass. The waterproof coffin hung poised over the vault on suspension ropes, and after Reverend's final "ashes to ashes" it was lowered and disappeared into the ground.

"Well, that's it," said Jasper, turning away quickly.

"Yes, now let's—"

"Back to the church," Maureen said.

"I want to see the town."

"No, we're supposed to eat again," I explained to Jasper. "Come on."

The Sympathy Committee had brewed fresh coffee, and the leftovers from this noon were laid out: cakes, pies, and bowls of Jell-O. E.J. wasn't among us, for his nephew had to catch a train in Missouriville—a likely excuse, I thought. More probably, a last chance to see Betty Kinwald before departing for California. Had he actually intimated that Betty would try to look me up?

"I can't eat another thing," Jasper said, pushing away from the table. "Let's take a walk."

I informed Maureen we'd be gone about an hour.

"Don't run him around too much, August. He's old and he's got to take it easy."

"That's not his way."

Uncle Jasper was dying for a couple slugs of whiskey, so we headed for Meecher's Tap, which, under another name, had been operating since the 1880s. "Oh, I love this place, yes, sir. Had my first drink of hootch right here." We stood at the bar and cocked our feet on the brass rail. "When I was bartending the thing I liked was the good stories you hear."

"Men talk when they drink, all right."

"Rumors, gossip . . . the real goings-on, you know what I mean? A good country lawyer—he'll tell you the best tales you've ever heard."

"Most of 'em can't keep their mouths shut."

"That's the legal profession—one drama after another. Often thought *I* should've been a lawyer. But I learned plenty about the law just listening. Like . . . there was this young fella"—he grabbed my sleeve and lowered his voice—"took his girl into a cornfield, was having his way with her, see, but he promised he'd pull out in time."

"Famous last words."

"So he'd gotten right there to the point—but not over the point—you understand? Just hanging fire in there and real, real still. When a pheasant hunter comes stomping through the corn and steps right on his ass . . . driving it home. He was gone in her, just like that! *Now* the question was—when she got a baby—was it the hunter's fault, since he was the agent responsible? Isn't this an interesting case? The fella didn't want to marry the girl—couldn't—was already married, and he didn't want to pay for the kid's maintenance. Claimed in court the baby wouldn't't've been conceived if the hunter hadn't stepped on his ass. Have you ever heard of a case like this before?"

"No, I never have."

"How d'ya think it came out? Who won?"

"The father had to pay—not the hunter."

"Right! And you know why?"

"*He* had his thing in her—not the hunter."

"Right again! August, you'd make a crackerjack lawyer! Ever consider it? Maybe go to night school, study for the bar examinations? You sure don't seem like any farmer around here. Why'd you come back to work the land, anyhow? I left all that drudgery years ago, and I'm not a bit sorry."

"I may not be here . . . all my life. Might just take off and be gone like E.J., one of these days. Spend the rest of my years in California sunshine." Effortlessly, I could reveal to Jasper every secret longing I had, should such confessions be necessary. He looked at me from the serene distance personal freedom gives one. He'd nothing left to lose except his life.

"Another finger?" I asked him. "Make it two and a couple glasses of water," I told the bartender. We toasted each other and moved over to watch a pinochle game in progress.

"I *like* this bar, I really do. Hasn't changed one bit, far as I can tell."

"Around here, not much does."

He mentioned the ridge of trees a mile north of Kaleburg, still standing—just as when he was a boy, only now huge. He was trying to capture or measure the implication of this distance: the trees, himself—then and now. With what sextant could he draw a line to the heart of the mystery? Cast an eye down Kaleburg streets to Meecher's Tap. Farmers still gather to play cards, sip beer, tell stories. The dark, stained tables in the rear and these oak chairs made by a nineteenth-century cabinet worker, the black-walnut bar with beveled mirror—all the same, even the brass spittoons. The customers possess the faces they've always had and guttural German accents still hover in the air. Only *you* have changed.

"Same's ever," he muttered. "Just the same."

"Jasper, I wouldn't be saying this if I hadn't had a couple drinks, but I've a funny feeling nothing in my life is *ever* going to be the same again."

"Just because you're buying another farm? That'd be *more* of the same, I should think."

"I don't know *what* I mean, exactly."

"Why'd you bring it up, then?"

"I do . . . but I don't know how much to tell you."

"Oh, it's a woman. No man talks that way 'less it's a woman."

"Yeah, in a way—only not what you think. I'm involved all right, but—I guess I'm too drunk to make sense."

"You need fresh air. Let's go for a walk. Awfully stuffy in that church, I thought. Gave me a headache, but it's gone now."

I paid for the drinks.

"Poor Winnie, dead and buried. Miserable little thing, wasn't she? And I hear she didn't get on with that big silent husband of hers."

"You know that already?"

"I'm not shy about asking questions."

"He couldn't keep his pants buttoned, and *she* found out."

"So she killed herself, like everybody says."

I nodded.

"Let's drink up." He downed another finger and pushed a fifty-cent piece toward the bartender. This dividend of booze seemed to cheer him. "One loose cock in the barnyard and you're in trouble. Why . . . up home a guy by the name of Zucker had a reputation for getting himself into trouble, mostly with other men's wives. To look at his three-hundred-pound spouse, you could understand why. Folks said the only way he could manage it with her was dog style. He probably spread that story about himself—just like him to. Anyhow, he took a fancy to the eighteen-year-old daughter of the meat-locker man. Zucker kept thinking of reasons to open his compartment. Put in quarters of beef or came with arms full of sausages for cold storage, but the one in his pants he couldn't put where he wanted. No matter how often he went to his locker, he never found the girl alone—her dad kept such a close watch. And no wonder! Tits you never seen the like of—oh, my God! She drove Zucker wild. He filled his compartment so full of meat he didn't have no excuse to come to the locker plant anymore, except to take out steaks, ham, and rib roasts one day, bring 'em back the next. You never *seen* such traffic in meat, and yet the one piece he was after he couldn't get. Her dad pretended he didn't know what was bothering Zucker, and right in front of him he'd kiss and squeeze the girl, even fooling with her tits, the way a father can. Sort of laugh at Zucker for how hot and bothered he was. But one day Zucker finally caught the girl in there alone, and he went for her like a bull in springtime. When the father burst in on 'em—with a witness, of course—Zucker had the girl up on the butcher's block, hand under her dress— and as the old man told the judge, Zucker was 'all the way to her what-cha-may-call-it.' The charge was attempted rape and the girl won a handsome settlement, enough to pay for four years of college. Suppose she used the same methods on her college boy friends—think how far she'll go! Oh, if only you live long enough, you see everything. How things turn out, I mean. I'm crazy to know that!"

"Come, let's look over Kaleburg, if we're going to."

We toured the new Sale Barn, inspected the old ball park, which was in poor shape and showed the decline of semipro baseball in the boondocks. He peered at the glistening yellow boards of the new bowling alley and glanced in the door of the Cornflower Ballroom.

"Now, Jasper, tomorrow you can roam around some more, but right now we'd better get back to pick up Maureen and Sheila."

"I'm leavin' tomorrow on the morning train."

"What's the rush? You just got here."

"I seen all I want to. Ain't anybody left who remembers me, anyhow." He laughed, cheerfully accepting it.

"Just haven't found 'em yet, that's all."

"Who, for instance?"

"Smilin' Larsen."

"Where's he at?"

"Used to work in the Produce House. I'd see him when I brought down a crate of eggs, but lately he's not lookin' too hot."

"Sick, you mean?"

"Kidney stones, then ulcers. Had several operations. Wife died not long ago, and then he had trouble with the oldest boy —caught stealing a car. Sent to the reformatory down at El-dora."

"That *is* tough luck."

"Oh, you ain't heard the half of it. So many debts he's near bankruptcy, but he can't sell the house because his title ain't clear. And now they tell me his youngest girl got scarlet fever and it left her deaf."

"Lord! And he was such a smiling lad when I knew him. *No, thanks,* I don't want to look him up."

On our way to the church we strolled past a vacant lot with a boarded-up front. "Used to play a funny old bowling game here —right behind that fence. Know what I'm talking about, August? *Sien zu dem alles* they called it. Meant something or other in Low German. Three fair-sized wooden pins sitting in a bed of sand, with a single smooth plank in front of them. Every man in the game had to throw down a dime or a quarter—then you had a chance to roll the ball down the plank toward the pins. You lost if the ball fell off the plank, or if somebody else knocked over all the pins. You could buy back into the game by paying double ante."

"You bowled a lot?"

"No, but I'd watch by the hour. Stakes way up to fifteen, twenty dollars."

"Haven't played it there for years."

"Whatever happened to all those guys, I wonder."

"I wonder, too," I said smiling. Jasper caught my look and burst out laughing.

"Funerals! They never teach us anything, do they?" Another hearty laugh.

In the back seat of the Chevy on the way home from church, Jasper tried to fool around with Sheila, but she'd have none of his avuncular teasing. "She's so tired," Maureen explained.

"I'm not, either. I just want him to keep his hands to himself."

"Oh, oh! Oh, oh! Now she's giving it to me!"

Once home, Jasper changed clothes and put on a pair of my overalls to help with chores. He talked all the time—about impromptu horse racing on dirt roads with teams pulling empty hayracks, cockfights in out of the way barns, the day Jesse James's boys robbed the bank and shot up the town, the prairie fire that destroyed ten square miles in 1892, the last raid of the Sioux Indians, and the tornado that changed the course of the Missouri River. It was nearly dark by the time we returned to the house with the milk pails.

"I can't get Sheila off to bed," Maureen told me in her tired voice. "I *know* she's exhausted but she won't budge."

"I'll try." I found her curled at the end of the sofa, head half hidden behind a *Collier's*. "Up to bed, Sheila—this very minute!"

Slowly, she lowered the magazine, eyes dark and face very pale. "I'm going to telephone the sheriff."

"What*ever!*" Maureen said, behind me.

"The sheriff?" Jasper snorted. "To help you go to bed? He's other things to do."

"I'll get the law on you if you dare touch me!" She scowled, furious.

"Sheila, if you don't want a good licking, you'd better do as I say."

"For somebody who set fire to a house, that's not—"

"Stop it now!" I shouted, hand raised.

Sheila leapt from the couch to escape me. "There's a criminal loose in the house, and I'm going to tell the sheriff! I'm going to tell! I'm going to tell! Can't you get that straight?"

"Sheila! Child!" from Maureen.

"Who killed Aunt Winnie? Answer me that!"

"Sounds like some radio program," Jasper said. " 'Mr. District Attorney.' "

"All right, dear, all right," Maureen soothed, "maybe it *was* wrong of us not to say. She did away with herself . . . set fire to the kitchen and suffocated."

"I don't believe it."

"We knew Winnie should have a regular church funeral, so we gave out the story it was all an accident. Now that's the whole truth. I suppose, since you're a big girl, we ought to've told you."

"Yes, Maureen, for heaven's sake, you should have!" said Jasper.

"Especially since Sheila was so close to her."

"I still *am* close to her."

"Of course, none of us are going to forget her *ever*," Maureen agreed.

"That's not what I mean."

"It's bedtime, and this is no way to make yourself feel sleepy," I said.

"How can I sleep—with the voices telling me these things?"

"Voices?" Maureen and I spoke simultaneously.

"The voices said what happened over there. E.J. hit her on the head and knocked her out, then set fire to the kitchen. And on the night of the wake Dad lit a match to the whole thing because he wants to buy the farm and make it all different. You're together in this—and I'm gonna phone the sheriff."

"You do a crazy thing like that," I warned, "and I—I don't know—what measures we'd have to take."

"You'll never put *me* away! I'll see to it *you're* put away first!"

"August, don't threaten her," Maureen said.

"What'll we do with her?" I was alarmed by this sudden turn for the worse and knew that if she kept up her ravings I'd have to use her insanity to shut her up. Somebody might wonder if there was anything to what she said.

"Now, I've a solution," said Jasper.

"You do?" Maureen looked dumbfounded.

"Both of you go to bed and I'll sit up with Sheila. Answer any voices that might speak. How does that sound?"

"It sounds crazy," said Sheila.

"Indeed it does," I murmured, "but we'll take you up on it. Let's go to bed, Maureen."

After closing our bedroom door, I said, "Hope it works! Anything!"

"You're to blame."

"Okay . . . now what?"

"After what you pulled last night! So many unanswered questions, yet you go along just like always. If you were deliberately trying to drive the girl mad you couldn't think of a better way."

"No matter how I explained things, you'd never believe me."

"No, not anymore. I surely would not." She opened the closet door and undressed behind it, then climbed into bed. I kept my back to her and did the same. When I reached to snap off the bed lamp she said, "Keep it on awhile."

She opened the Lenten booklet, white cross on a purple cover, and began reading aloud in a low, liturgical voice—something she'd never done before. The sentences made an impregnable wall, a Maginot Line of the word of God. She flung each phrase about the passion of Our Lord and Saviour Jesus Christ as if throwing lances at me. All of it glanced off, each line fell away; I buried my head in the pillow and feigned sleep.

Next morning, Sheila refused to rise. "How late did you stay up with her, anyhow?" Maureen asked Jasper.

"Half an hour, no more. Anyhow, I'm all packed and ready, so I might's well go up and say goodbye." He started up the stairs calling her name gently.

"He's wonderful with her," Maureen said. "He'll make her snap out of it if anybody can."

"I wish he wouldn't leave so soon."

"We haven't even had a good visit!"

I glanced uneasily at the clock. "He'd better do the trick. I was going to drop him off at the depot before going to the bank to sign those papers."

"You're ready with the money?" Her tension eased; I could feel a softness in her. My duties at the bank suggested a hopeful future, advancement in life for us. Hard work, yes. But physical labor would become a vehicle for her martyrdom; she'd throw herself into farm chores right alongside me, and in this way, yoked in harness together, we could step forward. My eager concern over closing the deal today was also testimony to my interest in keeping our alliance intact. We hadn't been honest with each other about ourselves, but buying this farm nailed down our outer circumstances even tighter. Whatever the mystery of my peculiar behavior the last days, she must have thought at least this farm buying was normal, out in the open.

Clumping on the steps. "Here they both come," I said.

"Sheila—what're you doing with your coat on?" Maureen asked.

"I'm going with him."

"That's what the girl says, but since I can't push her into my suitcase, I don't know how we'll manage it."

"Uncle Jasper, take me with you! Please! Please! You see what it's like here. I can't live in this house anymore."

"First, your orange juice." He handed her the glass. She drank but wouldn't sit down. "That-a-girl."

"Have your breakfast, Sheila," Maureen said, pulling out her chair at the table.

"You'd hate it in my town."

"I would not."

"Golar is so small we don't even have a school. You'd have to ride the bus ten miles."

"I'm through school, ready for work."

"At thirteen?" I asked quietly.

"Anyhow, my landlady wouldn't allow me to take on a youngster. No children, in her house."

"I'm not a child! Do I look like a child?" She pushed out her chest defiantly as if daring me to look at her breasts. I did.

"Uncle Jasper, don't pay *any* attention to her," said Maureen. "August will drive you to your train and that'll be that."

"If you won't let me go with Uncle Jasper, I'll phone the sheriff and have him arrest you.'"

"You keep this up, we'll have to take you to Doc Shepley."

"Oh no, you won't! I know the tricks he pulled on Winnie. How she looked when she came back from Omaha after shock treatments. You won't get *me,* I tell you."

For a minute none of us spoke, figuring the silence might soothe her.

"I know . . . Sheila, listen: right now I can't invite you up to North Dakota. It's the middle of your school term—it wouldn't be right. Maybe, come summer . . . I'll write. Your folks could put you on the train. For a visit."

"Is that a promise?"

"Cross my heart." And he did.

"Say it all, then.

"Cross my heart . . . and . . . hope to die." But those last words were barely audible, he resisted them so strongly. "Now, August, let's go." Sheila remained home.

We left the house quietly. On the way he told me he'd meant the invitation; perhaps when Arlene was around to help. At the depot we tore open the delicate moment just a little, in saying goodbye, for both of us sensed we'd never speak again. But openly acknowledging such an intimation was no way to deal with it. A clap on the back instead, a hearty hail and farewell. I couldn't hang around for the train—and in fact was eager to cross the tracks before it pulled in and cut me off from the town—otherwise I'd never arrive at the bank on time.

Both E.J. and Wolbers were waiting impatiently. We joshed with each other in the fake way people do when some important matter is at hand. "Well now, here's the deed," said Wolbers, shuffling papers, "and these are the transfer documents. Now I need *your* signature here," he said to E.J., "and *yours* right there."

"That all?" I asked, returning his pen.

"No, not quite."

"All we're lacking is a check for fifteen thousand," said E.J. dryly.

"Oh, yeah! That's right!" I pulled open my checkbook and wrote with a trembling hand.

"There! Now, August, you're twice the farmer you were." Wolbers tugged at his white shirt collar, which seemed too big already for his chicken neck.

"Two things a farmer has to remember—and he'll be all right," E.J. said. "Tell the truth and shut the gate."

I laughed nervously and Wolbers looked puzzled. It seemed a peculiar thing for E.J. to say.

"Guess only farmers like me 'n' August can understand *that* . . . about remembering to shut the gate. Why, that's funny. Takes a lot of years of things going wrong . . . pigs trampling gardens or gettin' into the oats. Everything on a farm is controlled by gates."

"Guess so," said Wolbers, at a loss.

"Tell the truth and shut the gate—right, August?"

"Yeah, that says it all."

Wolbers stood up so we'd get the idea we were supposed to leave. "Let me know your address, E.J., soon's you get located out there."

"Oh, sure."

"We'll be seeing each other—before you go," I said, not wishing a full-scale salute and farewell.

"August, one thing . . ." Wolbers waved E.J. off, as I sat back down. "How're you fixed for seed corn? Hope you're planning to take over E.J.'s spring order."

"Sure, I'll try A-Maizing, though I've always done pretty well with Pioneer." I even agreed to buy emulsifier, to give the kernels a boost if the rains were late.

"We're happy to have you take over the mortgage, but don't get in too deep, buying machinery. We sure don't want to have to foreclose."

Wolbers couldn't resist patronizing me, now that the bank had a piece of me. I resolved to pay off the mortgage as fast as possible in order to be my own free agent again.

On the way home, passing the farm that was now mine, I noticed the dealer in secondhand farm machinery loading a truckful of E.J.'s stuff. I might've found some of that equipment useful—but speaking up for it now wasn't worth it to me. I slowed at the road gate, came to a full stop. The absence of the house suggested to me that the barn should be removed, too. The buildings and feedlots took up a precious two acres. I wanted every last reminder of this place as a homestead removed.

Virgin land—right here! Lord, what a crop of corn I'd grow. I could see the heavy tassels on ten-foot stalks nodding in the overland wind. Those plants would feed on the decayed life of centuries, just as I expected my life to feed upon the compost of yesterday's memories—Winnie and all that had happened here properly forgotten as I worked away to make the land bear. There was always this consolation in the energy cycle of the earth. Half a billion years ago a vast inland sea covered this spot, the only life then a tiny sea lily and a few mollusk species and lichen. I thought of those vast reaches of time whenever I found the print of a seashell embossed on a pebble, looking like the crinkled cheek of a child after sleep. Of course, the virgin land here would peter out after a few bumper-crop seasons, but for years the corn would always look greener, stand taller. Eventually these two acres of soil would become much like all the rest; by then what had happened here would have passed from my memory, too—because of what working on the land did for a person. I'd have joined my life energies to the land's purposes—unless by that time I was six feet under, really *of* the soil.

The implement dealer drove away with a wave of his hand to me, and I climbed out of my car. For an hour or so I mooned around the place, feeling strangely at home—and surprisingly excited by the prospect ahead. Unlike the family farm, which had come to me through Father, this land was much more mine because I'd made it so. Foolishly, I even reached down and began pouring soil through my fingers, smelling it. I could do any ridiculous thing here because this farm belonged to me.

It was noon and dinnertime when I arrived home, mail tucked under one arm. Sheila at the table looked at me scornfully, her hair a mess, and several pimples had come into prominence on her cheek and chin. Her heavy thighs were tightly encased in her favorite green wool slacks. "Well, we're in business now, Maureen. I bought the farm."

"I know . . . E.J. stopped to say goodbye. Sold all his machinery and he's not getting a *thing* for it. The harrow only brought ten dollars. He paid ten times that for it."

"So he's gone."

"And that settles it," said Maureen. "He'll start a new life and we'll start ours."

"Nothing's settled! Don't kid yourselves," said Sheila. "There's still me. *I'm* still here."

I wouldn't take up that rag to chew. I'd had enough. "Jasper got off okay, I think. I couldn't wait for the train." As we began to eat I reported the last story he'd told me: about the bulldog-and-badger fights that used to be held under the bleachers of the ball park. Sheila became interested.

"Which one of 'em won?" she asked.

"Usually the badger because he could hug the ground so close no dog could get at him."

"Did the dog want to *kill* the badger?"

"It's instinct, you know," I said quickly. "The men watching bet on which animal would come out alive."

"Those were brutal times," said Maureen. Signals with her eyes—not a safe subject.

"And what about school for you this afternoon?" I asked.

"Oh, not today," said Maureen.

"All right—I'm not going to fight about it."

After eating I escaped legitimately to my work in the barns with the manure spreader. Three hours later, having been immersed in a world of animals and excrement, I felt serene, completely forgot the problems in the house. I might have parlayed my good mood if I hadn't made the mistake of looking in on wife and daughter before picking up the milk pails. I saw them on the sofa in the half-light, as if they'd been turned to stone: Maureen hovering, head lowered in concern; Sheila cowering, frightened and unhappy, under the maternal wing. "Isn't it time for Sheila's Indian Chief to come on the air?"

"I think it is!" Maureen said, falsely cheerful.

Sheila glowered at me, didn't move from the couch.

"Shall we tune in to Big Chief Bluewater—or are you going to?" Maureen asked softly.

"Woh-woh-woh-woh-woh!" I slapped my mouth in a war whoop, but she wasn't amused. Her addiction to that radio program was such that I knew she'd hate to miss an episode. The program, beamed from Chicago, was sponsored by an obscure breakfast cereal which we'd finally found in the city. After sending in three box tops and a quarter, Sheila received a red felt-covered booklet of passwords and signals. Last summer the Indian codes and rituals had been a favorite imaginative pursuit. She tiptoed around the grove, acting out ceremonials in the way of an only child, assuming all the roles herself.

"Ho-wah-ho, sawaka!" Maureen said, lifting three fingers, thumb and little finger joined, in the tribal benediction. "Ho-wah-ho, sawaka!"

"Be-nee-no-nee-nah," said Sheila finally, slipping off the sofa and running to the radio.

Maureen and I exchanged glances of relief and moved into the kitchen. "Any prayer," she said. "Or pagan words . . . anything that'll work!"

What worked for conversation that night at the table was our newly acquired land and how we'd manage to farm it. The more I warmed to the subject, with Maureen, the deeper became Sheila's silence. "We're counting on you to help, Sheila," I said, "soon's school's out this spring. You're old enough to drive a tractor. How about it? I'll teach you."

"Cheap labor, huh?"

"We'll figure out a wage, don't worry."

"How much?"

"A dollar a day."

"What hired man would work for that?"

"If you're able to work like a hired man, I'll pay you more."

"Everybody in this family has to pull their own weight," said Maureen. *"I'm* not working for wages."

"You're a fool not to ask."

"We're all in it together, don't you see," Maureen added.

"Not me. I'm not part—of anything."

We turned on the radio after supper in order to stop further dialogue, but when the programs ended at ten with the usual news about the wars in Europe and Asia, we stood up and declared it was time for bed. Sheila had her jigsaw puzzle spread out on the card table in a corner—a Swiss Alpine scene with several key pieces missing, though she refused to recognize that possibility. "Not till I've got it—I can't go to bed." She hovered over the problem, trying to make everything interlock, as if to solve the mystery of the universe. Maureen was too weary to keep on, said good night. I was afraid to leave the girl alone, for there was no telling what she might get it in her head to do. I read *Wallace's Farmer, Capper's,* and *Farm Journal* cover to cover, all the way to the truss ads. By midnight, when I could scarcely hold up my head, she still sat there puzzling herself over Switzerland. Suddenly she swept all the pieces to the floor and scampered up the stairs. "You pick 'em up in the morning —remember," I called.

Saturday and Sunday posed no threat of school; as a result, Sheila returned to "normal" with miraculous ease—so much so that Maureen and I were convinced she'd merely been putting on a show. Saturday night we shopped for groceries without incident, visited with neighbors on the street and in parked cars;

Sheila accompanied us without acting strange in the least. Sunday we all attended church, and later, after chicken dinner, I slept most of the afternoon with the radio going full blast in my ear. Some of our favorite programs were on that night, especially Charlie McCarthy, and Phil Spitalny with his All Girl Orchestra—most of them playing violins or harps. But the newscasts were grim, Panzer divisions were sweeping across Europe. The fact that only girls were left to play in an orchestra seemed depressingly appropriate.

Monday morning Sheila refused to eat breakfast, for she knew that at the end of the meal she'd have to start for school. Maureen drew up a chair and placed a comic book near Sheila's bowl of Cream of Wheat. "Now eat and read—go on." She thrust the spoon in Sheila's hand as if the girl were three years old. I watched more in pity than in anger. After endless cajoling, she was finally ready to be driven the mile to school— a distance she used to walk in the company of the neighbor children. We'd taken to driving her lately since she threatened to run away. How she hated that country school!

After delivering her, I swung past E.J.'s farm to indulge in a bit more proprietary dreaming. I kicked a few charred beams of the house and calculated the best way to remove the foundation bricks so that they could be used again. As I prowled around the place, a car drove into the yard. For a moment I didn't recognize either the vehicle or the woman driving it. She stepped out, sunlight on her blond hair, looking at me without a smile.

Betty Kinwald.

"Hello." And my first good look at her. About thirty— maybe older—the cool, direct manner of a woman who knows the world regards her as desirable. "Well, what brings *you* back here?"

"Came by, hoping to see you." Very matter-of-fact, a neutral voice. She slammed the door and her beige expensive coat swirled. She wore neat city galoshes.

"E.J. said you might." I moved closer, warily.

"Oh, he did?"

"I guess we haven't properly met."

"No." She extended her hand.

"So you're Betty Kinwald."

"August—right?" A silken shake, then she withdrew. "Forgive me for not recognizing you."

"How do you do?" I tried to keep it light, but my tight, nervous voice betrayed me.

"Not very well, thank you. Got a lump the size of an egg here—still." She touched her scalp gingerly.

Why had she come? "I'm sorry . . . I don't know what else to say."

"Surprised, huh? To see me." Teasingly, she leaned against the fender and folded her arms.

"Not really. E.J. said—"

"You know why?"

"Some kind of explanation—you'd want."

"That's what I had in mind."

"Well, I don't know where to begin."

"I mean—leaving me in there—running off."

"I know! It was your screaming started it."

"But what were you doing—hiding in there?"

"I wasn't hiding. The electricity was off."

"You know what I mean."

"Let me ask *you* what you saw there behind me—that made you scream."

"Behind you?"

"When you threw the lighter . . ."

"Nothing."

"There wasn't . . ."

"You standing there . . . and your shadow. It scared the bejesus out of me." She turned slowly to look at the ruins.

"If you hadn't thrown your lighter—there wouldn't've been a fire."

"No excuse for the way you lit out—and in *my* car. Me with only one page of ration coupons left. I could press charges, you know. Maybe I should've."

"Oh, you don't want the publicity, I should think." I had her there. Just the right squeeze to put her in her place. My remark kindled some kind of fresh interest. She looked me up and down, provocative—theatrical, something she'd seen in the

movies. A come-on but also a watch-out! I leaned against a
fender, casual as Gary Cooper. "Just looking over my farm
here . . . bought it last week." My voice had a hayseed crack
to it.

"Yeah, I heard."

"Imagine you sort of expected to go West with him."

"That's a nasty remark. Nasty as this bump on my head."

"Sorry."

"For your information, I'm not interested in picking up and
moving away."

She put on a brave front, but I remembered her anguished
"I'm scared, Jack." And "I wish we'd been more careful."

"I can't very well ask you in, but . . ." I turned to the
charred rubble.

"You could show me the barn instead."

I looked at her sharply. Her expression was surprisingly innocent. Didn't she know the salacious slant of that timeworn
phrase, "show you the barn?" "Not an animal there, not even a
cat."

"No swallows?"

"Not back from wintering—not till the mosquitoes and flies
come out."

We walked slowly toward the barn, side by side. What did
she hope to accomplish, driving out here to see me—on her last
ration coupons? The unmistakable drift of this meeting baffled
and stirred me. I felt peculiar about her, as if ours was a long
acquaintance already. She and I were the only ones, now that
E.J. was gone, who knew precisely what had happened here.
We were paired by that fact. I thought it odd she refused to
admit Winnie's ghost had spooked her, although in retrospect
the notion did seem crazy. That weird, powerful sense of a
presence could as easily be explained by my overworked imagination.

She questioned me about the barn, was surprised to learn I
planned to tear it down.

"I'll use the lumber elsewhere."

Having always lived in the city, she had the urbanite's fascination with—and romantic view of—country matters. Small-

town folks looked down on us, but from the distance of a city our lives seemed attractive, perhaps because there was nothing abstract about our labor. We produced food and fiber. We made it possible for people to live on cement streets in brick houses, far from any growing thing except a patch of lawn, a tree or two.

We moved from cow shed to cattle stalls to pigpens and on up to the hayloft, still furnished with leftover bluegrass in dusty piles here and there. A large cobwebbed window looked out over rolling prairie fields, as if the barn builder had cut a view for himself just for the hell of it. I wondered as we talked if she relished this chance to inspect E.J.'s stamping grounds—something she'd not been able to do while Winnie lived. And yet everything in her manner suggested E.J. was far from her thoughts now.

"What caused the bust-up, anyhow—between you two?" I asked finally.

"Not what you think."

We sat down gingerly so as not to send up a dust cloud. "How do you know what I'm thinking?"

"Not because of—the accident."

"Accident?"

"You know how it happened—he told you."

"Mmm."

"Even before all this, things were . . . you know . . . sort of not very good anymore."

"How long'd you two been—?"

"A year or so. A year and a half." She picked up a strand of hay and began to chew it, suck it. A very well-formed, sensuous mouth. "Mostly he'd come down to my place."

"Ohio Street."

"Yeah, you been there."

"Every front door looks like the next—can't see how you know which place is yours."

"Easy"—she smiled—"if you've lived there five years."

"You were born in the city?"

"I can tell you want my life history."

"I'll swap." But should I? Even as we talked easily and

moved toward friendship, I knew something wasn't at all right.
She had a special motive for driving out here, only a few days
after E.J. had gone; some purpose. But I couldn't hang back
just because of that. The spirited way she went about her business (whatever it was) attracted me. I'd been at the mercy of
forces beyond my control for so long—the weather and how it
affected the crops, and strangling family circumstances—I
couldn't help but admire a free agent who acted intelligently,
with a purpose. Here was someone used to shaping her destiny.
I'd met very few such people.

"What do you want to know?" she asked.

"Anything you feel like saying."

"All right . . . I married at sixteen—no, more like fifteen
and a half. Had to. What else—when you're pregnant?"

"You've a child, then?"

"I do—and I don't."

"Meaning?"

"I had her for a while, but my ex went to court and got her
away from me."

"How could he do that?"

"I'm a bad woman, see. Not fit to raise my own child, because I don't belong to a church and I occasionally have men
friends. Visitors without a chaperone present."

"Terrible."

"The judge decided against me—took the girl away. Lives in
Minneapolis, with *him*. She's fifteen and a half herself right
now, and I worry a lot about her."

"That's rough on you."

"I made him pay. My lawyer got a good alimony settlement,
so I manage okay, without having to find some crummy job.
Provided I don't marry."

"What would happen then?"

"I'd lose alimony—everything."

"A perfect setup for E.J. . . . I see. He couldn't marry, either."

"The son of a bitch had it all figured out."

"How'd you two meet, anyhow?"

"There're not many guys around these days, and he's a good

dancer." She'd gone stag to a dance hall across the river from the city, in South Dakota, where the liquor laws were loose. "He knew how to . . . give you a good time."

"But you wouldn't go to California with him?"

"And never see my daughter? Lose alimony? How could I?"

"He asked, though?"

"He knew I'd say no. Now, tell me about you."

I started at the beginning, with childhood, then the war, trying to make myself interesting, even a little cosmopolitan—not just some hick—but as I spoke something outside myself asked *why*. How could I imagine she cared to know anything?

"I've not gone into those early years in a long time!" Not since Maureen and I met, when both of us spilled out our tales. I wasn't telling it the same way now, for I saw it all differently. There'd been nothing so brave about my enlistment in the Army, nothing so patriotic about wanting to bear arms. It was mostly a splendid chance to leave the farm. I strove to make myself independent if I possibly could, follow some other line of work. The war justified it, made my break from the land easier to explain. My father didn't call me a *Dummkopf* or undercut my lofty spiel about service to one's country, only gazed at me with sad eyes, saying, "Be careful, August, and don't volunteer for anything . . . dangerous." How could I respond to such a wish, when I was going overseas to shoot and be shot at? If he'd been the tyrant father I once imagined him to be, I'd have seen to it that I proved my independent manliness by hitting the trenches in the front line. Instead, I discovered a talent for storekeeping and spent my service years as a quartermaster helping to outfit the doughboys leaving for France—and I never filed up the gangplank of those troopships myself. A family in Mineola on Long Island took a liking to me; I spent weekend passes with them, as if it were my second home. They adopted me as part of their war effort and fed me because they couldn't cook for the starving Belgian children. It was a wonderful time of my life. I hated to have the Armistice end it all, because I surely didn't want to go home. "You can understand why."

"I think so."

"The whole notion of having a future laid out like straight corn rows . . . it felt like a heavy weight on my life."

"I see."

"But why'm I telling you this?"

"Probably because I asked."

"Why don't *you* tell me more."

"I have to be getting home."

"Not yet . . ."

"But aren't you hungry?"

"I can always eat . . . that can wait."

"I have a couple sandwiches in the car."

"All right." We stood up, freshly aware of each other. I'd no idea of the time, we'd been in so deep. All quite natural and innocent. Circumstances had put us together this way and there was little we could do about it, if we'd wanted to. The surface of our lives had broken open; we were up in clear air, taking great gulps. How long would it last?

She unlatched the car door. "There're a couple bottles of Schlitz in the pouch here. Only, watch when you open 'em, they'll spray all over."

"I'm trying to imagine you making this sandwich. What you were thinking about . . . what you had in mind."

"Eating 'em alone . . . or maybe not."

A car drove by on the road. Betty quickly slipped behind the steering wheel, so her face wouldn't be visible. Just as if we were an illicit pair already. Although she'd been left stranded, here I was in E.J.'s place. All too obviously. The notion seemed more amusing than erotic; I wouldn't be sucked in this easily. I watched her snap open an enameled compact and touch her cheeks with the powder puff; then she repaired her lipstick with a carmine tube. She reminded me of other women I'd known in my bachelor days—girls on the wrong side of respectability, refreshingly coarse about the facts of life, healthily blunt. One had to be wary of such women since they were stray cats from respectable society and had learned meanly how to survive. Betty Kinwald seemed a mature version of these females—precisely what I needed. Not a tired bride of Christ or a hysterical adolescent virgin—but a straight-shooting, open-eyed companion who knew the basic way the world runs, and wouldn't forget it.

"Don't go!" I said, with an urgency that surprised us both, when she put the key into the ignition.

"I have to get back."

"When'll I see you again?"

"On a nice day . . . for a drive."

"That suits me to a *T*. Tomorrow's going to be another good day."

"I don't know about tomorrow."

"You promised."

"Why not . . . then?"

"What time?"

"Oh, don't hang around. It's hard to say—when."

"I'll be right here."

She looked me directly in the eye. "Where's all this getting us?"

"No place. That's what I enjoy about it."

"I drove out to give you hell—but you sweet-talked your way right out of it."

"We got interested in other things—about each other. That's all."

"You still haven't said—what's really the matter. You didn't get as personal as me."

"I won't talk about my wife, if that's what you mean."

"Wouldn't be loyal of you. I see."

"I don't want to hear my own words. Because then I might start believing they're true."

"It's so bad?"

"We're always at each other and nobody wins, ever. It never stops."

"Not even in bed?"

"Especially not there." Now we were naked to each other. People tell strangers everything, their close ones nothing. I could have said a lot more, but only if we were parting forever —and I knew we weren't. Tomorrow I'd spill out what reticence held back today, until at last Betty would know more about me than I knew myself—viewing me from outside, having perspective. I wasn't ready for full disclosures yet. I needed time to think about Betty and try to figure out what she was up to, playing cat and mouse with me here. I liked the game but didn't know why we were at it.

Saying goodbye, we shook hands, a serious seal on the diversion we'd both enjoyed. A friendly, solemn gesture. But this wasn't the moment for promises.

Soon after she'd gone I realized it was time to pick up Sheila at the schoolhouse. She came running out of the building as if the other scholars were after her. Hopped into the back seat without even looking at me and crawled under the robe. I drove away without offering the other pupils a lift. Sheila scorned such hospitality—wouldn't have it. For a moment I could think of nothing to say, didn't know how to return to my old life.

"What happened to you?" she asked.

I turned, startled. "What do you mean—am I late?"

"You look different."

I glanced into the rearview mirror. "I do?"

"Yeah . . . sort of excited."

"Well, I've got a new farm! Been there all day—so busy I even missed dinner! Don't know what your mom is going to say."

Sheila fell silent, as if the jiggling from the rough road had induced a trance.

Of course, Maureen was extremely put out that I hadn't shown up for the noon meal. "I waited round till after two—for you."

I apologized and explained that I'd been out measuring the limits of the land.

"Does it have to be surveyed?"

"No, no. I was . . . checking the fences, seeing what the ground is like, different places. It's almost time for the disc and harrow. I can hardly wait to start planting."

"This year, I don't know, August, but I feel . . . like something's changed for us."

"I said that already!" Sheila opened a Pepsi for herself. "Didn't I, Dad?"

"The new farm . . . and all that mess behind us," I said.

"If only Jasper hadn't left so soon. Might've been my last chance to visit with him, old as he is."

"I'll be taking the train to North Dakota. Any day now. He promised."

"Sheila! Not *six* cookies. You won't have an appetite for supper."

"I better start chores." If I stayed here much longer in the glow of my body, they might perceive halo lights around me. I hadn't felt so good in a long, long time. Once outdoors I could let my joy go free—only myself out there and the wide, beautiful world. The doubleness of my life now seemed to match exactly the yearning I'd been feeling lately; an appropriate reason for it was here at last. Undoubtedly, white-shirted bank embezzlers behind mahogany desks felt much the same way, as respectful customers came and went, and community trust welled up high—to ears which never turned red in embarrassment.

The following day Betty didn't arrive until midafternoon, and I wasted hours hanging around the barn, waiting for her. I didn't even devour the bologna sandwiches Maureen had prepared, thinking I'd share them with Betty. Now, however, I was soon due to retrieve Sheila from school. "What took you so long?" Irate as any husband.

"Did I say a certain time?"

"No, but I thought . . . yesterday . . ."

"Oh, that was yesterday. Today I had quite a bit to do."

I wolfed down a sandwich as we walked toward the barn. I knew perfectly well she was playing me for a sucker, but *that* didn't help any. The idea of this attractive young woman—here beside me, strolling toward the barn—was enough to excite me to the point of speechlessness. I took her arm as we stepped over the sill. Since she'd bothered to drive all this distance when there were plenty of would-be suitors in the city (the Air Force base could provide hundreds), I knew I must be on guard. Of course, I could be wrong to be so suspicious of her. The farm setting and me in overalls, hungry for her attention, might be arousing her. In some city girls I'd encountered a peculiar lust for a rank-smelling body and a perverse pleasure in the odor of manure on a farmer's boots. It'd happened a couple of times; they liked it dirty. Also, a lot of women were merely attracted to a working man whose muscles were hard and appetites crude and abrupt; they were the kind I used to take standing up in the alley behind the dance hall.

I watched her climb the hay-chute ladder ahead of me, my nose almost under her skirt. I felt like grabbing her at the top and finishing off in the hay but held back because I figured she probably expected it. I'd not get compromised this easily until I understood what she figured was in it for her—much as I wanted her. By delaying I hoped to see more of her hand. I kept talking, simply sticking to my role as host, as if our cozy contingent situation here hadn't given me sexy ideas. She grabbed my arm for support as she settled onto the cow lap robe, which I'd spread over the hay. When I didn't follow up with a counter caress of some sort, she looked at me warily amused. She knew I was holding back for some reason—that I hadn't accepted everything she said, or how she presented herself.

I maneuvered back to our beginnings, sensing the clue lay there. "I keep wondering what you meant when you said, 'I'm scared, Jack.' When you thought you were talking to him on the phone."

"His prison record. Investigation would bring it out."

"Thought you sounded anxious for *yourself,* more'n for him."

"That, too."

"Like—you knew you were losing him."

"I told you, I wouldn't go off to California with him or anybody—and forfeit alimony. No man's worth *that!*"

"You sure got over him quick."

"It started to go sour, some time ago."

"How?"

"Why does this interest you so much?"

"You're here, aren't you? How'd you get here—that's what I'm trying to understand."

"That I'm here should be enough."

"Not for me. Not after the way E.J. pulled me into his life."

"What went on between Jack and me shouldn't concern you. It's all past history."

"So quick? How could it be? I was going along minding my own business, when suddenly he grabs me and pulls. Now I don't think anything's ever going to be the same again for me."

"Don't you hope that'll be true?"

"Yeah, everything was *too* much the same. I've certainly changed that! I may not be gone to California, but I'm off and running—sort of."

"I believe you are." She smiled and grabbed my forefinger.

"Leaving my wife—and Sheila, too—as much as I can. I mean, I'm not taking up with them in the old way. As if I expect to alter things. Know what I mean?" I withdrew my finger as if I hadn't noticed her grasp. "Suppose you couldn't. You seem like somebody always able to work things out to suit yourself."

"Selfish, huh? Well, maybe."

"I intended it as a compliment."

"How do you mean, you're leaving your wife?"

"The way *she* left me. Just drop everything—down the gully between us."

"But Sheila?"

"That's another story. She's probably waiting at the schoolhouse for me right now."

Having a girl almost Sheila's age, Betty wanted to know the whole tale from the start, and I told her because perhaps I'd hear fresh advice on what to do. The "voices" business didn't interest her so much as my notion that Sheila felt sexual currents between us. This gave her new opportunity to allude to my attraction for women of all ages. I didn't follow up, or respond.

"You think she'll grow out of it?"

"Her mother could help—more'n you."

"But Sheila runs rings around her. Maureen is completely befuddled. Doesn't know what to do, any more than *I* do."

"August," she said, shaking her head wisely. "You're not running away from *any*thing." She shook out a Lucky Strike, oblivious of the incendiary surroundings, but before she snapped open her lighter, I suggested we go outside. "I don't want you to burn down the barn, too!"

"Why the nasty crack?"

"Fire is fire . . . that's all."

She lowered herself on the hay-chute ladder, step by step, to the bottom.

I pulled out my pocket watch. "My God, it's after four! Sheila's through school."

"Maybe today she just walked home like an ordinary kid."

"Not likely."

As we moved toward the car, I heard an auto coming and quickly turned my back to shield Betty from the road. She made the most of my suitor-like gesture—all the excitement of a clandestine affair. "So, when're you coming out to see me again?"

She wouldn't say.

"Or would you rather I drove to *your* place, since I can always fill my gas tank from the tractor barrel?"

"How'd you explain a trip to the city by yourself? Don't they always want to ride along?"

"I could manage, don't worry. I'm as good at deception as anybody." Infidelities begin long before the sex act itself; in a way, I was her lover already. "So, when're we going to meet?"

"Give me time."

"Tomorrow—the next day?"

"Tomorrow I can't."

"The next day, then. You come here, or phone and I'll be right down to Ohio Street."

"We'll see . . ." With a smile and a wave she drove away.

When I arrived on the school grounds I couldn't find Sheila. I looked in the outhouse, peered through the schoolroom windows. The door was locked—the teacher had left, too. I hurried home, and as I drove into the yard, Sheila met me at the sidewalk gate dressed in her tight-fitting overalls and lumber jacket. "So you walked home?"

"No. Bummed a ride with the teacher."

"*She* brought you home?" I didn't like the idea of someone outside the family getting mixed up in this. The teacher was already put out by having to deal with Sheila's peculiar behavior. Today's extra nuisance would only alienate her further.

"Well, you didn't come and didn't come. As we drove past I saw another car in E.J.'s yard. Who was there?"

"A salesman. Talked my head off."

"What was she selling?"

"Oh . . . the Avon lady, you know. On her rounds."

"She didn't come by here."

"Well, maybe tomorrow."

"I asked Mother."

"Asked her what?"

"If that's who the Avon lady is."

"Thought you said you 'n' Miss Jesperson just drove by . . . how could you see anything?"

"I didn't see much, case you're worried." She gave me a hard look that shot right through me. Just like her to catch the drift of things quickly. It's with girls this age drunken fathers get carried away and go too far—all the way. They're responding to something; it's not merely a matter of incestuous rape. I felt Sheila's interest in me as strongly as if she were the "other woman." Now she'd no longer think only of sicking the sheriff on me for house burning. My new crime was philandering.

Maureen emerged from the house. "What's taking so much time over there?"

"Oh, you know, it's all new to me. Have to get acquainted with the layout."

"And . . . the Avon lady," said Sheila.

I laughed. "Yeah, she talked a blue streak, but didn't sell me anything."

"Most of those products aren't for men. I'm surprised she tried."

"Didn't realize it was so late."

"After this, *I'd* better pick up Sheila."

"She should walk—now it's warmer."

"No, no!"

"I really don't mind, August, if the car's left here for me. You could run over to E.J.'s on the tractor, couldn't you?"

"Good idea." That way I'd be free, no boundaries on the day.

Like a man given enough rope to hang himself, I had ample hours for waiting—but Betty didn't show up. Rain in the afternoon was a possible excuse. Nor did she appear the next day, or the one after that. I wondered if the telephone number in the Missouriville phone book was safe to call, or if someone living in her apartment (who, though?) might be suspicious if I rang her.

On Friday afternoon at two she finally drove into the yard, and in answer to my indignation said, "What're you so sore about?"

"I've been lurking around this barnyard for days! I can't even get into the fields, like I'm supposed to. Just say *when* . . . is that too much to ask?" I rolled open the barn door and told her to park the car inside. "So we can forget about it."

"You *are* nervous."

"Precautions, that's all." Even by hiding Betty's Chevy, we weren't free of danger. On one of Maureen's chauffeuring trips she might drive into the yard to find out how things were going. Or some neighbor might drop by. The danger of discovery lent a keener edge to our meeting.

Not that anything definite happened. My noncommittal bantering brought her blooming toward me, completely alert. Our talk and cautious maneuverings served as foreplay. Were I young, I'd have grabbed her at once and taken her against the fender before another minute passed. But middle age is a time for savoring, and I relished the prospect of what lay ahead. Made everything last as long as possible; that way the future remained exciting with possibilities. I'd waited a long, long time, and now that someone new had entered my life, I wouldn't hurry the pleasure. Whether in the long run she'd be good or bad for me, now she was bringing about my wonderful rejuvenation. Ever so easy, ever so gently, I let it all happen.

Once she touched my bare arm but drew away quickly when I didn't follow up her move. She was unwilling to gamble on an unmistakably randy gesture which I might turn down—because then she'd have to leave in a huff. Clearly used to being in control, she was baffled by my ability to maintain the upper hand merely by not progressing with the seduction. Shy, or such a gentleman, or whatever. At times her irritation almost surfaced, then subsided. She realized she might spoil the whole thing.

I still wondered *why*. Did she find me interesting because of my connection with her absconded lover? We shared secrets— were new shoots growing out of dead connections. If it hadn't been for him . . . and if she hadn't, if he hadn't—how we went over it all again and again! I lay on my back in the haymow like a callow youth who couldn't proceed.

A car drove by and I stiffened. Not my Chevy—I'd recognize the motor sound anywhere, just as I'd always know the bark of our dog Shep. She laughed. "You *are* afraid."

"Remember, you're the Avon lady."

"Next time, it should be my place. You'll feel safer away from home ground."

No, I'd be even more on guard. "A school day would be best. Sheila's watching me pretty close."

"Since you've caught her interest, maybe she'll forget herself a bit." Sheila was merely going through a particular time all girls experience, Betty felt. "It's so scary when you start the bleeding. I remember how I felt. But pretty soon she'll be looking at herself in mirrors, putting on lipstick, and thinking about new dresses. Wondering who's going to date her. You'll see."

"I hope you're right." But I knew it was too late for Sheila to return to such a state of innocence. She'd never be an adolescent like that, for she couldn't believe herself attractive—not even in the eventual possibility of it.

We parted with a friendly handshake, me the first to pull away. Afterward, I worked like hell to calm myself down, but I was in an agony of sexual frustration as strong as a young man's. Maureen served as surrogate mistress. I forced myself upon her, much to her dismay, but she always gave in because she accepted her Christian vows of marriage. It was lonely copulation—dreadful that two people could be so close and apart at the same intense moment. I slept so deeply most nights

Maureen could scarcely rouse me next day. My once suspiciously faltering heart now seemed as true and strong as everything else in my body, all equipment in good working order. I awoke with a feeling of nameless happiness. In that moment when dreams are recognized as such and slip from one, I took on my life with gentle elation. I had a secret! Not just the sneaky matter of carrying on with another woman. No, my secret was that I was alive.

"You're working too hard over there," Maureen said, alarmed by my heavy sleep.

"Oh, it's not hurting me."

"Never seen you so tired nights."

"This is an awfully busy time of year."

When Betty had her daughter home Easter week we couldn't meet, and then I truly paid attention to field work. Sheila settled into farm solitude during school vacation, Holy Week, but refused to attend Good Friday services with Maureen, nor would she accompany us on our usual shopping expeditions at Schmidt's grocery. We finally bundled her off to school the Monday after Easter—an hour late, improperly clothed in a cotton shift, anklets, and black patent-leather high-heeled shoes. Maureen and I abandoned the fight over what she'd wear if only she'd agree to attend school at all.

At three-thirty Miss Jesperson drove Sheila home. I hurried up from the barn when I recognized the car and saw Miss Jesperson pulling Sheila up the walk. I'd never seen the placid woman so upset. Her reddish hair, high in an upsweep, was slipping out of the tortoiseshell combs and coming undone— she was like a brown thrasher aroused. "I want to speak with the two of you—privately."

"Oh, dear, Sheila, what've you done?"

"Let me alone!" Sheila ran upstairs and slammed her bedroom door. Maureen hesitantly ushered Miss Jesperson into the living room. "Care for something? The coffeepot's on."

"No, no, thank you, I've got to be off. Dismissed school early because—we couldn't go on." Earlier in the day Sheila hadn't asked to leave the room in time. "She—had an accident. Dress all wet down the front and back."

"Oh, no!" from Maureen.

"Well, such things *could* happen even to a child her age. But when I asked why she hadn't raised her hand sooner—to leave the room—she said she'd been afraid to."

"Afraid to ask permission?" I asked, for then it could've been the teacher's fault.

"No! Afraid to go out alone—to the toilet. Now, did you *ever?*"

"She was just *saying* that." I smiled, shaking my head.

"But she . . . made a mess! Now, I can't have a child in school who's afraid to run to the outhouse. I'm speaking to the county superintendent because we can't go on like this. Sheila must withdraw from school."

"Wouldn't she lose the year's credit?" Maureen asked. "And there're so few weeks left in the term."

"Then this afternoon she wadded up balls of clay and slung them around the room. I made her stop and asked why she was doing such a thing. You know what she said? That everybody was laughing at her and telling wicked stories."

"I suppose they *were* talking," I said. "About her wet dress."

"No, she *always* thinks the kids are talking about her. And there's the voices—you know about them?"

"It's just her manner of speaking," said Maureen.

"Frankly, it's none of my business, but I think you folks've spoiled her rotten. What she needs is a good spanking. Needed one for a long time, 'n' I've just been itching to let her have it."

"Such methods . . . are old-fashioned," Maureen began, "and we don't believe—"

"I know you don't. It shows! You've never laid a hand on her. I could make her stay after school and haul buckets of coal from the shed, make her sweep the floor and spread compound —but *that's* not punishment for her. She likes it. Everybody gone except her 'n' me. And I'd probably end up driving her home to boot! If this was the old days, I tell you, she'd have a mighty sore bottom! Far as I'm concerned, she's expelled."

"You said you'd speak to the county superintendent," I reminded.

"I'm in charge—it's my decision. Sheila's not to come back till she's learned to behave. The other kids—I have to think about, too. Sheila's ruining their education, taking over my schoolroom. I can't have it."

"You know about . . . our sorrow . . . She was awfully close to my sister, her Aunt Winnie, and I don't think she's over it yet."

"Oh, I know, and you have my sympathy." She paused, softened. "I didn't say Sheila would fail the year. She's done enough good work to pass even if she misses the last stretch."

"The funeral and all—it wasn't good for her. We noticed—didn't we, August?—how she changed. So upset. The thing is, Miss Jesperson, we don't always get dealt good things in life—sometimes it's pretty bad. Maybe if Sheila stayed home a week, say, and got rested up. She might—"

"No, no, she's just back from vacation."

"Could she do schoolwork at home?" I asked. "That would keep her busy." I was alarmed by the notion of Sheila hovering close; she'd find out about Betty in no time. From now on I'd *have* to see Betty in Missouriville, for there'd be no other safe way to manage our trysts. My self-concern took over completely, and I hardly listened to the two women. This much I'd learned from Betty: in all new developments, look out for number one. If you don't, no one else will. I'd not relinquish my new private life for anything.

After the teacher left, Sheila opened the hall door and Maureen cried, "Oh, child—what next?"

"You monkey, you worked things out just fine, haven't you?"

"The old bag."

"You're impossible!" said Maureen.

"I can do a lot around the house to help. *Now* I'll have a chance to finish the afghan."

"I wish I'd never started that afghan!" Maureen had been on it a year; now Sheila would become the happy home weaver, working away in a quiet corner.

"Or that jigsaw puzzle," I said sarcastically. "Now you'll have time to solve *that!*"

"What're we going to do with her, August?"

"She'll have to tend to her arithmetic and write English themes, just like she was in school. If I have to pick up her homework myself, I'll see to it she keeps on."

"I thought you wanted me to do farm work."

"Later, after school's out."

"You'll be planting corn before then."

"You can't plant corn. You can't even run a tractor."

"You said it was time to teach me."

I'd never seen her saner. The baffling thing about Sheila was the way she sometimes seemed the most rational person in a room. What we termed "crazy" was just an intelligence too strong and direct to take. But on the sick side, her calm sense right now derived from elation at the thought she'd *never* have to leave the farm again, never have to see any other people besides her parents. She was ours again as if she were a baby three weeks old. She offered to be my right hand in field work, if only I'd agree to sequester her safely out of the world's way. Our isolated farm situation made such a strange solution to Sheila's life possible. If I were not a farmer but a banker like Wolbers, she couldn't be pulling this on us. She'd know—that we knew—her family life was merely part of a larger society into which she must soon enter. But here instead of people we had animals and the land—and she'd make the most of it.

How smart she was—and how crazy! I also guessed she viewed her return to babydom and dependence as the one way to hold this family together indefinitely. We'd be locked in our parental duties forever. Nothing would ever change. I couldn't help but think this unconscious desire came from her sense that I was moving farther and farther away from Maureen. She'd noticed how carefully, grudgingly, we spoke to each other —unless the topic concerned farming. Events of the week of Winnie's death were never discussed—couldn't be—and I refused to give an accounting of myself, even in private. From that separation the other steps came, each growing wider, Sheila caught this drift and now, with her mad scheme to cling to us, was determined to keep us all together as a family, hidden as if in a cleft of earth.

In the bright, clear weather of May I worked long hours getting the crops in and could not keep on the lookout for Betty's car. I awaited a letter suggesting a time to meet in her city flat —and always opened our box on the road before Maureen or Sheila got there, sometimes receiving our mail from the carrier himself. Perhaps there was some good personal reason—her mother living in a back room—or a nosy landlord—which prevented her suggesting a rendezvous.

Then one noon hour she phoned, lying to Maureen on the party line, identifying herself as a secretary in the Livestock Commission office in Missouriville. Would I drive down this afternoon about three o'clock? I took over. "Three o'clock, you say? That'd be fine. I suppose it's about the account on my last shipment of hogs?"

Sheila said she'd ride with me, see a matinee movie and stage show. Maureen brightened. "Sure, why not? I'll come, too."

"No, not this time. Tomorrow maybe—some rainy day. A movie on a fine afternoon like this? Something unhealthy about it."

Maureen agreed with me at once, rather to my surprise, and Sheila didn't stage the tantrum I feared. "Daddy's got important business today. Has to see that we get every penny coming to us—to meet mortgage payments. It's not like the old days."

I put on my best Sunday suit but wondered if I'd look too farmerish once she saw me standing in her hallway. My sandpaper hands, callused from work, hung out of my sleeves. I'd taken a quick bath because the natural odor of me—perfectly okay in E.J.'s barn—might put her off if encountered too strongly in a city apartment. Maureen approved of my ablutions because I was pulling on clean underclothes and a shirt which she'd labored to wash and iron. She figured I had to feel right in order to deal on an equal basis with the Livestock Commission people.

By the time I reached Ohio Street and parked at the curb in

front of her door, my palms were sweating. I was awfully apprehensive about the whole thing. Like all farmers, I was naturally more on guard in the city, but now I suffered from a failure of confidence in myself as a presentable person. Our being together had been such a boon surprise—and part of E.J.'s farm setting. Perhaps her city look at me would end the affair for good.

Dressed in boudoir finery, she opened the door; and most of my fears faded. All the shades were pulled down and the pinkish lamps in her living room glowed softly, quickly exciting me. I took her in my arms as if it were the most natural thing in the world, kissed her; but our embrace was awkward (we'd waited too long?), somehow not intimate. I smiled when I realized *she* was just as nervous as me. We had a glass of sherry and talked over what'd happened since we'd last met. She'd been in Minneapolis—difficulties with the girl, but nothing serious. I didn't press. Something in her story didn't seem right; she seemed too offhand, unconcerned. I missed the honest, on-the-line streak in her and was too much aware that she'd made her flat into a seraglio in order to arouse me—doused herself in perfume, calculating what the heady aroma would do to my senses. Her frilly gown, nothing a housewife wore in the afternoon, was part of the vamp image. I asked for another sherry, but she looked at her watch.

"We've plenty of time, haven't we?"

"Oh . . . I hate to think about it, but . . ."

"Let's *not* think or talk, then. Let's—" I reached for her, kissed her, and she responded warmly. We moved quickly into the bedroom. She turned back the sheet while I hastily stripped. When I tried to untie her long sash, she pushed my fingers away. I thought her resistance part of the game but it turned out she meant it. She'd keep the gown on. I was in no mood to argue—ready, any way it was to be, with clothes or without.

No lover in the throes of it has a sense of time. I was mostly out of my head for the duration, but with that same animal ear which remains alert even while we sleep, I became aware of some sort of noise in the hall. I reared back from her and turned, just as a flashbulb exploded in my face.

I yelled and leapt from the bed, only to hear the front door shut even before I got into the hall. "Who the fuck was *that?*" I shouted. She lay under the sheet, eyes wide, fearful. "Who *was* he?" I grabbed her shoulders and began shaking her. "What're you pulling on me, huh?"

I knew precisely, even while I raved. She climbed out the other side of the bed. Back turned, she adjusted the sash on her housecoat. "So this is all it means—a trick for blackmail! E.J. was right about you—he warned me."

"No trick."

Trembling with rage, feeling humiliated and ashamed to be caught in this cheap, hokey business, I drew on my clothes, eager to hide my body from this wicked deception, as Adam and Eve fig-leafed themselves after having sinned in the Garden. "What then—if not a trick?"

"Call it insurance." Her voice and manner possessed some of the steely coolness it had the first day we met. Silken cat with claws; *now* they were sharp and in view.

"You won't blackmail me, I can tell you."

"One guy ran out—leaving me—do you blame me for taking precautions this time?"

"Precautions!" The word was a tacky reminder of condoms and diaphragms. I almost blacked out as I leaned over to tie my shoes, heart beating wildly off rhythm. Serve me right to have the postponed heart attack here and now; this time for real. "I ought to beat you up!"

"You wouldn't do that."

No, my melodramatic threats were just part of the act she'd started here.

"Not to somebody in *my* condition." She pulled the gown open and I saw the unmistakable bread-loaf look of her stomach. She managed to keep her condition hidden from me until this moment. "Five months. You'd've noticed any minute . . . if you'd had a chance to."

My fury was doused in astonishment. One glance at the white belly mound and I knew why Winnie had rushed E.J. with a drawn butcher knife. Why Betty came to the farmhouse that dark rainy night saying, "I'm scared, Jack." And "I wish we'd been more careful." Also, why E.J. had lit out of this territory so fast—leaving *me* like a cuckolded husband to deal with the problem. The shocking methods Betty used—straight out of the tabloids and Grade B movies—were understandable. I'd seen decoying mother pheasant hens limp away from their brood with pretend broken wings, willing to die as a prey of the hunter if it would spare the chicks.

"But *why?*" I said wearily. "Why should *I* be the fall guy in this? I'm going home."

"We've something to talk about first."

"If you think blackmail will work, you've got another think coming!"

"Oh, that's *your* term. It's just . . . with this camera evidence . . . my lawyer would say we've a case."

In those years the newspapers were full of breach-of-promise suits against playboys. No man could lead a girl down the garden path and have sexual relations without paying for it—in marriage preferably, but otherwise through financial indemnity. Betty got her cues from all this.

"I'll tell Maureen about you—right now, today. What do I care? My marriage can't get worse. And we've got Sheila to worry about." As I knotted my tie in the dresser mirror, I looked at her. "So . . . never mind the blackmail stuff. I don't care how much of me the picture shows."

"I didn't mention blackmail. You did." She lit a cigarette and strode quietly about the room, Jean Harlow fashion, voice flat and matter-of-fact. She wouldn't look at me, though. " 'Insurance' is my word for it."

"What I mean is, I haven't a reputation I'd pay money to keep up. I don't give a fuck what people think of me. They can all go to hell."

"I'm not speaking about 'reputation.' "

"What's this, then, with the camera? Or is he one of your lovers, too?"

"Oh, stop raging like a jealous boy."

"I'm not going to be so easy to trap. I've a lawyer, too."

"August, really I'm sorry about this—more than you can know! I didn't expect to get so fond of you—so I kept putting it off. But do I want a baby? Did I want *any* of this to happen? Yet it *has,* and somebody's got to pay."

"It's not my kid. Go after E.J.!"

"You know the story there."

"That son of a bitch! I've got nothing to do with your baby."

"You do now."

The very thought of our lovemaking with another man's child in her womb repulsed me. "I'm not responsible—I won't be!"

"I have to receive support *some*where."

"I don't suppose you ever considered working for a living, like the rest of us?"

"I've worked plenty! Keeping house, having a child, taking care of men. But I get paid in shit from guys like E.J.—and my ex. He's gone to court and stopped alimony. I'm broke."

"How could he do that?"

"The judge believed his tales about me. The law hates 'bad' women like me and thinks *he's* very noble, raising our girl all by himself. So, I've been cut off—and what'm I gonna do? I only wish E.J.'d agreed to pay for the abortion months ago, when I wanted him to. But he wouldn't."

"Why not?"

"You can guess."

"Didn't think it was *his?* That what you mean?"

She nodded.

"Did he have any reason for—?"

"It's his, all right. That was just his excuse. I tried to think how to force action from him. Nothing worked. And now I'll never hear from him again."

"That's no reason *I* should pay!"

"Somebody has to. How'm I gonna live?"

"It's not my problem."

"You're like all of 'em. I knew you'd say that. Still wonder why I had the cameraman in here?"

"Why the hell didn't you have a picture taken of you and E.J.? Get the whole goddamned thing straight?"

"He was too smart."

"Thanks."

"I might've got him to take responsibility—somehow—but his wife's death botched the whole thing. Set him free."

I didn't admit I'd once had the notion I was set free by that death, too. "You'll just have to have your lawyer trace E.J. Bring a court action." I turned to leave.

"Wait a minute. You'd better hear what I expect . . . from you."

"Far as I'm concerned, it's goodbye."

"I'm only asking what should be coming to me, that's all. What E.J. should be providing. Give me what you'll make farming his land. Say, two hundred a month, at the start."

"Two hundred! I'm mortgaged up to my ears, and there won't be any cash from crops till after harvest. You're crazy!"

"I'm not interested in details. You'll have to work that out yourself. Two hundred will do for right now, but later it'll have to be more. When I go to the hospital, you'll have that bill, too."

"Don't be ridiculous, Betty. I'm sorry about your situation, but I'm not in a financial position to help. Don't try any funny stuff—I've got a lawyer, too, you know. You'd just get into more trouble than you're in already."

"I may be in trouble—but you're in it with me."

"We'll see." I hurried out, and my brave words died like skywriting because I couldn't imagine spilling this sordid tale to Bernard Nemmers, any more than I'd been able to go to the sheriff with the truth about Winnie's death. What help could I expect from my lawyer, when she possessed a picture that proved my intimacy with her? The judge would never believe the child wasn't mine, if it came to court—wouldn't much care —since the law always tried to find fathers for bastards. The fact was, I'd been philandering with the woman and she had proof, just like the gold diggers in those awful movies. She intended to make me pay for every second of my pleasure, and the law was on her side. Pretty expensive fucking! At that rate I might've had the highest-priced whores in the world! Two hundred dollars a month and maybe more later as the child grew— years of it! What Indian rajah ever bestowed more on a harem girl for her favors?

There was a slim possibility that the flash picture might not turn out; but two days later in the mail she sent an eight-by-ten photograph, me buck naked and facing the camera as I reared back from her. I tore the image into a hundred pieces and ground the fragments into the roadside mud. A futile gesture. Later in the day, when I could think of no way out, I wrote a check for two hundred and posted it. At this rate my bank account would dwindle so rapidly I'd barely have enough for the down payment on a shipment of Wyoming feeders I'd planned to buy in early fall—unless I borrowed on my life insurance. I'd have to go steeply into cattle and hog raising in order to make enough money. Hopeless though I felt, there was also a strange sense of relief, now that I knew exactly how things stood. After a turbulent spring of death and love, I'd found a solid, new level and had my life in hand once more. Now I must accept the situation and figure out ways to keep going financially—make the best of it.

The neighbors helped me tear down the barn and clear away the house rubble on E.J.'s old farm; we pulled out the scrub grove with a drag line. Even with all traces gone of a settlement on this piece of ground, I felt what'd happened here had left a scar on me which nothing could eradicate. There were limits to what this or any land could do for me, but I'd no course open except to give myself to working these acres as if my very life depended on it. Because now it did.

III

Times Between

The growing season moved greenly into our lives, entangling us, saving me. Maureen and Sheila's victory garden surpassed the effort of previous years, and, as a sign of its importance to our finances, was located on a piece of cornfield that I deemed my best land. They harvested every available wild and domestic fruit, canning with Karo, honey, and the extra sugar the OPA allowed. The demands of the fruitful earth and the conditions of war held us in pattern: we could only abide and keep marching. What a relief not to have to think about anything! Each fireside chat from the President seemed an intimate communication, for our daily efforts had suddenly joined the nation's.

Sheila's queerness subsided with her summer labors, much to our relief. Maureen took her to Sunday school and church regularly (I spent the day un-Christianly and farmed), and the two of them frequently drove to town on shopping errands. We no longer possessed the strength to try to make Sheila over into something she refused to be. Since it was impossible to find a hired man, I relied upon her more and more, especially with the cattle- and hog-feeding chores. She seemed noticeably at ease with animals and never slipped up on what I told her must be done. I said to Maureen I'd rather have Sheila helping than most hired hands I'd known.

"Don't tell her, August. She'll use your praise to keep from going to school this fall."

"I'll not force her, if she doesn't want to go."

"But to stop—at *her* age?"

"Frankly, I need her. That used to be good enough reason for anybody."

Labor Day came and we'd still said nothing to Sheila about school; she seemed exhilarated. I put her on a modest salary—not even a dollar a day—but all I could afford. With the baby's arrival, Betty hiked her charge to three hundred a month. I kept telling myself to negotiate this figure, find out just why Betty thought she needed so much, but that would mean actually seeing her, and I still felt too rooked for a meeting—too angry. I wouldn't be able to keep my temper, might slam her around.

Finally one day I just walked into her apartment and sat down with her at the kitchen table, very businesslike. I wrote on a yellow legal-size tablet exactly what I had in assets and liabilities, something I'd never done for Maureen. Betty listened, jaw set tight. She fed the baby first on one breast, then on the other, as if to demonstrate her mother obligations, because of which some man must pay—any man.

Driving home after that futile session, I steered into Kaleburg's Main Street and parked in front of my lawyer's office. But my limbs wouldn't stir. I was unable to get myself out of the car, for I couldn't imagine speaking of this seamy business to Nemmers. I felt too shame-faced for such disclosures, still had too much pride. Several friends walking by waved to me, and one woman even asked if I were waiting for Maureen. Finally, I started up the motor and drove home.

If prices hadn't rocketed upward because of the war, I'd never've been able to keep ahead of my bills. Because we spent virtually nothing on ourselves, Maureen figured we were becoming rich and took a modest, secret pleasure in the notion, particularly when she saw me poring over my accounts, night after night, plotting ways to keep from going under. Once she ventured to offer investment advice: "Shouldn't you be buying war bonds? Better interest than savings accounts, isn't it?"

"Hate to tie up my money."

"With the government behind the bonds, at least we know they're safe."

In all community bond drives I avoided pledges, though one's patriotism had to be demonstrated, since *Bund* sentiment before Pearl Harbor made everyone now feel nervous. To any bond salesman who tried to pressure me, I'd haul out my history of service in the World War. "I've done my military duty —don't talk to me! *That's* more than buying a few war bonds!"

With my farmer's allowance of gas through C ration cards, I was able to drive to Missouriville and check up on my other household. Betty's boy, Richard, proved to be a vigorous, healthy little bastard, cute as could be. When he grabbed my forefinger, rough as a corncob, and squeezed with surprising strength, I knew he was making his deep connections with me, the male parent in his life, however my actual role was defined. I found it difficult to feel antagonistic toward his mother in the presence of that happy, blue-eyed gaze.

My proprietary, unannounced visits started in a vindictive spirit of seeing to it I "got my money's worth," since I paid the tab for the whole setup. I had a right to barge in, drink a cup of coffee, and play with the baby if I felt like it. Actually, I needed relief—and an alternative—to my strict, grueling routine, and this change of households relaxed me. I noticed a flicker of amusement in Betty's eyes when I brought Richard his first rattle and showed him how to use it. She knew I was succumbing to the child—a most natural and predictable outcome. Thus far our relationship was detached but cordial, something like that of divorced people who have the business of children in common. The baby, always in our presence, seemed the crucial monitor of our doings. We played out our roles before Richard as if he knew everything about us. For one thing, we had no illusions whatsoever about each other. Gradually the stripped honesty of our association seemed soothing, almost attractive. Church services brought peace to Maureen; I found it here. I even caught myself excusing Betty's trickery and the way she'd snared me, on the grounds of survival of the species. The presence of wonderful Richard explained the universe sufficiently.

Although Betty had such a powerful hold on my purse, I'd no claim upon her personal life; she made that clear. I wondered about her social affairs, if she had lovers, other women friends, family anywhere. Who entered this apartment in my absence, sat in this chair? Once while I was there the phone rang. She picked it up and said quickly, "I'll call you later," and set the receiver down.

I wanted to ask, "Who was that?" but knew I couldn't.

Looking at her, I sometimes vividly recalled our abortive moment of lovemaking and realized that only our fanatic adherence to a code of tolerable behavior prevented an onrush of our past selves. She drew out her full breast to feed Richard in my presence, holding up the nipple like a rose, looked at me and smiled, sexual pleasure almost a blush on her cheeks as Richard began to suck. How mundane but strange to sit in the brightly lit kitchen over coffee and chat about Richard's wispy coil of hair. Had we not touched each other too deeply ever to withdraw this way? Who were we kidding, anyhow? I felt certain she entertained such thoughts, too.

One afternoon I reached out blindly for her when I was about to leave—without even planning to—an abrupt hallway embrace not unlike our first on this very spot. She responded warmly, and in a minute we were in the bedroom, wordless and flushed, hardly able to tear our clothes off fast enough. Later, when she reached for a cigarette, she said she'd wondered why I hadn't made an advance long before and could only conclude I was still deeply angry.

"Yes . . . I was. I am." I'd held out as long as possible in order to keep free of further and as yet unknown complications —only at last to sink deeper. How had I ever imagined I could keep away indefinitely? Three hundred a month she cost me, but now at last I was getting every penny's worth.

I managed a trip to the city every week, not always on the same day, sometimes making an excuse to Maureen but more often saying nothing at all. Betty would receive me as her afternoon gent, looking pretty and smelling grand, clean sheets on the bed and a bottle of whiskey nearby, radio playing softly.

We were well matched, since she liked it as much as I did and had no hesitancy showing it. I hadn't had intercourse with Maureen in months—probably never would again. Afterward, I always washed away traces of perfume and funky smells, before returning home, but Maureen had no interest in me physically and seemed to pay no attention. We lumbered into bed at night without a word of endearment or farewell and fell asleep like strangers on a train ride.

Having such a small but perfect accommodation—a few hours of happiness each week—I thought perhaps this amount of intimacy was all either of us could manage or actually wanted. It was leading nowhere. Our pleasure remained the sole purpose; nothing needed to be justified.

All through the week and all those other waking hours, I felt cheerful and strong, on an even course. I just hoped everything would last—and that I could keep paying for it.

On a single day in April 1944, I cleared three thousand dollars on a cattle shipment, but it'd taken a plunge of twenty thousand in borrowed money to bring it off. Wolbers at the bank, when I paid up on my loan, clapped me on the back and suggested I sign another note immediately, while my luck held.

"While the market's up, you mean."

"You're doin' swell—and ain't you glad you took over E.J.'s place?"

"So far it hasn't set me back."

He laughed at my cautious comment, took it for superstition —that I wouldn't tempt the gods by boasting.

When I informed Maureen of my new loan to buy more Western range feeders, she nodded approvingly, somewhat fearful, however, that I might be caught short on a down market.

"Not as long as the war lasts, don't worry."

Because feeding cattle by the hundreds was big business, I was respected in the community as never before. They admired my financial nerve and acumen—took it as a sign of my superiority. Every shopkeeper straightened up when I walked in. It amused me to note how people measured you upon a scale of supposed wealth. I hadn't imagined that blatant money-love was so prevalent, even among pious churchgoers.

Maureen gloated over what she assumed to be our accumu-

lation of riches, as if harboring some lovely secret she could tell
no one, not even me. My rude well-being was sufficient testimony, in her eyes. I was obviously in good health, contentedly
submerged in the deep, swinging rhythms of life. I've often
looked back on that time—heavy work, open appetites, sound
sleep—as a moment when all alignments were true, even
though the scheme of things rested on basic falsehoods.

Sheila in stocking feet measured five feet seven inches tall
and weighed one hundred and sixty pounds, mostly bone and
muscle. Her legs were excessively developed, her breasts heavy,
but all of her went easily into my overalls. Every morning at
seven and evenings at five she'd haul a tank wagon of chopped
corn and pitch it into the feed bunks for the white-faced
Herefords filling my cattle lots. When she was through she
helped me milk the sixteen Holsteins; never had to be told what
chore to do next. She dressed in a farmer's outfit constantly and
scorned all skirts, although for church she put on a shapeless
brown sack mailed from Sears. She hadn't a single girl friend,
and of course no boys looked in her direction. She remained
close to Maureen and me as if she were some offshoot still part
of us, not an independent organism.

What would the years do to her? I wondered. She was already a freak and becoming more so all the time. She labored
so hard outdoors we couldn't deny her second helpings at the
table or stop her between-meal snacks, though the excessive
food was making her monstrous. People were already accustomed to Sheila's oddness, however. One of the comforting
facts about small towns is that nothing's so outrageous it can't
finally be accepted. The parishioners in church didn't scorn
awkward Sheila shuffling into a pew next to her parents, nor
did they try to draw her into conversation or force her to asso-
ciate with children her age. Sheila's way was regarded as
Sheila's way—they left it at that.

But the minister, who mistakenly viewed himself as counse-
lor as well as pastor, asked Maureen in early September why
Sheila wasn't in school.

"She didn't go last year, either."

"But—why?"

"She likes it best at home, on the farm." Maureen knew she was caught. So long as no one said the obvious about our situation, we were safe in it.

"That's no life for her—a girl her age! She should be with the others."

"Maybe you're right, Reverend. I'll speak to August."

Naturally I tried to argue Maureen out of the notion. "Why spoil things, when everything's going well?"

"It isn't right . . . for us to use Sheila the way we are."

"She's happy—she loves farming!"

"But where's it getting her?"

"I don't know. Where's anything . . . getting anybody?"

"If this keeps on, she won't ever be able to leave the farm. She'll be here the rest of her life, working like a man."

"She'll never be Homecoming Queen, let's face it."

"But at school she'd meet others . . . socialize."

"Not Sheila—ever."

"She's young, her life can change. If we don't try to do something, I'll never be able to look Reverend in the eye."

"Oh, if *that's* your reason!" I turned away and glanced out the window at the trees, boughs bending to the insistence of the west wind. I knew that nothing I could say would stop Maureen.

Troubles came like crows to sit on our shoulders. Sheila kicked up such a ruckus I couldn't even manage weekly trips to Betty. We had to drive Sheila to junior high in town because she wouldn't ride the bus; and pick her up at four. In the afternoons she complained of headaches from having been cooped up all day, and she no longer helped with chores. Maureen volunteered, although women who'd do this sort of work she always regarded as lower-class. Pioneer forefathers worked their women this way, but for laudable reasons. Surely we'd made progress since then! Still, she tucked her dress into the overalls legs and tied on heavy work boots—Sheila's outdoor gear. But a bold steer could unnerve her and she was afraid of being knocked over by the unruly pigs, clamoring for the corn in her bushel basket. As Sheila took to bed with unidentified fevers and "female" complaints, Maureen gave up the role of hired man and became her daughter's nurse. I shipped two hundred cattle to market because I couldn't handle the work—and took a beating on the price.

The campaign to force Sheila's attendance at school ended in October. We formally withdrew her, hoping the action would pull Sheila out of her slump, get her out of bed and into fresh air again. But there was no immediate response, and by now Sheila had become an almost unbearable drag on Maureen. Whenever I returned to the house for dinner or supper, Maureen welcomed my appearance with a haggard smile. Now she could slip away—to the basement for clothes washing, or upstairs to dust the hall—anywhere to attain a little privacy and bask in relief, free of Sheila's constant demand for attention.

The girl's spiral became so bad we couldn't risk leaving the farm without hauling her with us, because she felt impulses to start fires. Voices told her to strike matches and empty the kerosene can. She didn't mention her Aunt Winnie by name, but I recognized the trappings of that spook. Sheila now refused to attend church with Maureen or shop with us or go to the movies, since all these activities took our attention away from *her*. Her passion to have us hover like brood hens seemed to grow. In order to buy weekend groceries, we'd all climb into the car, but only one parent shopped, the other stayed close to our monstrous baby. If an acquaintance stopped us to ask what in the world was happening to us, we'd say Sheila was having "a sickly spell" and leave it at that.

"What does the doctor say?" some would insist.

"Oh, the usual."

"What can be done?"

"Nothing more'n what we're doing, I guess." Impossible to explain these shut-lid days to someone else.

By letter I apprised Betty of my current difficulties and explained why I hadn't been down to see her, much as I wanted to. Having a daughter herself, I knew she'd be sympathetic to the problem, particularly if I continued to send that three hundred a month. How wrong I was!

Weeks passed, with Sheila more and more voracious in her

demands, more threatening. She spoke of doing away with her-self in order to make us suffer guilt over the way we'd treated her.

"Maybe Doc Shepley *could* help," I said to Maureen one day. "Sedatives . . . something!"

But when we tried to transport her to Shepley's office, she flew into a tantrum, weeping and screaming. "You're tryin' to put me away! I won't go! I'll jump out the car!"

When we telephoned and guardedly told Shepley our prob-lem he promised to be right out. "I knew he'd come," said Maureen, pleased that friendship and family alliances still held.

"We should have thought of him long ago."

"I didn't want to admit, I guess—how serious it is."

Like lying to the dentist that your teeth don't trouble you at all.

The presence of that white-haired old friend of the family pumped new strength into us. Somehow we'd triumph because all of us working in unison could surely conquer Sheila's de-mons. At first she scowled, remained silent there at the table as Shepley reminisced about Maureen's father and recalled poker-playing times they'd enjoyed. Just the sound of these tales filtering through the air over her head seemed to layer Sheila back into a place of security, firmly fix her once again in a shored-up family. When Jasper was mentioned, Sheila suddenly spoke, reminding us of his intention to have her visit him in North Dakota.

"Oh, that was way last year," said Maureen. "He's probably forgotten all about it."

"If so, we'll remind him," I said quickly. Maureen hoped to guard Sheila against disappointment, but I didn't want her spark of interest in the future snuffed out.

In his expansive, avuncular ease, perhaps Shepley reminded her of Jasper. He persuaded her to leave the kitchen and have a let-your-hair down talk with him in the living room. I walked to the window and emptied my head, looking at the parchment-colored oak and scarlet maple, serene in autumn sunlight. Soon I heard the doctor sending her outdoors, reminding her to but-ton up her lumber jacket, for the day was cold.

"She hasn't been outside alone for weeks!" Maureen said.

Shepley came into the room, lit his pipe, and puffed heavily. "What's all this about voices?"

"The voices tell her to wet her bed—or won't let her sleep—or say bad things about her. Whenever she hopes to get away with anything, she blames the voices," Maureen said.

"Oh, they're real enough . . . in her head," I added.

"Something about the radio?"

"She thinks the radio's on because she keeps hearing voices there." Maureen filled his coffee cup again. "We finally worked out a system. When it gets really terrible and she's bawling something awful, we pretend to shut off the radio."

"That stops the voices?"

"Isn't it awful? What should me 'n' August do?"

"A girl that age, she just might snap out of it."

"Don't say 'snap out of it'—it makes her furious," I said.

"The monthly bleeding still scares her. You should've explained it more to her, Maureen."

"I tried but she wouldn't listen. It embarrassed her."

"She ought to be in school with kids her age."

" 'Back to school'—that's no answer," I said. "You should know what we've gone through—on that score."

"And, August, don't . . . how shall I say it?—don't touch her so much."

"*Touch* her?"

"She misunderstands . . . your affection."

"She said that about me?"

"You've never even in fun, sort of—"

"The wicked child!" Maureen blushed and turned to the stove.

"These matters bother her, whether *you* think they're wicked or not."

"Where does she get those ideas?" Maureen shook her head.

By my lack of response Shepley knew I wasn't entirely unaware of her charges.

"I'll prescribe a sedative for nights, but pills are no answer, you realize. She's still upset over what happened to Winnie. Nightmares . . . can't get it out of her mind. Now, if I were you I wouldn't talk so much about that mess."

"We don't," I told him.

"It's not come up for months."

"Did Sheila take it awfully hard—do you remember?"

"No, right in stride—didn't she, August?"

"Well, not exactly. She thought *I* had something to do with the fire."

"She never cried over Winnie, that's what I mean."

Shepley scribbled a prescription, ripped it off his note pad, and handed it to me. "This isn't a cure. But a doctor's expected to do *some*thing."

After shaking hands with Maureen, he walked to the gate with me. "I'd've seen to it E.J. got what he deserved, if Maureen hadn't wanted that church funeral so bad. E.J.'d be in jail right now. You know what I'm talking about, don't you, August?" A squint-eyed, fiery glance. "Now he's disappeared, lost in California. A year and a half and the whole thing's blown over. A thing like that! And you're surprised Sheila's upset? *I'm* furious, too, just thinking about it."

"He was rotten to Winnie, all right."

"Rotten! He broke her neck!"

"Well, she was after him with a butcher knife—did he tell you?—that day you two went outside to talk?"

"Deserved the knife! Getting that woman pregnant!"

"Why'd he let Winnie know? Other times he fathered a bastard he kept quiet about it."

Shepley looked like a bantam rooster in a fight ring. *"He* didn't tell her. The other woman did! Drove right out to the farm and spilled the whole thing to Winnie."

"Are you positive?"

"That's what he said!"

"But why?"

"Beats me!"

No wonder Winnie had flown into a rage. What had Betty hoped to accomplish by such a confrontation?

"So, there's another of E.J.'s bastards somewhere in the countryside—and him gone to California, nobody knows where. If Winnie hadn't flown off the handle that way, he might've gotten the horsewhipping he deserved. As it is, he's away scot-free. Oh, it's not fair. Some folks can do the dirtiest,

damnedest things and get away with it, while others . . ." His
eyes dimmed as he drew up all his righteous indignation—he'd
lost his practice, his reputation—just for buying farms cheap
during the Depression. "Others get crucified for no good reason
at all!"

Now I knew what Betty meant when she said, "I'm scared,
Jack. . . . I wish we'd been more careful." Betty must have
thought she was being modern, straightforward, civilized. She
must have hoped Winnie would sue for divorce—hadn't
counted on such a violent, primal reaction. But Betty should've
known better than to imagine she had rights to someone else's
husband, just because he'd fathered a child upon her. But since
E.J. refused to pay for an abortion and disclaimed any responsibility, she must have become desperate. Action was necessary
because the problem was growing as fast as the fetus. She *had*
to find a way of taking care of herself and the infant; as it
worked out, she managed to do just that.

I probed my new knowledge for over a week, sucking on it
like a sore, speculating. Once I saw Betty, I'd have to come out
with it, let her know I knew everything about her role, at last.
Finally one day I managed to contrive an errand that took me
to Missouriville alone. I didn't telephone from a filling station
on the outskirts, partly because those of us who live on party
lines don't use the phone for anything but impersonal business
matters, never knowing who's listening in. Also, announcing
my arrival would give her time to prepare for me, and I preferred dropping in on my domain with the freedom of a lord,
unannounced. If my three hundred a month didn't buy me *that*
privilege, what good was it?

I noticed the nifty dark green Packard out front and wondered who could drive such a vehicle on his gas allotment. At
first my speculation stopped there, since many people lived on
this street; but when Betty answered the bell and almost shut
the door in my face, I knew the car owner must be her new
gentleman-of-the-afternoon. "I'm busy, August. I can't see you.
Why didn't you phone?"

Slam.

I stood there, cut to a weak-kneed suitor by her rebuff. Hol-

low in the middle—then a rush of anger. But if I stormed the
back door she'd probably phone the police. Worst of all, she
was wearing that frilly hostess gown, just as she did for me.
Same old tricks but a new man to play them on. I felt loathing
for myself—being gulled this way—but could think of no effective action to take. I glanced at my rough, unmanicured hands,
the "town" shoes with their too pointy toes, and felt myself a
rube. A city girl's turndown will do this to a country man every
time. Also, we were back to passionless basics: monthly support payments, dirty-picture evidence, and threatened legal action.

What did he look like, this new lover? I might hang about
and catch a glimpse of him, beat him up when he stepped out
the door, for he'd be too weak from screwing and whiskey
drinking to put up much of a fight, no matter how big he was.
But such schoolboy stuff would get me nowhere except locked
up in the city jail perhaps. I wrote down his license-plate number, just in case I'd need it someday, and drove home to my
brown, fallow fields. I felt the winter ice and snow coming to
cover me up.

For months the days passed in a routine established to contain Sheila's madness. I found release only in excessive labor
and purchased more scrawny Western feeders than a sane man
could handle; my pigpens were populated with Berkshires of all
sizes. All these barnyard creatures were eating and shitting and
moving inexorably toward the slaughterhouse. Because of a
bumper harvest, my granaries bulged with grain for this exten-
sive feeding operation. When the young range cattle trotted
down the chutes from the trucks and into my lot, they were
thin, wild-looking, all bone and rough hide; after a couple of
months on Iowa corn they turned sleek and firm-fleshed—but
never fat. I got rid of them before overweight set in by calculating exactly what quantity of grain produced the desired
poundage. When the gain was sufficient to return a profit, I
shipped them out at once. Sometimes Orvall Beams would tell
me, when I phoned to have him transport them to the stockyards, that their peak was still a month off. But I knew pre-

cisely what I was doing. I didn't care what the animals looked like or if some other farmer bought them to finish them off for top price (at a high cost in feed).

For evening chores that winter I employed a neighbor kid, Ralph Johns, who was a year younger than Sheila and considerably less husky. "That cob can't do a man's work!" she said. "Why don't you hire *me* instead?"

"Okay. I could use both of you."

She claimed she could outperform Ralph, and I said, "Prove it."

They worked well together in silent rivalry but seldom spoke. Ralph would scoop away at the silage on one end of a load, Sheila on the other. When they came to the small mound remaining in the center they'd divvy up, finishing with a laugh of triumph, each scrambling for the honor of having the last scoopful. Sometimes Ralph stayed for supper, and we enjoyed the novelty of having company at our table, although he blushed a lot and was too shy to say much. Still, I could imagine Ralph twenty years from now, after his father retired—this guy would likely become one of the ablest farmers around. There were great satisfactions in having a son take over and carry on what had been started. These dreamy speculations were easier for me than having to confront the probability that Sheila would be right here twenty years from now, and I'd be a gray-bearded old-timer still trying to take care of her.

Sheila stopped the prescribed pills when she began doing farm work again because she said they made her feel logy, and now she needed all her energy. She'd about exhausted her supply, whatever they were. We couldn't have gotten more from Doc Shepley in any case. He died of a heart attack in February. Not many mourners showed up for his funeral, and even the elements conspired to keep people away—we had our worst blizzard that day. Maureen and I spoke of finding a new doctor, but who'd ever be such an intimate friend that we could truly expose the miserable inner life of this family? We seemed condemned to isolation, stewing in our own troubles. However, we felt we were "in it for the duration," as servicemen said. The heavy war effort helped carry us along, put a framework to the struggle, as if our nation's ultimate victory would liberate us. I put off attempting any solution to my problem with Betty and simply tried not to think about my ignominious role in helping her lover thrive. But I knew I must do something about that soon—perhaps stop payments and risk legal consequences.

In early spring Maureen complained she "wasn't feeling right," kept losing weight and had a sallow complexion. The hysterectomy three years earlier had been ordered upon discovery of cancer of the cervix in an early stage. The surgeon assured us that this operation would very likely halt such activity in cells elsewhere. But now, without mentioning it aloud, we both wondered if this could be another flare-up. Instead of entrusting her health to some new internist, Maureen asked me to drive her to the big fat brothers who did a thriving chiropractic business in Marion, South Dakota. "They can cure any ailment, people say." And best of all, they were complete strangers.

After a good bone-cracking treatment, Maureen felt much invigorated, but the beefy chiropractor who worked her over noticed a lump in one breast, urged her to see her physician at once. We drove directly to the emergency room of the hospital, and the doctor on duty recommended a mastectomy—for both breasts, it turned out. The young surgeon, who thereafter became "our doctor," told me not to despair, since the operation had been performed in time and would probably stop cancer from spreading. "Your main problem will be to convince the patient *she* should have hope."

A smart young man. "I know, she'll be of two minds about that." She'd always half wavered between the choice of heaven and earth; this calamity would seem the occasion to opt for eternity.

Taking pen in hand as if drawing up a solemn will, I wrote Betty what had happened, explaining that my present family circumstances made further payments impossible. "I'm sure you'll understand." (Not in the least—I knew!) "Furthermore, I gather from our last brief meeting on your doorstep that you've made other arrangements. I wish you happiness. Yours truly . . ." Crossed it out. "Yours cordially . . ." Crossed that out, and on a new sheet copied the letter down to "Yours sincerely."

The following week I received one of those threatening official letters from her lawyer. Unless payment for the last three months, plus this month, was delivered to his office by the day after tomorrow, he'd bring a court action for child support. Perhaps at that point I should have waited it out, called the bluff—faced the consequences if there were to be any. But I didn't feel I had the strength in me (emotional or financial) to handle a lawsuit, and so I paid up by cashing in my life insurance policy.

With Sheila now nurse as well as hired hand, Maureen and I capitalized on the new situation, which accorded heavy responsibility to Sheila. Once a child truly comprehends that one's parents are mortal—even on the way out—adulthood arrives, compassion begins, and the flow of family love now turns the other way. Maureen, face held up like a frail pansy, asked silently for pity from her daughter: you have all your strong, young life ahead of you—think a little, therefore, of me.

Reverend Kallsen drove out to visit Maureen twice a week, as if to prepare her for the grave. The lopping away which had taken place seemed to her a grim metaphor of what lay in store: she'd be cut to the quick, finally; it'd be over. Maureen behaved toward Sheila as if the girl were an ordinary daughter upon whom a mother could lean—and she'd have to take the burden.

"August, maybe we should go to California, the little time I've got left."

"You shouldn't talk that way—'little time.'"

"Sit in the sun, enjoy ourselves."

"Oh, you don't want to pull up roots—not now."

"I mean it. Settle in Long Beach or somewhere. Just live off the rent of these two farms—why not?"

"But what about *me?*" Sheila said angrily.

"Oh, you'd come, too."

"I don't want to live in California! I like it right here in Iowa."

"Don't worry, girl, we can't afford to go."

"Oh, I'm sure we can *afford* it," said Maureen, with the secret, almost naughty smile that broke whenever she speculated on how rich we were.

I felt like a scoundrel. "Hospital bills, these doctors—they set us back quite a bit."

"Why shouldn't we have a little retirement pleasure?"

"Plenty of years ahead to think of that, Maureen."

"For you—maybe—not for me."

"Cut it out, Mom." That very phrase so often used against Sheila, she now turned upon Maureen.

"You think there's plenty of years? I don't." She appeared capable of saying anything that came into her head. Such a burst of honesty was like a loose billiard ball in a game. Where might the ball hit next?

Sheila glowered at her mother, hated the sound of this talk. If Maureen forced us to quit the farm, where would that leave Sheila? Normal parents frequently voiced the assumption that their children would be grown someday, fly from the family nest—but we never could. We weren't allowed to say that one day it'd be time for Sheila to go. Or for us to.

Maureen's wistful speculations brought back a flare-up of the old trouble. One afternoon Sheila smashed a whole set of glassware merely because her mother criticized the way she washed dishes. Later, she drove the tractor in road gear across a stubble field until the wagon behind wrenched loose and smashed up in a gully. Given Sheila's size and strength, these mad tantrums were ominous. Were we heading into an even accelerated nightmare of trouble?

"It won't do for me—just to lay around the house," Maureen said. "I better get back on my pins, take up where I left off."

I let her try because it was obviously good therapy. The necessity of taking her life in hand once again because of Sheila was her particular way of using circumstances for her ultimate personal benefit. I used the demands of the land in this way. And Sheila used us.

We saw very few people. When the neighbors helped us shell corn, or if I lent a hand in their endeavors, nothing about our situation was ever asked. Perhaps only Ralph knew of our locked-in lives, and he wasn't talkative, minded his own business, lest he be out of his part-time job. Our shopping trips to Kaleburg were swift and businesslike, one of us on the errand, the other home with Sheila. Church services were out entirely, for Maureen couldn't face the queries from the curious congregation or visit naturally with any woman afterward. The minister, knowing Maureen wasn't exactly a patient anymore, crossed her from his sick list and ceased his house calls. The truth was, in order to accommodate Sheila's insanity, we became a little crazy ourselves. Oddly enough, we were used to our sealed-off existence; it was as if we inhabited our own sanitarium. The farm became our perfect sanctuary.

"How blest we are—that we own our land," Maureen often said. "We can just be here by ourselves if we want to. Nobody need know anything about us. It's all *our* business."

But every acre was mortgaged to the limit, and my name was on staggeringly high short-term notes. Even a brief hospital stay and surgeon's fees would put me under. I feared the end of the war, a dip in the high prices—catastrophe! But Maureen gazed pensively from our kitchen window at the distant fields surrounding us and felt safely enclosed. She believed in the land: it was there, and the deed was ours.

All this time I brooded over what might be happening on Ohio Street. Was the Packard friend still paying afternoon calls, or had Betty kicked him out in favor of some other stud by now? And me paying for it! I agonized over how I could resolve this unfair use of me, and yet I'd become almost paralyzed by my state of inaction. Put in sixteen-hour workdays; tried not to think about it.

Finally, I couldn't stand the numbing sameness of our routine a single day longer. "We're getting too worn down," I said to Maureen on a fine Saturday in May 1945. "Let's go to town tonight just like there's nothing unusual about us. Make nothing special of it. Go to a movie with Sheila—the seven o'clock show—then do our shopping at Schmidt's and come home."

The boldness of my plan lay in its ordinariness. We didn't say a word to Sheila but she caught the note of something different. After Maureen finished baking, cinnamon and raisin coffeecakes cooling on racks atop the stove, she glanced at the clock and announced she'd be the first to bathe, then she'd fix supper while we had our baths.

"So soon? Why?" Sheila asked.

When I lifted the milk pails off their high hooks and headed for the cow barn an hour earlier than usual, she said, "What *is* it? You two going someplace? You both gonna leave me here?"

"No, you'll be right with us," I replied. "Going to town, that's all."

"Not me. I can't."

"We'll see."

After supper our struggle with Sheila began in earnest. "We *must* shop, you know," said Maureen, "and Saturday night's a good time. Have to have food or we can't eat."

"Farmers don't need to buy food."

"Who says?"

"I'm *not* going to town, but I'm afraid to stay here alone."

"You don't give us much choice, do you?" I said.

"No, why should I?"

"If we make it to town by seven, we'll go right to the movies," Maureen said.

"Been a long time since you've seen a movie, hasn't it?"

"Now, girl, help me wash these dishes."

Sheila subsided more quickly than I expected. Our spirits lifted—we felt freshened—like having wind blow across alfalfa. We savored, astonished, the kind of peaceful unconcern most families enjoy doing ordinary things. Soon we were dressed and ready to leave. At the moment of departure, Sheila drifted away into the farthest recesses of the living room. I knew I'd have a difficult time pushing her across the doorsill. If it hadn't been for Snowball, who dashed into the kitchen when I opened the door—and Sheila rushed forward to catch her—perhaps we wouldn't have gotten the girl out of the house. Sheila snatched up the lean old cat, spanked her head with two light finger taps, traditional reprimand for misbehavior in cats, and carried her outdoors.

On the road to Kaleburg, Maureen didn't let the conversation lapse, as if her words were a net holding up the illusion that this was a normal Saturday night. Parking was difficult but

I found a space two blocks farther away than I'd hoped. We had to walk up Main Street to the theater, past the shops, nodding to people along the way. Maybe to them we looked like an average, fine little family.

The clock in the Catholic church steeple showed five past seven, and it was never even a minute off. By now we'd missed the newsreel, and we'd be too late for the advertisements and previews, though perhaps still in time for the cartoon before the main feature. Sheila knew we were late—and why we hurried so.

"I'm sure we'll get there before they start Mickey Mouse," said Maureen, sensing how important this might be for Sheila —or perhaps giving the girl a cue as to how she might disgrace us.

The ticket-selling matron under a beaded globe, her cheeks brightly rouged, epitomized the theatrical world there in her stall. I'd never once seen her in ordinary daylight on the streets of Kaleburg or buying a dozen eggs at Schmidt's.

"Did we miss the cartoon?" Sheila shouted, just after I purchased the tickets.

"Shhhhhh," from Maureen.

The woman in the booth bobbed her head, smiling, and leaned forward to speak through the hole in the glass. "It's half over, dearie. Run right in."

"We'll see it all when it comes round again," I said to Sheila quickly.

"No, we're too late. I won't go in!"

"Come *on*," Maureen whispered fiercely. "It's Abbott and Costello. You *know* you like them. They'll make you laugh."

"If I can't see the cartoon, I don't want to see the movie."

"You'll watch all the Mickey Mouse *later*," Maureen said in that low, breathy, stern voice, a mixture of exasperation, love, and determination, which she always used with Sheila in moments of trial. That particular tone bespoke the locked nature of their struggle, the tic-tac-toe of emotional involvement. Never-ending, always branching out to further contests.

"I won't!" Body rigid, she held her arms awkwardly, the way a gorilla walks. "If you make me I'll scream.

"August, do something with her. I haven't the strength."

"Enough of this nonsense, Sheila!" I grabbed her arms and shoved her toward the draped entrance. Just as she opened her mouth to yell I clamped a hand over it and pushed her out of the lobby into the street. This intractable, enormous girl, my own flesh and blood, locked in warfare with me. Once outdoors she went limp, almost clinging to me, as if now that I'd mastered her I could go ahead with whatever violation I had in mind. In that single moment I was so overwhelmed by my life I felt I couldn't struggle free, ever.

Seeing Sheila subdued, Maureen quickly embraced her, held her up while I stepped back inside for a refund on my tickets. The woman counted out my change with a good-natured shrug, but when she pushed the coins toward me she winked and smiled—all but twisted her finger above her hair in the whirligig sign of madness—the conspiracy the sane share over the heads of the mad. If I could've gotten at her I'd have slapped her face and willingly joined the legions of crazy people.

My strange family waited for me under the marquee lights. Farm women in nearby cars leaned forward, taking it all in, and for a second I glimpsed wife and child with an outsider's eye. How queer the two of them looked, huddled together, bereft of the ease the rest of humanity enjoyed without giving it a thought. For one long green moment I imagined what it'd be like to escape to California—grass-widowing Maureen, leaving her to cope with Sheila; leaving Betty and the boy and the three-hundred-dollar-a-month obligation.

But I walked toward them. "Guess we'd better place our order at Schmidt's," I said. "Let's go."

"Sheila wants something to eat."

"We just had supper. What do you mean?"

"I wish now . . . I wish maybe . . . we'd gone into the show."

"No, too late, Sheila," I said.

"You should've *made* me."

"Your father surely tried!"

"I don't know why I wouldn't go in there."

"Enough shenanigans for one night. You'd pull something else on us once we got to our seats."

Sheila said nothing in reply to me. When we came to the

yellow-and-red popcorn wagon I bought three bags. Munching the kernels as we ambled along, I felt we were almost ordinary again. Maureen nodded hello to several acquaintances in parked cars. All evening a good many women watched the passing scene from parked cars while others paraded the sidewalks—both segments needed to make a festive Saturday night in town.

"How *well* you folks are lookin'," said two churchwomen, coming abreast of us, as if such blessed words could cure us.

Maureen stopped to chat, and Sheila became restive. Suddenly she dumped her popcorn on top of her head. The buttery, mallow flakes tumbled down her hair, over her shoulders. The visitors fled quickly. Maureen slapped Sheila's face—quick and hard, the jabs of a boxer trying to keep the blows from the referee. "You wicked child! *Why* did you do that? August, get the car—hurry! We've got to take her home right now."

As if *that* would be punishment! No, she meant, since we'd disgraced ourselves in front of the town we must carry ourselves off in shame.

I bought a few essential grocery items while Maureen and Sheila waited on the sidewalk outside Schmidt's, Maureen facing the wall so that nobody she knew passing would have to speak to her. Her sense of public shame wasn't shared by Sheila, who stood beside her mother quite unconcerned, face and hair greasy from the butter, staring defiantly at anyone who looked sharply at her.

When we reached the car I spread a blanket on the back seat so that Sheila's hair wouldn't spoil the plush upholstery. She was quite cheerful, hoped to mollify us, and asked me why I thought a Buick better than a Pontiac. I refused to answer. As we drove along she began singing softly:

> We meet, and the angels sing . . .
> The angels sing the sweetest song
> I ever heard.

She'd won and now savored her victory. Surely E.J.'s life had been tyrannized by Winnie's tantrums in this same way, but good Lord, I hoped I wouldn't have to kill the girl in the end—that she wouldn't drive me to it, in a rage. More likely, some dark night I'd take off and never return home. I had very strong intimations that someday my life would be totally different, or was it merely a hopeful straw to grasp? Now, after these many years, I understand that if you live long enough one's circumstances usually become very different. Survival is one solution—the passive answer—when everything seems too much.

Maureen's hand tentatively pressed her chest, as if she were still surprised to find such flatness there—nothing with which to nourish the enormous baby in the backseat.

"Winnie said popcorn gives you the bellyache. She'd never pop any for me."

"She said that?" Maureen replied evenly. "Maybe it isn't so good for little girls. You were only twelve when you stayed with them—that summer."

"I remember everything, and don't you forget it!"

As soon as we entered the house, Maureen heated water and shampooed Sheila's hair. I tried to read a farm journal, but couldn't. I glanced into the kitchen and saw Sheila's head part-way in the oven, drying her hair—and thought of those who turned on the gas cock and did away with themselves. Every time I looked at her these days, some monstrous notion popped into my brain. I retreated to the living room and snapped on the radio. "The Grand Ol' Opry" from Nashville, Tennessee. Saturday night and these damn hillbillies! What a way to live.

At breakfast next morning Sheila refused to use the nickel-plated knives and forks because "it makes the food taste funny." Only our best Rogers silverware would do.

Maureen flashed me a wry look, and I recalled the family tale that Winnie was such a princess she'd only eat with silver utensils. "That's our Sunday set . . . for company. It'll get scratched if we use it too often."

"Phooey—this fork makes me sick. I feel like throwing up."

"If she won't eat with our forks, let her use her fingers like a baby," I said.

She did. We paid no attention as she plucked at her scram-bled eggs, whimpering now and then.

Since it was Sunday, Maureen laid out the Rogers silver and

damask cloth at noon, just as if guests were expected. By sticking to the Sunday ritual dinner, we hung on to our normal
selves, believing that someday reality would catch up with us
and we'd become a standard family again.

In order to avoid a ruckus from Sheila, Maureen set out the
Rogers for supper as well, and at breakfast next day we were
still using silverware. The result was, Sheila thought of a new
condition to impose upon us. As Maureen gathered up the
Monday washing, Sheila informed her she wouldn't consent to
have her clothes laundered along with ours in the usual way.
"It's not sanitary. Do we eat off the same plates?"

"Then *you* wash them!"

"I won't use the Maytag if it hasn't been sterilized."

"Do it any way—I don't care!"

"Where's a washboard?"

"I don't know. I threw ours out years ago, before you were
born."

"What'll I do?"

"Whatever you want! I'm still weak, Sheila, you know that."

"I think it's time to call a halt to all this," I said, walking
away from her, pulling Maureen by an arm. I hoped Sheila
would feel the weight of our withdrawal; I closed the door.

"There's only one way left to us," I began.

"Not the asylum, August, no. Not to my own flesh and
blood. I couldn't stand it. I'd rather be her nurse and work-
horse, I really would."

Sheila flung open the door. "What're you saying about me?"

"That we can't take care of you anymore. Somebody else will
have to."

"I knew you'd try to put me away." She glowered at me.
"You son of a bitch!"

"Sheila, please! I swear we won't do it, not while I'm alive."

"*He* should be put away for setting E.J.'s house on fire."

"That was so long ago you don't remember what happened,"
I said.

"Put me in the booby hatch, and I'll tell the police everything
I know about you."

"Hush, child."

"I *will!* You think I'm just saying it, but I'm not *just saying it!*"

I could effect no change if Maureen wouldn't cooperate; Sheila would continue trampling over our lives.

I left the house in defeat, temporarily cutting off the problem as I slammed the door. The house held all my miseries. I strolled across the new-green lawn and gave myself over to enjoying the bright, splendid day. The pale leaves of the trees seemed to exude a sweet, delicate perfume, the true odor of fresh air. I felt the intimate warmth of the sun on my arms and face, a delicious wash of spring heat. Oh, it was a beautiful day, the sky flawless all the way to infinity. I felt poured into the morning, into the simple good fact of a perfect day in May. Grateful to the land—and forgave it for its terrible indifference.

One day in mid-August we'd just settled down to the noon meal when a large truck drove into the yard, much to Maureen's annoyance. "When we're about to eat!" I pulled on cotton socks and work shoes (in summer I walk barefoot indoors, refreshed by the cool floorboards). "Do you have to go, August? Your dinner'll get cold."

"I won't be long."

"How do you know? Anyhow, Sheila 'n' me won't wait."

I found Shep standing on his hind legs growling into the faces of the occupants of the bright red truck, his toenails scraping the door. "Down, Shep! Down!"

Over the cab, *Johan's Acres,* a sign in gold script garnished with trumpet vines, each letter with an angled shadow, as in German hymnbooks. A stout middle-aged woman smiled and stepped out to the knobby running board, certain of her welcome. "You're August, aren't you?"

Might've gotten my name from the mailbox, the way salesmen did. "Yeah."

"I'm Arlene—Jasper's daughter."

"Oh, my God, Uncle Jasper. He never writes anymore."

"You don't . . . don't know?"

"He's dead?"

"Last year. I thought I wrote."

"First we heard about it."

"Oh, I'm sorry."

"So'm I."

"He had a good long life, and the end was quick. Sure hope we're not droppin' in at a bad time for you folks." Arlene's tiny musical voice came through valves of fat. She was dressed in dark blue gabardine slacks, the kind wives wore on fishing trips with their husbands. Her tortoiseshell glass frames matched the hue of her freckles and her arms were deeply tanned. I noted a certain resemblance to Jasper around the eyes, all the rest hidden by fat. Her rope-colored hair was held down by a field of bobby pins, a hairdo that would easily go under a babushka, never be any trouble.

"Want you to meet Karl. It's his rig."

"You settin' up for the carnival in town?"

"That's the idea." A tinkly laugh breaking from her.

Karl rounded the truck fender and we shook hands formally, his "How do you do?" faintly accented. A handsome middle-aged man, tanned face almost leathery under a yellow mesh hat with a brim that drooped like a thin meringue. Pale, aquamarine eyes—striking in his dark face.

"We're in the middle of dinner—come inside and have some."

They said they'd eaten, apologized for arriving at the wrong time.

"Why, now that you folks are going to be here workin' for the carnival, I hope—"

"We don't work *for* the carnival," said Karl.

"We work for ourselves, he means."

Karl nodded gravely, removing his hat. The sun fell full upon him. He looked reserved and dignified as an Indian chief.

"Just thought while you're in Kaleburg you might's well stay by us. Plenty of rooms upstairs and you're welcome to all the meals you want."

"Gee, thanks, but we—we got our set way of handling things when we're on the road."

"There's not a decent place to stay around here."

"We don't put up at hotels," said Karl almost sullenly, and he firmly replaced his hat.

"We camp out—you know?" said Arlene. "There's always a camping place for carnival people."

"Why not pitch your tent right there in the orchard? Have meals with us or not, however you wish."

Arlene grinned—this was "family" talk, the way it should be. "Karl, you think we *could?*"

"A faucet there behind the house . . . outhouse to the left, near the lilacs. All the conveniences." And I was thinking: any diversion for Sheila, something special for Maureen to think about, particularly now that Jasper was dead, the last of the generation ahead of her. "Should think you'd like to get away from carnival life a bit, if you can."

"What makes you think that?" asked Karl.

"I didn't mean . . . only . . . when you got *folks* in a neighborhood you might's well make use of 'em." Show people were always suspected of being good-for-nothings, else why'd they go in for such a nomadic life? But clearly, carnies had their pride, too. "What *is* your act, Arlene?"

"A mechanical farm—Karl made it."

"Johan's Acres, named for my father," Karl said, jerking his thumb toward the sign. "All packed away now. Or plowed under, however you look at it, *ja?*"

Czech? Hungarian?

"When we get set up I'll let you folks in free," said Arlene.

"Wait'll Sheila hears about this."

"Oh, I'm eager to meet my cousin Sheila."

Karl abruptly climbed back into the truck. "Not now."

"You decide what you want—about the orchard," I said to Arlene.

Returning to the kitchen, I told Maureen the news about Jasper. "I *knew* that's why we didn't get our Christmas card."

"What's this about a carnival?" said Sheila.

"Why weren't we notified? What other relations did he have?"

"You can ask Arlene."

"Why'd they come out here now? I'd like to know." The disreputable carnival aspect bothered her, for what would people think if they heard Arlene was "relation"?

"I invited them to stay with us."

"Without even consulting me?"

"She didn't take me up on it, don't worry. Might camp in the orchard—I suggested that."

"Some life . . . a wonder she's stuck with the man this long . . . living like Gypsies."

"Can we go to the carnival tonight?" Sheila asked, and I tried not to look pleased.

"You bet! Wouldn't miss a show like that."

"Jasper, too, always liked to keep moving. Arlene must take after him. All these years, Jasper'd rather live in some god-forsaken North Dakota town than near the only relatives he had left. And what'd he get out of it? Nobody even went to his funeral, none of his kin."

Out of curiosity I drove to Kaleburg after finishing my coffee to watch the carnival set up. I offered to help Karl but he insisted I stand well to the side. For a heavy person, Arlene moved around easily, hauled sandbags, anchored guy ropes. The canvas lay spread out flat on the cement street, and finally Karl crawled under it. He didn't thrash around but went exactly to the center—like a worm in a kernel, he knew what he was after. Muffled shouts from him to Arlene as she yanked first one rope, then another. The tent lifted up and she made fast all the ends. When the thing was standing its full height, she joined her husband inside, both of them laughing, as if they'd done something wonderful.

Stringing the lights would take a while, Karl said, since they had to hook up to the generator provided by the road-show company. They didn't want me hanging around any longer, so I left them with one last reminder: "You *will* stay in the orchard tonight?" I was surprised how much this meant to me. Perhaps if they didn't camp out there I'd do it myself.

After a few beers in Meecher's, I drove home by way of E.J.'s acres. I parked in the roadway of the empty spot and now in my imagination relived horny moments in the barn that had never happened but probably should have, while I had the chance with her. The corn growing where the house once stood was several inches higher and deeper green than the rest, verifying my knowledge of what would happen on that strip of land

—mocking me in its very predictability, for nothing in my own affairs worked out as expected, no matter how hard I tried. Even now this land I'd bought would go back to the bank soon unless some miracle saved me.

As I washed up for supper, Maureen whispered to me, "Sheila's eager to go to town—can you beat that? I suppose she hopes to kick up a fuss where other people can watch."

"Oh, what the hell . . . we'll give it a try."

Although we arrived in Kaleburg a little late for the free show in the center intersection, we hadn't missed much of the program. Four chow dogs dressed in human clothes walked around stage on their hind legs and sat in chairs. Sheila from her vantage point on the top step of the Farmers' Savings Bank had a good view. "The father looks just like you," she said.

"Yeah, barking all the time."

Next came three dancing, leaping tumblers, constructing pyramids out of themselves. They were followed by a couple of unfunny clowns who had the hard task of announcing that this was the end of the free acts. Boos and hisses. Many farmers had traveled miles for these fifteen minutes of free entertainment and felt there should have been more. Loudspeaker music drowned out the angry shouts, and the Ferris wheel began to turn. The merry-go-round heaved out a beer-hall tune as it wheezily started up. The crowd broke apart, many people hurrying to be first in line for tickets at the ride concessions.

When I introduced Maureen to Arlene, who took tickets beside a hollow, painted post at the tent entrance, her disapproval of Arlene's spangled costume was clearly evident. White platform shoes with the toes cut out, black slacks—the kind of outfit cheap women wore when they palled around with men in low bars. Sheila was much less shy than I expected and mightily interested in Johan's Acres.

Suddenly I felt a strong hand on my shoulder. "August! *Here* you are!"

I recognized the voice and turned around uneasily. "Hi, Bill."

Wolbers stood there like the sheriff himself. "Been tryin' to get hold of you for days. Didn't your wife say?"

"Oh yes, each time," she said earnestly, alarmed. But she had no suspicion I was six months behind on the mortgage.

"Let's go inside the bank, once."

"August, is something wrong?"

"You 'n' Sheila attend the show. I'll pick you up later."

Trapped by Wolbers and led away, I had the notion, as Arlene put her arm around my wife and child and ushered them into the dark tent, that I'd never lay eyes on them again. But, of course, I wouldn't be hauled off to jail—I'd only lose that extra farm I'd taken on. Once inside the quiet, cool building, which had the musty smell of money, I explained that I'd used the mortage payments to buy feeders. Wolbers shook his head grimly, recalling our negotiations for that loan—he hadn't realized where my initial deposit was coming from. "That's no way to do business, August, and you know it. You have to keep up the monthly charges."

"I tried to."

"I realize you took a beating with your stock last winter, but you can't salvage things *this* way. At the bank's expense."

"Every penny's going out—it seems."

Wolbers scratched his bald head, turned away, embarrassed. "I notice by your checking account, you *do* pay a lot every month. Is that woman a doctor who—"

None of his damn business. "Psychiatrists cost a hell of a lot." Although my canceled checks to Betty were carefully hidden at home, sneaky Wolbers had noted the transactions as they came through the bank. "And then Maureen's medical bills. These doctors will skin me alive before they're through."

"Is she—the woman—doing any good for Sheila?"

I opened my hands and shrugged. "Who knows? But what else can a fellow try? For your only child."

"Maybe you're extended too far—considering the circumstances."

"Yeah, I might just let E.J.'s place go."

"You may *have* to."

"Does that mean foreclosure?"

"I've got my board of directors—they tell me what to do."

Clearly, they already had. I stood up. "Long's I keep my own land, still, that's what matters."

When I found Maureen and Sheila, they were both full of details about the mechanical farm, the girl's enthusiasm so bright I felt a sharp pang of happiness. All the way home she spoke of the miniature animals and how they moved. "I want to see it again."

"Sure—tomorrow."

Later, as Maureen and I undressed for bed, Shep began barking. "They're going to camp in the grove," I said.

Lights out, we stood at the windows watching. I heard the floorboards creak overhead and knew Sheila was posted at a window, too. The big truck, running lights ablaze, backed up as Arlene gave directions in sharp little cries. Karl kept the head lamps on, even after shutting off the motor, as if they were on stage for us to see. The two of them cast large shadows on the raspberry bushes, and every time they moved, ragged images spread out from their feet. Karl lit a kerosene lantern and hung it from the bough of an apple tree. They stretched a tarpaulin from the open rear of the truck and attached it to a branch. The rolled-down canvas suddenly became an annex to the truck, with the truck box a kind of second story, where they probably kept cooking equipment and bedding. A man like Karl, capable of fabricating an entire farm, would surely have his gear stowed in a cunning, orderly fashion. No doubt Arlene loved this quality in him—that he could carry his house with him, neat as a snail; they could be mobile and yet have all the necessities right at hand.

When Arlene moved toward the house with a flashlight, we dropped into bed, but a few minutes later the glow on our curtains was gone. Karl had turned off the truck lights. I couldn't resist sneaking to the window to glimpse again this caravansary in the orchard. They'd taken over a random spot and made it their home, favoring a branch here, a knob there, and the matted grass underfoot became a fine mattress for their sleeping bag. They tucked themselves into this hitherto anonymous patch of earth as if they owned it—which they *did* for the night

—and surely their acquaintance with this land already surpassed mine, even though I owned it and had lived here most of my life. Clearly, I'd never guessed the full possibilities of those apple-tree boughs or that springy green grass. The owner was like a host plant, always more used than using; never taking advantage of what was right nearby, available. So what if I lost E.J.'s farm tomorrow—in time I could even be reconciled to abandoning this one. These acres weren't the center of my existence, after all, merely one angle. I knew the limits of this land—and that my life went beyond them.

I watched Karl unroll the sleeping bag, thought how pleasantly cool it must be close to the earth. Not too many mosquitoes either, this year. They'd sleep refreshed by a gentle western breeze, while Maureen and I in this dark coop could scarcely feel a breath of air.

Arlene disappeared into the truck, no doubt to undress. Karl said something, his deep voice a buzz. Then he laughed. She echoed him, a musical lilt. I envied the easy companionship revealed in that lighthearted exchange.

"August, come to bed."

"Guess they're settling down okay."

"If they want to sleep in the grove like a couple of tramps, when there's a bedroom upstairs they're welcome to—that's *their* hard luck."

I didn't say what I thought of their luck; nor was I able to pull myself from the window. Karl bent over a white enamel washbasin set on top of a campstool, removed his shirt and sloshed water over his muscular chest and arms, thorough in his ablutions as in everything else, and dignified. Too dignified to have me and Sheila spying on him. I knew why I stood there and what Maureen had given up trying to see: right out in the apple orchard a man and wife were together on an ordinary domestic evening, completely in charge of their circumstances, masters of their frugal equipment. Karl refused to accept any suggestion of dependence upon objects, possessions, places. He'd never allow the earth to make that fatal claim upon him. He and Arlene simply alighted for an evening, enjoyed their temporary spot, were off next day. Simple as that. They could take and let go. Something I'd never learned to do. I'd spent too much time trying to accumulate a mass of stuff, as if money or landownership could ever be a bulwark against the turning years and my slow attrition. All these seasons of work—I'd merely been passing the time. But Karl and Arlene lived in a very different way. After they'd gone tomorrow I'd find trampled-down grass, like the matted lair of a rabbit or pheasant. Tonight they were paired as affectionately as a couple of birds, mindlessly consuming their life by pleasuring their way through it. The land and orchard for a brief moment wore the shape of these human possessors, but by evening this evidence of how the place had been used or claimed would be gone.

Nothing in my life matched this deft, effortless success. These people grasped their days but understood the necessity of each release. They let go. And it was *this* which I knew I must learn to do.

Karl blew out the lantern. His white back was still visible against the leaves, and then the rest of him as he removed all his clothes and sponge-bathed at the basin. I hoped Sheila at an upstairs window was taking a good look. Someday a naked man like him might come toward her; let her think it possible. Oh, please, God, why couldn't it be for Sheila, too, as it is for others? The white body in the grove vanished.

"August, what're you brooding about?"

I turned from the window. "They've a good life—those two."

We awoke hearing voices outside the window, knew we'd overslept. Maureen swung hurriedly out of bed. "It's Sheila out there, isn't it?" She grabbed her clothes as if the house were on fire. The sound of her daughter's voice would pull her from the grave itself. "Eight o'clock! I suppose Sheila's bothering 'em."

I pulled aside the net curtains. "She's with Arlene on the back step, playing with Snowball's kittens." The grass in the shade was gray with dew; the girls' bright yellow and deep red slacks ornamental as flowers.

"Suppose we'll pay dearly when they leave—she'll be that much worse." Picking up brush and comb, she leaned close to the triptych mirror and stared at her stark, morning face. The sight half paralyzed her. I hurried outdoors to do the chores; fortunately, only two of the Holsteins were giving milk just now.

Later, when I entered the kitchen, Maureen stood at the stove fixing breakfast, Sheila and Arlene were at the table. "Karl'll come by when he's through packing up," Arlene said to me, after silvery good-mornings.

"Every day—you both must get tired of it," said Maureen.

"*I* wouldn't!" from Sheila.

"Why not leave all your gear set up, just like it is—until tonight?" I asked.

"Who knows? We might have to sleep someplace else."

"I thought you said the carnival was here through Saturday," said Sheila, clearly upset.

"Oh, honey, we are! I mean, something might happen to the farm and we'd have to fix it. Might not get back here. If anything breaks, Karl's got to mend it before the next day's show."

"Mom, Arlene says *I* can help them."

We looked to Arlene for confirmation and she nodded, elbows firmly on the table, hands under her chin. All merriment and ease.

"So I'm off to town today." Sheila snapped the elastic band of her left puffed sleeve, which was too tight.

"Okay by me." I turned away so that my relief wouldn't show. Never before had she expressed such a clear wish to be independent. Cutting loose at last.

"Your father and I'll have to discuss this first."

"Nonsense, she's going. Right, Sheila?"

Karl glided past the kitchen windows. His step on the porch was toe-first, silent. "Oh, there you are," Arlene greeted him. "Smelled the bacon?"

He nodded gravely to each of us and took his place. Throughout the meal he replied to my general queries about the carnival but didn't give more than polite answers, his mind on the day ahead. By ten they were ready, and Sheila climbed into the truck cab to sit between the two adults. "Best thing ever happened to us," I murmured to Maureen as we waved goodbye. Then I turned toward the house to fetch my car keys.

"What? You're off, too?"

"Been meaning to get down to the city."

"A hot day—for a trip like that."

Freed by Sheila's independence, I suddenly felt able to care for my own well-being at last. I envisioned myself eloquent on the subject of finances, Betty listening, understanding. If the farm had been E.J.'s legacy for what he'd left behind—and me the stand-in father—now both ceased to exist in that way.

"Will you . . . be back for dinner this noon?" Knowing I wouldn't be.

"Sheila won't either." I shook my head.

"Then I won't fix anything. Not hungry much these days." Her hand groped for her chest, feeling the emptiness there since the operation.

"By noon you might be." Some phrase had to be patted into shape between us before I could leave.

I drove the whole distance in a state of mounting excitement, sure of my success. Even if she refused to accept my arguments, she'd have to understand I'd do nothing further. Let her lawyer unleash his attack. I felt ready.

Instead of the guarded, hostile greeting I was prepared for, Betty welcomed me with a warm smile. Before I knew it, Richard was perched on my knee—a healthy, beautiful child. We had coffee together and all plans of attack vanished under the seductive onslaught of domestic ease. I felt right at home, as if I were an old-time sea captain returning after a long voyage.

I realized Betty must be between men just now, that she was playing me for a sucker, but I couldn't resist her lively response to me. She drew the shades as soon as Richard fell asleep in his afternoon nap, ran a bath for me, and perched on the toilet seat as she talked—about the boy, movies she'd seen, nothing that mattered. I kept warning myself I shouldn't be succumbing, but my body wouldn't listen to my head, and soon we moved naked into the bedroom. Fell upon the sheets, bucking and plunging for all we were worth, until I thought her shuddering cries would wake the kid. Later she murmured all those complimentary things a man likes to hear, which I accepted as my due.

I told her about the arrival of Arlene and Karl, Sheila's unexpected attachment to her cousin, and how encouraged I felt.
She pointed out that each time my straitened circumstances
gave way a little, I became my own man again, but when bound
to Maureen's illness or Sheila's tantrums, locked into an emotional obligation or family pattern, I couldn't move or grasp my
own life. "You come to me when you feel alive again—simple,
isn't it?"

"You make it so." I ran my hands over her whole lovely
body. I wouldn't spoil this day by dragging out tawdry matters
of foreclosure or haggle over support payments. Perhaps in a
month or two my situation might improve, and in the mean-
time, how many afternoons with Betty did I have coming to
me? I could manage to squeeze another six months out of
Wolbers somehow, another three hundred dollars for Betty—
from somewhere. It was just money. Whereas this was . . .

I awoke hearing Richard in the hallway outside the door.
Betty swung her feet to the floor, drew on her fluffy housecoat,
and suggested a fresh pot of coffee. "Great idea!" I felt a rush
of happiness—brimming up, almost flooding my eyes. "Let's
go!"

Returning home at five, I sensed Maureen's resentment; she
looked as if her day had caved in upon her. Sheila had phoned
to report she wouldn't return until the show closed tonight, and
then she'd be sleeping in the tent with Arlene and Karl.

"They don't mind?"

"It was Arlene's idea."

"What a picnic!" Cooking over Sterno, plucking a few
nearby raspberries for breakfast—a lovely, vagabond life.
Later, when they arrived, I was too sleepy to watch them set
up.

In the morning Sheila informed us she'd joined Johan's
Acres for the duration of the carnival. "Why not?" I said
quickly.

Then, on the last day, Sheila and Arlene proposed that we
allow the arrangement to continue. "Let her come with us—
she's such a help!"

Sheila would travel around the Middle West with Johan's Acres? Deliverance! I couldn't believe my ears.

"Go with them?" Maureen asked, dumbfounded.

"Oh, please, Mother!"

"We'll have to . . . think hard about this."

"I'm starting to pack. I'm leaving, I tell you. We're setting up in Worthington on Monday."

After Sheila'd gone upstairs, the four of us stood awkwardly in the kitchen, eyeing each other. Karl rolled a cigarette, licking the frail edge with a deft tongue; Maureen stared at his slithery tongue, bothered by it. Sheila would be sleeping every night in a tent with this mysterious carnival man. Would it be safe for the girl?

"We can surely trust Arlene to see Sheila's okay," I said, reading her thoughts. "So there's not much to talk about—I guess she's going."

"But when'll she come back?"

"Whenever she wants to," Arlene said. "Next week, if she's had enough by then. Or next month. We'll pay wages for her."

After more reassurances, Maureen capitulated. She called up the stairs, "It's all right, Sheila . . . with us."

"Of course, it's *all right,*" she hollered back.

When the carnival contingent had left for the day, I walked out into the hazy, humid morning, the sky a watered-down hue, the trees dull-colored and heaving in the south wind. Thunderstorm coming. I attached the mower to the tractor and cut weeds along fencerows, immersing myself in a jungle of steaming corn plants, marijuana, and towering ironweeds. The dreamlike hours dissolved into a blur of being, and only the heat of the sun on my back, my parched throat, and the aching muscles of my legs (from sitting too long) made me stop and take a rest. I swilled down half a jug of water and lay exhausted between two corn rows, grasshoppers looking me over. By noon the mere exertion of walking brought sweat to the brow; in the west, blue-black clouds were piling up, there was distant thunder.

"It's coming fast," I said to Maureen when I entered the

kitchen. I hoped we weren't in for hail. My oats was all set up
in shocks and I'd been waiting for the neighbors to finish theirs
so that we could proceed with threshing. A heavy rain with
wind might delay harvest even longer. But there was always the
sweet consolation of an extra empty afternoon with Betty.

I checked to see that all the barn doors were rolled shut, the
machines safely stored, although in two minutes a tornado
could wipe everything away—something no farmer ever forgot.
In Kaleburg the worst weather seemed no match for the solid
brick houses and concrete streets, which was why so many
neighbors retired there, hankering after this false reassurance
that nothing could get at them, do them in.

The rain was brief, little more than a settling of the dust, but
sufficient to end farm work for everybody and warrant a large
crowd for the last day of the carnival. I filled a twenty-dozen
crate of eggs to use in barter at Schmidt's grocery store. Since
Maureen had no interest in coming along, I hastily changed
clothes and made the trip alone. I hoped to glimpse Sheila at
the Johan's Acres exhibit before she noticed me—so I'd have a
sense of what she was like away from home.

From behind the beer signs in the window at Meecher's I had
a good view of the street carnival. Arlene at her tent entrance
wore a gray tunic with silver whip trim, but I saw no sign of
Sheila. I ordered another Blatz and remained at my post. Suddenly Sheila emerged from the tent, dressed in pink circus
tights, a ballet skirt, and a tiara of brilliants on her head—she
looked enormous. And yet, I'd far rather see her dressed this
way than in overalls and work shoes.

"Go right on in," Arlene told me as I walked up. "It's just
starting."

Spectators stood at a rope around the display and looked
down upon it. I wiggled forward until I had a good view of the
flat, laid-out farm. "Buffalo Gal" from the Victrola seemed exactly the kind of music Jasper used to play on his violin. The
miniature carved animals moved to the beat and the thread-
and-pipe-cleaner trees swayed as if the music were wind. Fields
of ample space with minute, orderly plants, fences, birds on telephone wires, nests in plum brush. I'd expected an elaborate

dollhouse of a farmstead, but Karl's creation seemed to emphasize the outlying acres—which dwarfed the buildings in the center and made them seem an outpost on the plains. The binder in the oats field seemed to cut the fuzz and a swarthy hired man who looked like Karl lifted and set together thatches of shocks. In the meadow bearded grandfather and teen-aged grandson were making hay in a bower of green. The mossy velvet slough sparkled with wild roses and dandelions. Bells tinkled on little horses pulling a hayload of gray-green Spanish moss.

Everywhere on Johan's Acres things were happening, and I felt as frustrated trying to take it all in simultaneously as I did at any three-ring circus. Twenty-five cents for seven minutes of scrutiny, and then Sheila like a movie usher stepped forward to turn on lights and show the customers out, unless they produced another quarter to stay for a second viewing. When she spotted me I winked, made no other sign that I knew her—which clearly pleased her. The new customers arrived, Sheila doused the lights, and the zing-zing music started up, gay and confident as only distant years are always believed to have been—when fears of disaster were nobly compounded with the pioneers' lofty aspirations. A man could measure himself against hefty obstacles, tangible risks—and the triumphs, if they came at all, were sweet and complete. To be a pioneer! Measure up or be broken in two.

A raw-faced farmer at my elbow turned to me and said, "Never seen anything prettier—have you?"

"More than pretty."

"That's what I mean." His color-bleached eyes turned back to look some more.

Between the clear absence of life on this farm and its simulation, our very days seemed demonstrated, though not quite clearly defined—no solid statement to grasp. We had to keep standing there, looking and looking, doomed never to come to the end of our fascination or the unraveling of the puzzle. Even if I stared for hours at the enameled chestnut roan, it'd never wander from its path up the lane, any more than the child at the churn by the stone well could ever succeed in making butter. None of the activities on this farm ever ended (or even began), they just went on and on. A world that looked full of life and yet was completely dead. We gazed upon it from outside our own personal struggles. "So that's it . . . what I've been in"—able to sense the design from far off, just as Karl, who created all this, maintained toward Arlene and his exhibit here a charged distance, as if he'd gone through the agonies of closeness and was already beyond them. Here was an eternity of soil without the pressing thrust of nature and one's own involvement in the struggle. Looking down upon Karl's farm from up here, *you* had nothing to do with it. An immortal world that scarcely seemed to concern you. Oh, what relief! Karl and Arlene's life was characterized by this same burdenless quality; I was delighted Sheila would now be joining them. All of us were released from our particular confinements. We could move now without bumping against limits; we could live freely as never before.

"You know," said the farmer next to me, "it's . . . it's . . . words can't describe."

The roan reached the barn door at last. All motion stopped as if the wind had gone under, and then the lights came on.

"Don't try. Show's over."

I V

Since Then

We traced the route of Johan's Acres through two-for-a-nickel tinted postcards Sheila mailed once a week from the Black Hills, the Bad Lands, the Corn Palace at Mitchell, Chimney Rock in western Nebraska, with no space for her to write more than "I like it real well" or "Arlene and Karl are fine, say hello." We posted letters to General Delivery in dozens of towns throughout the West, only a few of them ever reaching her. When she sent word from the Ozarks in September we guessed she was heading South for the winter, following the migrant-bird route as well as the carnival circuit. "You think she'd come home—if I got sick again?"

"None of that, Maureen. Don't pull sickness on us, just to close us all in." Twice a week now I enjoyed Betty's favors, randy as a youngster, and I didn't want anything to interfere.

"Can *I* help it?"

"Try." I was tough on her—for her own good as well as mine, but we both knew something was physically wrong, the disease still there in remission. She shied away from doctors, not wanting particulars.

Sheila phoned Christmas Day from Oklahoma City, the con-

nection so full of static we could scarcely recognize her faraway
"Merry Christmas."

"To you, too!" we both shouted into the speaker.

Maureen explained we hadn't known where to send her
Christmas present. "Your *present!* Your Christmas gift!" But
she couldn't make herself understood. "Well, goodbye then,
Sheila. Thanks for calling. And Happy New Year."

I'd heard enough of her news to gather she was operating the
truck on a bona fide driver's license granted by the state of Arkansas. She'd been saving her wages to buy clothes when they
reached New Orleans in early February.

"Never a word—when she'd be home," Maureen said wist-
fully, as if she'd forgotten what we'd lived through.

"No . . . why push it?"

"I suppose not till summer. Carnival time here."

Over the holidays Betty's daughter lived with her and I was
to keep strictly away, lest her ex make trouble about the "decency" of Betty's home life. Even phone calls seemed incon-
venient, and I only tried once, to ask if the bracelet I'd sent arrived. The first two weeks of celibacy made me feel depressed,
but gradually I got accustomed to it.

In January I expected to be summoned as soon as the girl returned to school, but no phone call came, and Betty wasn't
home when I rang. I held the three hundred dollars until I
could deliver it in person—which of course led to the quarrel. I
must not imagine my seeing her had anything to do with just
cause for the regular monthly payment. "The two are two separate things." Her bills were long overdue and in the future I'd
better remember to fork over the cash on the first of the month.
Her squint-eyed glance and businesslike voice shriveled my
ardor. I could now foresee, almost with relief, what it'd be like
to have this relationship ended for good.

Ready to call it quits. We made up finally and in bed I forgot
the harsh words, but later a new soberness settled over me. The
connection between money and affection had eroded my
blinder-eyed reach for her.

During Mardi Gras (we figured Sheila was in the midst of it,
in New Orleans), Maureen suddenly became very ill, and I

rushed her to the hospital. A quick operation for an intestinal blockage; the diagnosis: more cancer. "I think we got it all," said the surgeon, "but it's difficult to be certain." I notified Sheila by telegram, the last address we had, but obviously she was way out of reach. How could Sheila help anyhow? When Maureen returned home from the hospital I hired a practical nurse for a week; after that I managed by myself, eagerly filling a role destiny provided, just when I wondered how to stop my visits to Ohio Street. Maureen complained about my cooking, rose from bed—weak but determined. She'd obviously decided she didn't want to die just yet.

With the depression in crop and livestock prices following the end of the war, my financial affairs were in collapse. By the time Wolber's bank took final possession of E.J.'s old farm, all my equity had been used up in delinquent mortgage charges. In order to buy feeders, I'd borrowed on my land. Lost five thousand and had to rewrite the mortgage, went even deeper. Maureen didn't seem to remember I'd sunk her inheritance into E.J.'s farm and now had nothing to show for it. She knew the place was no longer ours but didn't grasp that her money had been lost. Her operation and hospital confinement coincided with these financial disasters in a way that seemed to be fate, not human misadventure and poor judgment. I hadn't the heart to tell her the very earth under us was mortgaged as steeply as the bank allowed. None of these buildings or any of these acres were really ours any longer.

As for the official, long envelopes from Betty's lawyer: I tore them to shreds without opening them. Like any gambler or drunkard, I couldn't stop the spiral; now I'd lost control and it was merely a matter of time before—what? Could worse happen? A slide to the poor farm, maybe. Some dreadful, destitute situation in which Sheila would have to come to the rescue. Children must take care of parents when they falter, fail.

It might be the best thing for her.

On Mission Sunday, the first of September, our church held a full day of services, with a picnic in Schumann's Grove, the collection-plate money for missions in the South Seas. We were away until chores time that evening. When Shep didn't bark as we drove into the yard, I knew something was a little different. To our astonishment, Sheila stepped from the front porch—a grown-up young lady, thin, healthy-looking, wearing a flowered skirt and blouse. Maureen threw her arms about her with a cry of joy, as if to reclaim her just because she stood so calmly independent of us. "Where'd you *come* from?"

"Why didn't you write?"

"I been waitin' around all afternoon. You been to somebody's family reunion?"

Finding the house locked, she'd hunted for the front-door key, usually slipped under a porch ledge, but she couldn't find it and guessed we'd agreed upon a new hiding place.

"You must be starved!" said Maureen. "And you're so thin."

She'd copped a few raw vegetables from the garden—tomatoes, carrots—and had feasted on ripe blackberries.

"Karl and Arlene just drop you off? Couldn't stay?" I asked.

They were hurrying to set up for the Labor Day fair in Norfolk, Nebraska. Sheila answered our queries calmly. No, she hadn't felt sad or lonely, just puzzled as to why her parents hadn't returned home from church. "Scared? Why should I be scared? I grew up here—it's our land."

We moved into the house, sometimes the three of us speaking at once. Never had there been such a rush of conversation between us. "Did I hear, you plan to go back to school?" Maureen asked.

"Starts after Labor Day—right?"

"What grade would they put you in?" Maureen wondered.

"We'll have to see. For the experience *she's* had, I bet they have her skip a couple grades." What else could they do with a sixteen-year-old?

"I'd be a junior?"

"Why not? I'll speak to the principal."

"Where are your . . . things?" Maureen asked.

"In that suitcase."

"Everything?"

"Can't take a lot with you, going from town to town."

"Bet you're glad *that's* all over."

"Not really. I just couldn't see any future in it."

"Sensible girl!" Scarcely able to believe my ears. It wasn't what she said so much as her reflective, calm manner. Somehow in the intervening thirteen months, she'd grown up.

We spent the evening as if entertaining a guest. Aside from her unfamiliar clothes, her speech had taken on the tone and inflection of Karl and Arlene. She spoke with a vaguely western drawl, had adopted Arlene's lighthearted ironic style. Relating her experiences on the road to us seemed to bore her—or perhaps the distance between that life and this was too wide to bridge. Also, if she made it all too understandable and vivid, her own sense of difference from us would be diminished. Her adventures had become such a strong part of herself we couldn't take them away from her by anecdote, the very telling of which would deflate her whole life of the past year. By keeping these matters to herself, she remained independent of us.

"Sleepy? Want to go to bed early?" asked Maureen, unable to think what else to say.

"*Ja,* a little tired."

"But you must be used to late hours, like all show people," I said.

"*Ja.*" She shrugged it off and mounted the stairs.

I phoned the principal at his home and made an appointment to see him in his office, next day, even though it was a holiday. I accompanied her as far as the door, but Sheila said she wished to handle registration herself.

When they emerged a few minutes later, the principal announced, "She'd like to be a junior. We'll try it—that's the right age for her, with the others." No examination was required, the interview alone sufficient, since she had high-mark report cards from grade school. Skipping grades was such a common practice that if it didn't work out she could drop back with only a slight risk of humiliation.

The first days she traveled by school bus, which stopped at our road gate each morning, but in the middle of October she said, "I know where you could buy me a secondhand Chevy—a '39—for a hundred dollars. Never had a valve job, runs good. I still got my Arkansas license, so I could drive it to school right now, then take the Iowa test when I get a chance."

"In winter—you'd really expect to drive?"

"I want to be on my own when we start basketball."

"Basketball?" Of course, they must have been coaxing her, because of her height. The Kaleburg team had reached the semifinals in state competition two years previously but hadn't done so well last year. Our boys were never much, but the girls' team was usually a house-afire.

A hundred dollars? I'd *have* to find it. I'd missed both September and October payments to Betty and no longer attempted to see her. I'd choose my daughter and attend to her needs, instead of my mistress's—and feel noble about it. Perhaps such loftiness of purpose wouldn't last, but the longer I kept away from Betty's bed, the more I built up my resolve to stop seeing her altogether. Because of my abstinence a familiar depression settled over me; were I a monk, the gloomiest sort of spiritual meditation would pour forth. I felt lousy. I couldn't free myself from my body any more than I could rid myself of the claims my possessions had upon me—particularly this very land. Sheila's arrival therefore spelled no deliverance, only a shifting of circumstances; the bindings still held.

Betty's lawyer phoned while I was out in the fields, and in response to Maureen's alarmed queries, told her how much money I owed his client. Later, I managed to calm her fears somewhat—she thought I'd borrowed money from a city shyster who now had me in his clutches. "No, I won't even bother calling him back. And as for these letters—" I drew them from the desk and tore them up.

Now Maureen remembered the five thousand from her inheritance and questioned me on how I'd lost it. All these years the one thing she hadn't thought to doubt was my financial acumen; henceforth, that too would be held in resentment against me. "Can he get a lien on this farm, August?"

"No, the bank's got me there—to the limit."

I told her of the mortgage for the first time, explaining that because of her illness I hadn't wanted to burden her with these doleful facts. She knew I was lying but didn't know what it meant, where the truth lay.

"Don't worry, Maureen. The worst is over, I think."

"Then we *can't* go to California . . . can't possibly!"

"No, there never was a chance we could."

"I like to know where we stand, that's all."

"I promised to take care of you. That assurance used to be enough."

"Yeah, before you . . . began keeping so much from me."

"Trust me."

"Not on your life! Not any more."

Meanwhile, Sheila sailed triumphantly above our mired existences. Didn't miss a day of school, performed brilliantly in her studies—top of the class. She never failed to show up for a session of basketball practice, even in corn-picking season, when her help with chores would have been extremely useful. I hired Ralph Johns again—to bring in the corn crop—and I sold it immediately to pay off debts (on the lowest possible grain market, alas). I managed to soothe Wolbers and the bank board, and I mailed three hundred to Betty in order to hold off her legal dogs a little longer.

Sheila's evening workouts with the girls' team spawned half a dozen close friendships. She experienced her first slumber party, then a Halloween costume affair, and often attended Saturday-night movies with her teammates—but still no boy friends that I knew of. A six-foot girl presents a problem for any would-be suitor except perhaps a very short man who likes to prove his virility by squiring around the largest female he can find. Furthermore, as center on the girls' team, she was a hotshot basketball player, better than any of the boys. She beat them in grades, walloped them on the hardwood court—so how could they approach her? The girls adored her for this. Sheila proved herself better in everything than any boy could ever be.

She took care of all her homework in study-hall periods, never lugged books home. Driving her Chevy back to the farm about nine-thirty after a night practice, wet hair wrapped in a Turkish towel ("looking like Carmen Miranda," Maureen said), Sheila'd fix herself a cup of hot cocoa and a sandwich, then go right up to bed, a book or magazine tucked under her arm. We owned the Harvard Five-Foot Shelf of classics by then, and Sheila's voracious reading was so contagious I started in too, and have seldom glanced much at farm magazines since.

All this time, Maureen was off her feed and ailing, but she refused to undergo a medical examination. "I'd rather not know. What could be done, anyhow?"

"But if it's something—to be taken care of now, we should—"

"Another operation? Not me. They've already taken all my removable parts. If it's started elsewhere, I can't help it—can't spare anything more of me."

"I could drive you to the Mayo Clinic."

"Maybe this new diet will help."

"It's just getting you more run-down. Nothing but fruit and bran! No wonder you've had diarrhea for weeks."

"Now Sheila's normal again, *that's* what matters."

"Getting away from us . . . seemed to do it."

Both of us knew it was more complicated than that. Long ago Dr. Shepley predicted she might "grow out of it," citing a possible imbalance in some vital secretions, which maturity would calm. "Let nature take its course." The body would surely act to save itself and attempt to right the disorder. Our incapacity to effect a change in her well-being seemed consistent with Maureen's fatalism about her struggle with cancer and my farmer's acceptance of the vagaries of the weather. No matter how often I rebelled against this demeaning submission to fate, circumstances always put me back into that narrow consideration.

Winnie's death and our deviousness with regard to it hadn't brought on Sheila's illness, but the episode gave her leverage, substance for her mad drama. She'd have found another issue just as well if Winnie hadn't died. One way or another she would use an event to flog us—just as we, in turn, made use of her craziness for our own curious purposes. Maureen could thereby become a martyr and lay her life upon the altar of the Almighty. And *I* could carry on my covert love life, shielded by half-truths easier to proclaim because my daughter's illness demanded certain responses. Possibly nothing we did actually made Sheila worse. We tightened ourselves into fixed positions, that's all. In her year away, whatever caused the aberration played itself out, as a disease occasionally will. Stability developed through no influence from her parents—if anyone, from Arlene or Karl. She'd done it mostly herself; one spark of will strong enough to assert itself. She chose to live sanely if she possibly could. Now it was our job to support her efforts in every way. We became "boosters."

Most of Kaleburg's ball games were on Friday or Saturday night, both the home games and those in consolidated schools in the country or in neighboring towns of the league. We were on hand for the opening whistle at each of them, no matter the weather, joining a claque of other parents, taking passengers in our car or hitching rides. We perched on narrow bleachers with all the other rooters and chanted yells directed by the cheerleaders. Even as we shouted in rhythm, our *rah, rah, rah* seemed a strange sort of cry to come from our lips, but Maureen and I could pretend—and while we were at it the whole thing seemed marvelous fun, a great easing into ordinary life. "We're just like anybody now," she told me, gasping weakly, hanging on to my arm after an exhausting *sssssssss, boom, bah!*

Given her strength, height, and cool head, Sheila became a star player, and the Missouriville *Press* wrote a feature story on her. In the reporter's opinion, if Sheila didn't make girls' All-State this year, she'd surely receive the honor her senior year. Thirty points in a single game was not unusual for her, though the final tally might come to only fifty points for Kaleburg. Her teammates on the floor would scream hysterically in a tense moment, but Shelia, their captain, tall under the basket, never showed a bit of stress. No game crisis upset her so much she couldn't function. After what she'd already been through in her life, this neatly ruled contest must have seemed simple child's play.

Joining the basketball fans as honored parents of the star meant prominence in local society of a sort we'd never had before. Women asked Maureen to card parties (she declined politely, not telling them she'd never played cards, didn't know how); shower-party and wedding-dance invitations arrived in the mail each week from people we scarcely knew. We were celebrities now, just because Sheila was.

"She's puttin' this little town on the map," the mayor told me, after a picture of Sheila appeared in the Des Moines *Register*. Weak though Maureen was, when the Ladies' Aid elected her president, she didn't refuse the honor and chaired her first meeting with the authority they all expected from Sheila's mother. "I never thought I could stand up in front of so many people," Maureen reported, "but I just thought . . . how would Sheila do it?"

At the annual meeting of the stockholders in the Farmers' Elevator cooperative, I was elected to the board of directors, even though I'd seldom attended meetings and had played no previous part in deliberations. Since only farmers ran the enterprise, no bankers or lawyers were present who might have vocally questioned my financial acumen or suggested out loud the real precariousness of my position just now.

That winter we fought snowdrifts to support the girls team engagements, all the way to the finals of substate, where our squad was unexpectedly knocked out of the competition. We were riding high in the euphoria of basketball, and even after the excitement subsided, Maureen and I held on to our curious, honored position in town. After years of almost total obscurity, we were now closely watched and approved of, greeted with smiles. They'd known all along Sheila was "kinda different," but her freakishness had turned out to be this wonderful thing. They were so glad for us.

The next big high school event was the Junior-Senior Prom, every class member obliged to attend. The dance committee, working to that end, paired up those students like Sheila who never dated at all. They put her with Ralph Johns, currently without a steady girl, because he was our neighbor and part-time hired hand. Sheila's pride could accommodate this arrangement because it wasn't a big-deal romantic thing, just a convenience to achieve one hundred per cent attendance.

In home ec. class Sheila followed a Simplicity pattern and sewed herself a green satin-taffeta evening gown. Maureen shopped for a proper wrap in Elsie and Marie's department store—found an off-white shawl. Except for the fact that Sheila didn't know how to dance, she was all set. With only a few days remaining in order to practice ballroom dancing, one of Sheila's girl friends came to the farm to give lessons, flipping the radio dial to find the right music. Sheila's instructor forced her to assume the woman's part, though she was so naturally used to leading, not following. "Take your signals from *him*," she said, fox-trotting Sheila across the dining room.

The evening of the dance, Ralph drove his father's car into our yard. He wore a dark, somewhat floppy-looking new suit, the "zoot" style of the time, and a bridegroom's white carnation boutonniere. He handed Sheila a two-camellia corsage encased in a cellophane box, clear on all sides, like a doll's coffin.

"Gee, thanks," she said. "How much did it cost you?"

"Now, Sheila . . ." Maureen blushed and shook her head, smiling at Ralph, who stood there looking miserable: a tall, gangly kid with large hands, thick wrists, and the big-boned frame of all his family, voice a deep bass. Though he hadn't any meat on his limbs, there was a strong masculinity about him. His pinkish, adolescent cheeks were bright from a close shave, and he'd doused himself in a pungent after-shave lotion. Standing under the kitchen light next to the table where he'd eaten so many noon meals as our hired hand, he seemed painfully aware of his awkward role as the evening's suitor.

Sheila in front of the hall mirror tried to pin on the corsage.

"Careful you don't stick yourself," said Maureen. She leaned over to rearrange the folds of the voluminous, slippery skirt. "How beautiful! Oh, you look just great, Sheila."

"Cut it out, Mom." She cracked her chewing gum.

As the couple departed, we watched from the windows. They were exactly matched in height. "Wonderful for Sheila, isn't it? Her first date."

"Yeah, he's a good kid—to do it."

Sheila wobbled on her high heels. Ralph opened the door, gripping her elbow for support as she climbed in.

"Wouldn't it be great if Sheila 'n' Ralph hit it off?"

"None of that, Maureen. Don't you even think it. Ralph can have any girl he wants, so I hear. Just broke up with his steady.

Before the night's over, he might be back with her. You know, kids that age . . ."

"Just so Sheila isn't hurt."

"She understands the score, don't worry."

But both of us did. We couldn't sleep. After the prom each year, the youngsters had a tradition of moving elsewhere for further celebrating until dawn. Usually they hit the nightclubs on the outskirts of Missouriville or drove across the river into South Dakota and Nebraska, where the liquor laws weren't strictly enforced. Nobody was supposed to go home to bed until sunup. Some kind of outlandish incident must take place, which seniors could allude to as they autographed each other's yearbooks. Often, alas, with too much drinking and fast driving, there was an auto wreck and a front-page write-up about hot blood and sudden death—to sober every household and instill fear for the lives of one's offspring. We knew Sheila would want the traditional "big night," but we scarcely slept until five o'clock, when Shep's barking announced Sheila's return. Groggily, Maureen asked the time, said, "Well, now it's over," and both of us sank heavily into unconsciousness.

We weren't particularly alarmed by the fact that Sheila sequestered herself most of the day behind her bedroom door. When she finally clumped down the steps to eat supper, I noted her ashen face, kidded her about being hung over, but got no response at all. She sat lumpishly, hollow-eyed, as if the spirit had left her body. Later Maureen reported having seen her satin-taffeta dress torn up the side, her dancing slippers covered with mud, and Sheila had savagely attacked her room, dumping everything out of dresser drawers. We carefully avoided asking anything about last night or if she'd had a good time. It'd obviously been disastrous.

I hung around Meecher's Tap, hoping to hear gossip of the high school class's shenanigans, but nobody produced any stories, and I could only bring up the subject once or arouse their suspicions that I had some motive. Ralph might have filled me in on what happened, but how could I ask without seeming to be an overly concerned parent? Nor did I wish him to think

Sheila's peculiar behavior today a throwback to her old difficulties.

Since school was over, Sheila had no fixed schedule to hold up her days. She slept late, read magazines and books on the porch swing, and moped in her room. I couldn't get her to don overalls and gather eggs or feed and water the chickens, let alone help with the milking. "Once you're rested, we'll start you on a summer program," I said, though I hadn't the faintest idea how to do it—or what I was talking about.

Necessity from another direction came to claim her empty time. Maureen's kidneys suddenly failed to function and there was danger of uremic poisoning—serious damage unless she submitted to surgery at once. We rushed her to the local hospital. Before going up to the operating room, she told me that if anything happened and she didn't come out of it, I must be sure to investigate her attic trunk before Sheila did. "There're some of Winnie's old letters up there. Never got a chance to destroy 'em, and I . . . I wouldn't want Sheila to read 'em and get stuck in that . . . in all that terrible business again. I always meant to burn 'em, just never got round to it."

"What kind of letters? Why didn't you tell me before?"

"Did *you* ever say anything? I kept 'em just in case . . . anything was investigated someday."

"You mean, you know something about what happened to Winnie and never said a word until *now?*" This was a sort of deathbed confession so startling I couldn't hold back my angry dismay. I knew I shouldn't upset her, when she was in such pain, but *why* had she delayed until what might be the very last minutes of her life to tell me what I ought to have known years ago? "Oh, Maureen, why didn't you trust me?"

"You can still ask . . . a question like that?" She shook her head, half smiling, without rancor.

"This is what comes of going separate ways, all the time."

"You should talk."

"Where are Winnie's letters? In your family trunk or in the old wooden one at the top of the steps?"

Secrets like this, of course, had to be tucked among her most personal mementos, her mother's fancywork dresser scarves, Sheila's baby boots, her own baby clothes, and all the other sentimental paraphernalia nobody in any household knows what to do with and cannot simply toss out to the Salvation Army. Sheila returned and we could say no more; shortly thereafter the orderlies wheeled her away.

Only one kidney was affected. They removed it and told us she'd recover. "Lot's of people are walking around with only one functioning kidney. Only thing is, she won't be able to drink so many highballs."

"That doctor's a card," Sheila said when he'd gone.

We'd been waiting the outcome five hours, pacing the hospital corridors. My livestock now needed attention, and I said to Sheila, "Come, girl, let's go home and do chores."

Much to my relief, she pulled on overalls, buckled herself into boots, and wrapped her head in a farmer's blue bandanna. My own girl again! She worked quietly, steadily, attending to the job at hand, knowing her strength was needed. Now she could stop brooding over the humiliations of prom night and shun whatever dark thoughts possessed her. The milch cows, reproachfully mooing—a low, painful music—stood as close as possible to the barn door, their udders heavy, eager for us to relieve them. "You're going to have to help me a lot, Sheila. I've taken on more livestock than I can handle, and I haven't the money to hire Ralph."

"That shit! Who needs him?"

"We don't. Not with you around to give me a hand."

While she pulled on the Holsteins' teats, I dumped grain in the bunks of the pigs and cattle. Somehow, I meant to sneak upstairs to the attic with a flashlight and start hunting. But we were due back at the hospital during the visiting hours between eight and nine, when Maureen would be down from the recovery room and expecting to see us. I stinted my usual rounds in order to finish before Sheila.

It didn't take me long to find the packet of letters tied together with household string. For some reason (to obscure the identity of the author?) the envelopes had been discarded. The letters themselves weren't dated. I read hastily through several sheets of schoolgirl chitchat and finally came to the one I hoped to find:

Dear Maureen,

Since I can't phone, and you won't come see me, this is the best I can do.

I met the woman yesterday. No kidding. I'm not seeing visions or anything, either. She drove out, knowing E.J. was away. Said she wanted to speak to me alone.

I told her to take her slut-filth out of my home. I don't speak to women like her.

Then she claimed she was having his baby, that E.J. had to marry her.

Marry you! I says. He's married to *me*. That'd be bigamy, didn't you know?

I chased her out of the house.

Don't ask what she looks like. A peroxide blonde whore. All look the same.

How can she prove it's his baby? She must have a dozen guys on the string. She won't get E.J., I can tell you. But did you ever hear the like?

I don't know whether to tell him she was here—or not. What do you think?

Love,
Winnie

I recalled how quickly Maureen had understood E.J.'s confab with Doc Shepley on the back porch that day of Winnie's death. She'd even suggested an illegitimate baby—much to my surprise—but I hadn't thought to question her later on this. Given her insistence on a church funeral, she wouldn't have told me much, anyhow. These were women's secrets, meant to be kept to the grave itself.

But this letter would save me! For one of Maureen's kidneys, now removed and gone, we'd salvage our farm. Oh, the truth was worth a piece of our bodies (what could I give?), and the truth would allow us to keep our land. I lifted the precious document from the trunk lid and rushed downstairs, hearing Sheila's clanking milk pails.

In the hospital room, with Maureen still drugged and scarcely aware of our presence, Sheila watched me closely, perhaps surprised by the uncontainable elation in my face. Every time Maureen opened her eyes, I said some fatuous thing like "It's all right! You're going to get well. We're over the worst." Later in bed at home I could hardly calm myself enough to sleep. Two unopened letters from Betty's lawyer lay in a corner of my desk, and heavier summonses were probably soon to come—but now they couldn't touch me.

After breakfast Sheila mounted the McCormick-Deering with the cultivator attached and headed for the cornfields. I said I'd go to the hospital alone for this visit. And I did pop in for a couple of minutes to say hello to her. Then, in order to be sure of privacy, I drove all the way to the city and found near the courthouse a photography shop that specialized in filming documents in a hurry. I ran through scenes of triumph: me at Betty's front door flinging the photographed letter into her face and saying: *You* had a cameraman, now I've got one, too. Show *this* to your conniving lawyer!

But I have little stomach for such theatrics, and now that Betty's con game had ended, saw no point in vindictive crowing. Anyhow, what would little Richard think of such bizarre behavior? I wondered in fact what she'd been telling her son to explain my prolonged absence. I was genuinely fond of the little guy and hated the idea of never seeing him again. Fortunately for him, he'd a mom who'd turn the earth upside down in order to care for his well-being. He'd do fine. When the photograph developer handed me the reproduced letter, I slipped it into a brown envelope and mailed it to Betty without a covering note. The case was closed.

I didn't let myself review the total cost of having allowed Betty to blackmail me successfully all these years. I'd taken too much sensual pleasure along the way to wallow, now, in remorse and self-recriminations. In time I'd come to forgive her —and myself—for the expensive escapade, because in the end things didn't go so far that I lost my farm, livelihood, everything. An act of God had pulled me out in the nick of time—a malfunctioning kidney! Odd, now Maureen's constant prayers seemed to work, in ways she'd never dream of.

I was kept too busy trying to remain abreast of the season to spend much time on reflection. When our invalid, Maureen, arrived home, I helped Sheila in housework, too. Father and daughter sweated out the days, side by side, long thoughts extinguished as we returned to the healing womb of mother nature in summer. We succumbed to the growing season and half expired there, gratefully laying our lives upon her terrible but nourishing breast. I hadn't felt so deep into life for years. I seemed to view everything afresh; I was young again.

After August threshing, it was time to think of Sheila's return to school—new clothes to buy, but Maureen was too feeble to help her shop. Also, I was due for a general reckoning at the bank (harvest-grain cash allayed their immediate questions), and I'd soon have to plan for winter cattle and hog feeding. Sheila offered to continue as my "partner" and scorned the idea of going back for her senior year.

Alas, I'd given her too much farm responsibility—it'd gone to her head. How could I argue with her? She knew all the weak points in my position: that Maureen couldn't manage the house yet, that I couldn't afford a regular hired man. As a team we were coping, so why change anything?

When the basketball coach learned of Sheila's decision to remain home, he showed genuine concern by driving out to the farm. None of Sheila's friends, the past weeks, had made any attempt to seek her out, not only because they knew she couldn't bear to face any of them after what happened prom night, but because in summer the concerns of the farm were radically different from the town's. Some of her cronies were hanging around the sandpit swimming pool, tending to their tans; others had summer jobs. The old basic differences between the two sectors emerged so strongly Sheila might as well have been living on another planet. Therefore, the arrival of the coach signaled something unusual—just as the appearance of the doctor might—a representative from that other-than-farm world.

But Sheila wasn't in the least moved by the unusual gesture, this coach coming to court her. All she told him was the same she'd said to us. In Iowa you don't have to attend school beyond age sixteen or if you've passed the eighth grade—and she was okay on both scores. The coach tried every line of persuasion he could think of, even suggesting that his career would miss an important leg up, if she denied him the chance of having his team win the girls' state basketball championship.

Sheila despised him for parading his personal job motives in order to arouse her sympathy. "If you're such a hotshot coach you oughta be able to train somebody else. And if you can't, why get praise for being a good coach?"

She was tougher than he and both knew it. I felt sorry for the guy. He was one of those wiry little athletes who sometimes chalk up a career out of sheer courage. He'd played quarterback on a college team, forward on the basketball squad, and Kaleburg was his first coaching job. In the midst of a game he always got very excited, paced up and down the sidelines, chewing gum and grinding a fist into the palm of his hand. His special success in handling the girls probably derived from his deep interest in and love for women (he had a wife and two girl-children), and the fans were always amused to see him hug his players and slap their bottoms as if he were managing a team of fillies. "The secret of coaching girls' basketball," he told the Rotary club one noon, when I attended as Wolbers' guest, "is knowing women and what to do with 'em." The men roared and he blushed at his gaffe. "You know what I mean— it's all in the handling." Even louder whoops of laughter. The likable thing about him was that his involvement with the girl players was free of conscious sexuality. He won their loyalty and love because he'd eradicated such thoughts from his mind and theirs—it was the game itself that counted. Occasionally he was in the girls' dressing room, with some of them in the showers, and I knew it didn't matter—there wasn't any scandalous talk about it. The girls took off their clothes in front of him as they did before their doctors. Basketball was serious business.

But he failed with Sheila. Angrily, he finally said, "What kind of life is *this* for you? You only get to play on a basketball team once—and if you miss out, you can't ever do it again."

"I'm not playing."

"So what *are* you going to do?"

"Farm. What's it to you?"

"Girls don't farm."

"What do *you* know about it? Where'd you come from, anyhow—Des Moines, isn't it?"

"Think it over, Sheila. I'll phone tomorrow."

"Thanks for the warning."

Her teammates were just as disappointed and thought *their* persuasion might be more effective than the coach's, but whenever they came out to see her she fled to the grove and perched for a long time on a stump in a chokecherry bush or wandered off across the empty, brown stubble fields, where the wind drowned out the sound of our calls, where she could be completely alone with the earth and sky, the way she liked it.

We kept on as partners in the farm enterprise, and after our corn had been safely picked before the first snow, with Maureen now up and able to cook and do housework, Sheila's help made it possible for me to feed more cattle than ever before. Instead of selling most of the corn crop, I saved it for the feeding operation. My aim was to recoup all money spent to support Betty and Richard, pay off the mortgage as soon as possible, and start earning for my old age. Or so I told myself. I kept wonderfully busy in any case.

Maureen comprehended little of the excitement Sheila and I shared in this joint venture to get the farm back on an even course. She knew a mortgage hung over us and a single year's crop failure could do us in, but the fact was, we seemed to be living much the same as always. Why the talk of crisis, then? What was the challenge? Why keep Sheila home this way, when she should be in school? She did her very best to pry Sheila loose from the land.

"Wouldn't you like to have a job in Missouriville—after graduating from high school? So much more interesting—it'd be—than stuck out here."

"No."

"Your father can't afford to pay you wages, but you work hard as any man. It's not fair."

"But I don't pay him for my keep, so I work it out."

"No child owes her parents for *keep*."

"It equals out, what I do."

"No, Sheila, you're giving too much, it's not right. You shouldn't just stay on here. Young people have to get out, make something of themselves. Maybe you should learn to type . . . for an office job, in the city."

"I'm not interested in typing."

"I'll send a letter to Elsie and Marie. *They* might know of a sales job down there. It's been *so* long since we've seen the girls. Wouldn't it be wonderful if you got a position in their store? With a discount for buying things for yourself."

"What'd I want?"

"Clothes—and, oh, I don't know what all. The store's got four floors of goods!"

"All of it junk."

"You could maybe live at the Y."

"You trying to get rid of me or something?" She stalked angrily out of the house.

"Don't press her too far," I said. "She's better *this* way than . . . like she was."

But Sheila's physical appearance became sloppier with every week passed in isolation. She wore only one pair of torn denim overalls, a stained T-shirt, lumber jacket, and tennis shoes. Her long, stringy, unwashed hair hung in her eyes. Whenever she had a chance to reach for the cookie jar, she snitched a handful and slunk away smiling. Her smooth-planed face disappeared in fat. At night she'd sequester herself upstairs rather than sit around with us, listening to the radio. She had her own portable up there and usually I heard music until after midnight, sometimes until dawn.

One day when I had to call the neighbors in to help shell corn, I made a point of asking Ralph. He hadn't come near our place since that May morning when he returned our disheveled daughter to us. When the other men trouped ahead to wash up for the noon meal, I saw a chance to speak to him privately. "There's no hurry, Ralph. Let's give Sheila a chance to run to her room—when she sees everybody coming for dinner."

Ralph was startled, almost wild-eyed—because I'd detained him.

"You haven't seen her since then, have you?"

"No . . . but I'll make it up to her somehow." He blushed deeply.

"Write her a letter maybe. Apologize."

"That wouldn't do no good."

"Want me to try to get you two together—have a talk?"

"Oh no, no, don't do *that!*"

"She won't bite your head off."

"I just wish . . . I could understand, how I got so drunk."

"So . . . that was it."

"Honest to God, I didn't know what the hell I was doing. I swear I didn't! Only when I realized, next day . . . when I sobered up, I—"

"She never'd seen you drunk and mean—was that it?"

He looked puzzled. Figured Sheila'd told me everything and now realized my ignorance. "No . . . not that." He moved toward the house, refusing to say more.

I felt numb with the weight of my awful surmise. That crude clown! Drunk and horny, he'd had his way with *my* daughter! How could he have done such a thing on the first date she ever had? I was filled with a new pity for her, felt lovingly protective. I'd happily keep her right here where such a violence could never occur again.

Maureen clipped a coupon from the AIB secretarial school, penciled in Sheila's name, and mailed it. One clear December day we drove to the city and pointed out the AIB building to Sheila, two floors of lights blazing in late afternoon, suggesting many girls at work over typewriters and shorthand pads. But Sheila wouldn't glance in the direction of Maureen's pointing finger. And when we met Elsie and Marie for coffee and pastry, Sheila refused to speak to these possible conspirators, even when they asked her direct, smiling questions.

Once we were back home, she pulled her old overalls off the peg. "I like it here."

"But you can't just stay on and on," said Maureen.

"I can't? Why not?"

"She means it won't get you anywhere, Sheila, in the long run."

"I don't want to *get* anywhere."

"Oh, why're you so stubborn?" her mother asked.

"It's my home, too, ain't it?"

"And *ours*. Ours . . . so long as we live." Maureen tried to keep the falling tone out of her remark, but self-pity was a useful resource. That she was doomed to die from cancer became coupled with an upsurge in faith, spoken aloud. "Let *Thy* will be done, O Lord." If she couldn't save Sheila's life by practical suggestions, perhaps it would happen through the help of God. She pushed pamphlets at the girl, tried to clasp her hands in mutual prayer—to all of which Sheila responded negatively.

"Don't keep doing that," I told Maureen privately. "It won't work for her any more than it's ever done with me."

But more remote, closed-off people than Sheila had been touched by religion, Maureen insisted, their lives transformed —even ignorant, naked savages in New Guinea, pictured in the films we viewed on Mission Sunday. The Holy Ghost could descend and inhabit Sheila, ousting the devils. Stranger things had happened.

Yes, we'd all known some of these strange things.

Maureen became so intent on her pentecostal mission that all we'd won in community esteem during the height of the basketball craze now seemed sinful, secular. What did the Lord care about basketball and which team won?

I laughed when she said that. "He cares plenty. Look what this nun in parochial school wrote in the paper:

Butch Beneath the Basket

"Hurling his body up towards the basket, he lays the ball in for two points. The other team takes the ball. The ball flashes to the forward, to the center, out to the guard, back to the post, and up that player goes for a jump shot. Swish, it's good!

"Mary, you, who gave your body totally to God and who always had correct relationship of body and soul, are the ideal physical athlete. Please give me a realization that my body belongs to God, a realization that perfect manipulation of my body shows forth God's glory. Mary, you who—"

"Stop it, August! You're just making fun of me."
"No—of this nun!"

Such petty interchanges filled in for the absence of outside conversation and no social life. Maureen received fewer invitations to "brush parties" and wedding showers, and she'd resigned from the presidency of the Ladies' Aid. We weren't seen much on the streets of Kaleburg. Our retreat from the community was known to everybody, in the same mysterious way that fish send impulses through the waters of a whole pond.

The only successful therapy for Sheila was accomplished by our domestic animals, whose appetites and bodily needs seemed to call out. She had a great deal of companionship in the feedlots with the cattle and hogs, who seemed to sense her recognition of a personality in each of them. When she opened the hen-house door a chorus of clucking greeted her, old rooster friends stepped forward. Although she might've figured she could escape from life altogether by drawing away from high school, family, all human society, these dumb creatures responded to her presence and she could not shun them.

Prices remained low all that winter, pork so cheap it hardly paid to raise hogs. I'd harvested a good crop of grain sorghum because I'd been tipped off by the county extension agent that sorghum was the coming cash crop in feeds. However, most of the stuff spoiled because its moisture content was too high and I didn't have electric or gas blowers in the granary to dry out the crop. Next year, what should I plant—and how much? It was hard to figure out the most advantageous way to fit into the government program. With tight acreage allotments, there wasn't much room for a good plunge in any direction. I met the mortgage payments without difficulty and even put by a little, but my heart had gone out of the economic struggle, now that the pressure had eased.

To have a daughter go bad on you . . . I would say to my-self, feeling a soft, sick spot in the pit of my stomach. But was I merely using Sheila as an excuse for my own lack of purpose, finding myself in a lonely, sexless middle age, with no prospects for change in sight? In the midst of strife at least I'd felt com-pletely alive.

Things remained in the doldrums for me throughout the next year, with Maureen and Sheila just the same, the evenness of our set ways now boringly predictable. I couldn't face an-other winter of this dull routine—something had to be done. Sheila mustn't stagnate this way with the old folks. I took the initiative in Sepember and enrolled her in the AIB secretarial school, engaged a room for her at the YWCA. Each stage of the plan, I told her what I was up to, and she didn't absolutely refuse to go along with these schemes. Perhaps she was weary of the rut she was in, too.

Maureen sewed name labels into Sheila's skirts, blouses, un-derwear. We hauled down from the attic two suitcases, began to pack, although I fully expected that at the last moment Sheila might uncoil from her lethargy and make a stand against being carted off this way. Perhaps *our* faith in her ability to take a new direction helped move her along toward it. On the scheduled Sunday afternoon of departure, the day before the start of her course, she climbed meekly into the rear seat of the car, next to the upended suicase that I hadn't been able to fit into the trunk. Without a word she slammed the door and we drove off, past all those too familiar landmarks of our life, out the road gate. Gone.

At the Y a white-haired, clucking housemother showed us Sheila's quarters: a small, bleak little room overlooking a sec-ondhand auto dealer's lot. "Nice and clean," said Maureen, going quickly toward the window, gazing at the sky. No pic-tures or curtains, just roller blinds, two iron beds, and a couple of chipped painted steel bureaus. The vinyl floor was lead-colored and would never show the dirt. "Your roommate ar-rives tomorrow morning, so pick the bed you want." And to us: "The girls like to furnish a place their own way—with drapes, pennants, toy dogs—*you know* how girls are."

Downstairs while I wrote out a check for the month, our chatty hostess talked about the many activities available, "especially for shy girls, like this one." She pinched Sheila's arm.

"Cut it out!" Sheila jumped away.

"Oh dear, did I hurt you? I'm sorry. Gail . . . Jean . . . come here a minute." To Sheila: "Now I want you to meet some of your new friends."

We kissed Sheila goodbye as if we were bussing a post. She glanced at me terrified, with half-angry resentment. I doubted she'd last one day.

But a week passed without a peep from her—no phone calls or letters. Then two.

"Suppose she's all right?" Maureen wondered.

"If she ran away, they'd notify us."

We finally telephoned the front desk and asked for the housemother, who assured us all was well, Sheila getting along splendidly. "I'll scold her for not writing."

"Oh, don't do *that,*" I said quickly. "Don't even tell her we called."

We had no news to tell our daughter. Nothing was happening to us. Instead of feeling relief over having Sheila embark upon a new venture, I found myself unable to take up the slack; I couldn't match her change with one of my own. My land remained as always, all about me, but shorn of its power to hold my attention. It might as well not have been there. I could've been a city factory worker or a nine-to-five businessman, for all the difference these hallowed acres made, and that was because I was no longer in any useful relationship with them. A skeleton of the old commitment remained—the mere bones of duty. I went through the demands of daily chores and the autumn harvest because these obligations had all been set up previously. I fell into the familiar round as if I'd lost all direction and could do nothing but follow the worn grooves. Since life isn't real unless one is conscious of it, and I wasn't much any longer, I folded myself under—just as in fall plowing the moldboard turns over the turf and buries the year's growth, the compost of one season nourishing the life of the next year. Would these fallow days do the same for me?

The passing time wore out my unease at the sight of Ralph Johns. Although I couldn't forgive him for his rotten behavior, now that Sheila was away it didn't offend me quite so much. Everybody stood guilty of some horrendous act. I could not bring myself to imagine his brutal assault upon her; therefore I refused to think about it and tried instead to see him only as the neighbor kid who helped out.

He'd arrive by motorcycle about 6:30 A.M. to start milking, grateful for the chance to keep at farming now that he was out of high school and supposedly all set to begin his life's occupation. Other farm boys headed for the cities by way of colleges and universities, but Ralph told me he preferred farming and didn't need the expense of an ag. course at Iowa State to tell him that. What he desired was the hardest thing of all to find: a piece of land to work. His father was far too young to retire; there was no family money available to buy property that might come on the market—and precious little opportunity to rent a strip, anywhere, with numerous part-time farmers coming out from the towns to work acreages wherever they could lease them. By working for me he kept a toehold on his farmer dreams, and I was attracted by this streak of ambition in him and sympathetic to his goals. Anyone as young as Ralph who knew exactly what he wanted was somebody to aid. I paid for his hire by embarking upon a more ambitious cattle-feeding program than I'd otherwise have started. I added ten Holsteins to the milch herd, too.

Maureen, who knew nothing of the dastardly incident, enjoyed Ralph's company that winter almost as if he were a son. For the noon meal he occupied the place at the table where Sheila would have been. Maureen heaped his plate with second helpings, unable to understand why he remained so thin, for he cleaned up everything she put before him. "Where does it all go?" she asked me once. "I know he works hard, but . . ."

"Runs around nights—that's what works it off. He's got quite a reputation for *that*."

"*Ralph?*"

"So they tell me."

"Oh, soon as he gets a wife and settles down . . ."

Then the thickening can come, the layers of fat to slow you down, smother you.

Outdoors in the midst of work, Ralph asked me more questions about machinery and farming than I suppose he ever put to his dad. I enjoyed teaching him what I could. In the spring he offered to lease the old barn, which we now only used for chickens, to raise thoroughbred pigs.

"Why'd you want it?"

For one thing, there'd be no influenza or cholera germs in the dust, since no hogs had been there for years. Also, he'd saved some of his wages and wanted to put his capital to work. "How else will I get started?"

I charged him a nominal rent and he bought three pregnant sows, all of whom produced eight or ten piglets. "Well, there's your beginning," I said, looking down into the pens at the grunting sows and sausage rows of babies. "Their beginning and *your* beginning."

Meanwhile, Sheila stuck to her new road, albeit with reluctance. After finishing the typing and shorthand courses, she landed a job in the popcorn plant: filing, handling bills of lading, and doing correspondence. When visiting home on weekends she refused to discuss her work or tell us about her evenings at the Y or say anything about her friends. *"Please,* let me get away from all that!"

We wanted her to conjure up scenes for us so that we could do our own imagining about the rest, but she never helped us out. She wouldn't allow us to take pleasure in the thought of her new, citified life. Sheila's healthy-faced look of a couple of years ago was gone entirely. She'd become sallow-cheeked, wan, heavy shadows in loops under her eyes; a wistful expression on her face unsettled me.

She thoroughly disapproved of the way Ralph had, as she put it, "muscled in" on us. When he sat at the noontime table and helped himself liberally to mashed potatoes and gravy, he carefully avoided her eyes. They not only didn't speak, they scarcely recognized each other's presence in the same room. He kept his head down and fork busy, while she, modest in appetite, distracted, only said yes or no if asked a direct question.

One Saturday in May she drove home to tell us she'd decided to quit her job and not go back to the city. It was a particularly gold-and-green day, the kind of joyous May weather that can break your heart.

"If you don't like that job, try looking for another," said Maureen. "Now you have experience."

"I hate sitting in an office all day."

"Plenty of things one has to do in life—one doesn't like."

"I hate the city."

"It's not much of a place," I agreed, "but you haven't really taken advantage of all that's there, maybe. You didn't see Sonja Henie when she skated in the Ice Capades, did you?"

"I hate the Y. It's so noisy . . . and my roommate snores all night. The food stinks."

"Isn't there a girl friend you'd like to room with?" I asked. "Get an apartment together, share the rent?"

"I'd rather live here at home."

"These days girls have to get out," Maureen began, in that false, guidance-counselor tone. "Go to parties, see other young people. It's not like when *I* was young. I had to stay home and take care of Dad when he was sick. I couldn't go out and land a job. You're lucky, Sheila—to be so independent. You don't realize how lucky you are."

"I could help farm."

"Ralph does that now," I said.

"I don't see why you got that guy. I could do all *he* does, better'n him. But you never asked me to."

"Everyone has to do what everyone's *supposed* to do," said Maureen.

"I'm not supposed to type, I can tell you. I'm cut out for farming."

"Oh, Sheila," her mother said, "we ony want you to be happy."

"What about that apartment idea? Think of the fun, cooking by yourselves, having your own place."

"You people don't understand anything. I give up."

She soon realized no one in Kaleburg was capable of under-standing, either. To townspeople who saw her in church Sundays, smartly dressed in the "new look," her dresses fashionably below the knee and low-waisted, hair combed into a chignon, Edwardian style, she epitomized the successful young woman of the day. Her pallor seemed deliberate, and next to red-faced farm women, almost exotic. Friends of Maureen asked if the Kaleburg girls in the city attending nurse's training, beautician schools, or holding office jobs ever got together? The way they breathily queried indicated they believed all these lucky young people were leading glamorous lives. Doing something different, striking off in new careers—a sure measure of progress. Generations were moving forward, on and out—and that's as it should be. Nobody asked if Sheila missed the home folks or longed to milk a cow.

The more she toughed it out, the easier it became for her. Whereas at first the local neighbors' imagined views of her life irritated her so much she'd make some scathing, sarcastic remark about "that crummy place," as the months passed she lit up with a little pride in her difference.

Weekends at home were like a rest cure. She took what the country offered with simple acceptance: ate homemade cottage cheese, drank brimming glasses of milk, consumed Maureen's butterscotch cookies and sugary Bismarcks. She slept late and spent hours taking care of her clothes: mending a raveled sweater, sewing on a missing button, doing all the repairs she never had time for in Missouriville. After a year and half of the dormitory atmosphere of the Y, she teamed up with two girls and rented a large apartment on a bluff overlooking the Missouri River. One a nurse, the other a legal secretary; both were pretty and didn't lack boy friends. We felt it only a matter of time now before Sheila met the person Maureen called "that special someone." But the months passed, and if any such male entered her life, we didn't hear about it.

Again, Maureen began to suffer such pains she consented to medical attention, and I drove her all the way to the Mayo Clinic, where they operated immediately for an intestinal blockage. "You're lucky," the surgeon told us later. "If it hadn't been for the pain, we might not have found the cancer in such an early stage. Now the chances look really good for you."

Despite Maureen's half-conscious wish to have her life ended, she still managed to save it at the very last minute. For both of us, her illness highlighted each passing day, made life consciously present once again. I realized we'd been slipping along, losing our days, shamefacedly saying "Time goes so fast!" as if it were something to laugh about and accept.

In the old-fashioned way for daughters, Sheila was called home. I thought we'd need her for a couple of weeks, but Sheila grasped this chance to make her homecoming permanent. She packed her car with all her belongings and returned to stay. "What're the chances for Mom?" she asked me privately. "What'd the doctors say?"

"Not so hot. It's likely to spring up somewhere else."

"I thought so."

"But don't let on. If she has the notion she won't get well, she'll just lay there and never get up. I know her."

Thus for the first time in her life, Sheila found herself on the other side of a conspiracy. We were in cahoots against her mother, for all the righteous reasons. Those paltry questions about whether or not Sheila was as truly happy as she might be were suspended, since she had years in which to be both sad and happy, whereas her mother was on the way out.

"One thing, Sheila, if you're staying for a while, you 'n' Ralph have got to make up. He said he was drunk. He's sorry, what happened."

"You *talked* to him about it? How could the son of a bitch have the nerve?"

"He didn't mean to hurt you. He didn't know what he was doing." I blushed, not knowing what else to say, feeling too much a culpable male myself to say anything more.

"He's got no business talking to you about what's strictly a matter between ourselves. Get it?"

"I won't say another word."

I'd read enough articles on the subject of fathers and daughters (even at that time, plenty more since) to know that we needed each other for all sorts of reasons. Sheila and I made a notably handsome, satisfactory pair. She managed the household beautifully: cleaned, cooked, washed clothes, ironed, and we usually shopped together, like an older husband with a young bride. Maureen in her easy chair by the radiator gazed at our newfound companionship with muzzy attention, half remembering her own years of housekeeping and nursing her father. Such affections were natural, maybe even for us inherent, given those long-ago pubescent encounters, vaguely sexual moments that so troubled me and which she always seemed to sense before I did. How else explain the fact that I didn't particularly miss my sexual life with Betty and scarcely thought of her, as if the affair had occurred to some other self I'd once possessed—a shadowy E.J. figure who was me and yet not me, some doppelgänger I'd exorcised.

One day after picking up my check at the Livestock Commission, I drove down Ohio Street, where Betty still lived (I examined each new year's phone book), hoping to glimpse Richard playing on the front lawn—before I realized he'd now be in school. Whenever a newspaper article told of a man's double life, I sucked up the details hungrily, wondering about this brother of mine who'd had wives in two different towns and only his death brought the widows and children together in a hassle over the inheritance. I knew all about these circumstances; I could testify.

I gave up trying to shape Sheila into something she refused to be. We were having it too good as it was. Why spoil the setup? As we glided slowly in the porch swing those hot summer evenings, Maureen long since in bed, we'd talk over the crops, gossip about the neighbors, discuss the animals, anything that came to mind, an easy flow. Only one topic—Ralph—was forbidden. She resented the fact that I hadn't kicked him off the farm, now that she'd returned. But since he'd spent a lot to build the pens for the farrowing sows, had installed lights, feeders, and even laid pipes to the waterers, I couldn't in fairness tell him to leave. We'd nothing in writing between us— neighbors didn't have to—you only got into contracts and trouble when you consulted lawyers or bankers. Honor among farmers was still a thing to pride yourself on, and I'd given my word to Ralph that his venture should be a continuing thing. I told him I'd no use for the barn, and his rent eased my insur-

ance bills. If he weren't occupying the space I'd probably have
to tear the old barn down.

Occasionally Sheila drove to Missouriville to visit her former
roommates, but never overnight because of the pigs and cows,
who were expecting her at the usual hour, and she had meals to
fix for her parents. Sheila returned home happy to engage in
all this work, as if she felt a capacity for complications and ar-
duous assignments, which needed to be borne out by events, for
in this way she proved the validity of her choice to remain on
the land. Now and then we'd take in a movie—just the two of
us, sharing a bag of popcorn—and we were often invited as a
pair to wedding dances. I taught her to waltz and schottische,
and onlookers would applaud as we came off the floor, we got
so good at it. Whether meeting us in church or in the grocery
aisles at Schmidt's, the many smiling faces seemed to approve
of our alliance. Men and women my age congratulated me on
having accomplished the very thing everyone secretly hoped to
do: I'd successfully snagged and was holding on to my own
offspring, saved, therefore, from the cruel abandonment by
children every parent seemed to suffer these days. Sheila and I
made an old-fashioned picture: dutiful daughter, grateful father. Our splendid way of coping with Maureen's illness in-
spired the neighbors. Loved ones could indeed help one another; it was heartening to see love and companionship in a
family win over adversity.

Whereas I'd once thought only some other Betty would do
for me, if I ever lost my weekly sessions in her bed, I was surprised to find myself content to forget the whole business of sex
and accept the appropriate comforts of middle age. Randy
skirt-chasing is for younger fellas, I half seriously told myself;
after all, I was old enough to be a grandfather. There was no
place in the scheme of things for lecherous old-timers—plenty
of youngsters around to carry on; nature would take its course.
Close to the primal rhythms in my very work, I couldn't fool
myself into thinking I could jump the traces—pretend to be
young—when the reality of time's movement presented itself in
every aspect of farm work. I was graying, getting heavier in the
stomach; I looked my age.

Perhaps if Maureen had gotten back on her feet and wrested control of the household from her daughter, my complacent live-and-let-live attitude might have been upset. We would have had to scrutinize Sheila once again and ask what she thought she was doing with her life, wasting it here on the farm in her childhood nest. But no such questions were ever asked again.

Maureen suffered a slight stroke that paralyzed her left side. Not seriously crippling her, just a numbness, an inability to make a fist of her hand, and when she walked she limped badly, unable to bend her knee. The seizure made her cling to Sheila even more, as a person drowning will clutch for whatever might be near—a birch limb almost out of reach or a log floating by. The familiar indulgences of the continually sick began to surface: a whining note in her voice, a faint dissatisfaction with everything and all of us. Something better than *this* seemed owed her. She was determined to exact payment of some kind from those of us near. Lying close to the radiator, covered with the afghan she'd woven in stronger years, in full sight of the gloxinias and double begonias flowering in the fernery of the south bay window, the Bible open on her lap, she'd fall asleep at last in the middle of the afternoon and wake with a terrible stab of understanding about herself, her "fix" (as she called it), and knew what awaited her one distant afternoon (how long?) when she'd never wake up from her nap. The terror of her understanding, though never voiced, filled the house. She realized to the full that she was on her way out—and that we were merely waiting for this to happen. Our false smiles were wearing thin, our phrases of reassurance becoming outworn; our patience was no longer what it once was. How she loved and hated us! "You two . . . you two!" she'd say, over and over.

The familiar bedroom dresser mirror confirmed her passing. She didn't flinch from her image but instead seemed fascinated, clinically interested. She'd stare at herself as if something had been peeled away and now she saw herself as she truly was—and always had been. Her hair was almost entirely white, her complexion yellowish, but because her skin was puffy there seemed to be fewer wrinkles. From a few steps back, she appeared to have no age lines around the eyes and mouth, as if she'd become beatified before her time and had been given the countenance she'd wear at the Resurrection.

Sunday church services became a rehearsal for her entry into heaven. Sheila on one side, me holding her lame elbow, we'd escort the invalid down the carpeted aisle to the very front pew. Maureen's eyes glazed over at the sight of the splendid altar with its white embroidered linen, gold cross, silver vases of multicolored flowers, brilliantly lit with concealed spotlights; it dazzled like the throne of God. She savored each weakly accomplished step as if she'd become the bride of Christ, treading a path toward some holy and final nuptials. The entire hour of the service she had a stunned, ecstatic expression on her face.

Afterward, as old friends inquired about her health, she joyously assured them she was "carrying on," forgetting now to ask them in return how *they* were, what worries they had, what misfortunes. She'd heard but scarcely comprehended that American troops were being shipped to fight in Korea, and our local draft board had snatched a few farmers' sons who'd managed to escape the quotas in the last war. She'd no interest in other people's troubles, no time for it. No matter what private disaster might have happened to someone the past week, the moral to be read from such a terrifying event didn't catch her attention because such wisdom couldn't be put to any use—to bolster a pet conviction or underscore a belief—not now, with so few months or years remaining in her life. She no longer needed any instruction, any guidance; no more evidence about people's lives could make a difference in how *she'd* live. Her illness in itself had become the prime news. She regarded herself as a living event, and though her friends might tire of hearing about her ailments and go on to fresher topics, Maureen could not.

As the months dragged on, much the same, I found my compassion beginning to numb—and so was Sheila's—in the way any nurse's must, out of sheer unconscious self-protection. We felt sorry for Maureen by rote. She was no longer regarded as wife, mother—only as our burden—and our circumscribed life could be endured only if we enlarged the limits of our days,

looked to our land and the business of farming it—concentrat-
ing afresh, applying the best husbandry we knew. Farm prices
rose nicely during the Korean conflict and I paid off the last of
the mortgage, burned the paper in a little private ceremony in
our kitchen. Free and clear once again. A fine property to turn
over to Sheila's sole management one day; she knew it'd be
coming to her, if she just hung around long enough. Secretly,
she must have been getting ready—not merely by becoming
used to the fact of Maureen's terminal illness, but surely by
noting my gray hairs and sagging body with a slight, satisfying
nod of acceptance. Someday.

I left the household on a brief trip West, for I'd heard the
best feeders could be purchased cheap on Wyoming ranches if
a man went out with a truck and picked them out. Orvall
Beams and I made quite a picnic of our visit to Cheyenne—a
lot more than I expected myself capable of, considering my
many years away from the fleshpots. Orvall knew all the bars
where women could be found, and we picked up a couple of
doozies with no trouble, though Orvall was so drunk he konked
out and I ended up with more than my money's worth, both of
them working me over. What a night! On the way home next
day Orvall pretended he'd had a fine time in the saddle and
that we ought to go on binges more often.

Knowing I'd be away three days, I'd engaged Ralph to take
over in my absence since Sheila couldn't manage the house and
chores all by herself. It was suppertime when I arrived home,
and as I supported Maureen in her walk to the kitchen table,
she said with a wink, "The children did real well while you
were gone." Loud enough for both to hear and catch her sly
meaning.

I looked at Ralph, grip on his fork the same as on a pitch-
fork, head lowered—then at Sheila, who served from the stove,
her manner grave and mature, not a flicker of response to this
teasing. In Maureen's ravaged face I saw the flash of mute
pleasure. They'd made up—Sheila'd forgiven him. And why
not? They knew everything about each other, so they might as
well come to an understanding. He'd been a brute to her, but

that was years ago; now she had him under control in a very special way. She'd inherit this farm. A bright prospect for *some* man, and it might as well be him! Having had first rights with her, he'd actually established a claim upon her person; anybody else would be secondhand. He'd taken the only virginity she'd ever have—they were joined by this fact, no matter how Sheila viewed it. There was almost something holy about their connection.

I looked at Ralph with new attention. Behind that stumbling, embarrassed manner, a tough, realistic kid lurked. I'd seen him lifting bales of hay on a sweltering day that would have given sunstroke to almost anybody else, his shirt off, stringy muscles pulling. He did what he pleased, could do anything. And a stud with the girls—it all figured. Now he'd played around enough to realize that he might just as well use the resources of his body to stake out a claim in life, not waste his favors on any Sally of the neighborhood.

"The children went to the movies, night before last."

"They did?"

"I didn't mind being left home alone."

"What'd you see?" I asked Ralph.

Cheeks flushing, he looked up at me, the father, and now his enemy. Eyes ablaze with nervousness. "Cowboy picture, wasn't much."

It's okay, okay, I meant him to know. You won't have to fight me to win Sheila. Go ahead and take her if she'll tolerate you. She knows your worst side. Please take her, only this time be gentle—promise? I could pronounce a satyr's benediction over this budding pair with no hesitation, for I'd just come from a romp with two broads in Cheyenne.

"I was asleep when they got home. Didn't see the time." A teasing smile.

"Was it late, Sheila?" She wouldn't look at me. "Not that it matters. You're a grown woman."

Sheila kept jumping up throughout the meal, finding an extra serving spoon or rummaging in the pantry for a fresh jar of jelly, her attention solely on our repast. When she asked Ralph a mundane question such as "More coffee?" or "Would you pass the cream?" I looked at the two of them, fragilely connected by these remarks, and mused over the miraculous way everything now seemed different between the four of us.

Ralph sensed he had our blessing but the courtship proceeded haltingly, for he wasn't free of his debt to Sheila. Coolly indifferent to his advances, she kept making him pay for his crime, as if she feared letting him get away with *that* might corrupt him into thinking he could always get away with anything. Unlike most young couples, who used the front seat of a car for their private sofa and first sex, Ralph and Sheila spent many evenings in our formal front parlor, neither necking, talking, nor playing cards. Just sitting rather stiffly side by side on the davenport, space for a third person between them—the ghost of virginal Sheila. Ralph usually wore a clean pair of Levi's and a fresh sports shirt, open at the neck, revealing his white T-shirt. His hair was always slicked back with Vitalis and water when he came to call. Given his open pie-face and long skinny neck, dangling heavy hands and clumsy feet, he made a rather unprepossessing picture of a lover. Perhaps Sheila thought so, too. I could scarcely believe his reputation for seducing girls. What did they see in him? He didn't seem to have the slightest notion how to proceed. But I knew I was watching the performance of a defused Ralph. An angry girl sat there glaring, defying him to woo her, scornfully waiting for him to try to show his stuff. Nothing shrivels a man's ardor faster than such female hostility—it wilts him at the roots.

The too loud, nervous tone of Ralph's rich bass, rising and falling, made me curious to know what they were discussing. Phrases I caught indicated it was farm talk. Maureen retired behind the open, unread newspaper and dreamed of the burgeoning happiness in her front room. I worried about the stalemate and could only conclude that Sheila's terms were unreasonably severe. Yes, he'd done a terrible thing to her on prom night, but since then he'd matured considerably and no longer drank so much. Having demonstrated his single-minded devotion to her, what more could he do? But Sheila's expression remained cold, impassive. Maybe she never in the world planned to marry him but was getting in her licks by putting him through his paces—to get even. Bored with the months of caring for her invalid mother, perhaps she looked upon Ralph's suit as a diversion in preference to the tedium that would otherwise be hers. What a laugh on him!

Ralph knew enough about women to realize how badly he was doing. Now he tried a public approach. These days it was sometimes almost as important to a couple how they appeared in the eyes of others as it was how they viewed each other privately. If enough people considered them "going steady," the weight of this opinion might finally clinch the match and lead them to the altar. Sitting side by side at the movies Saturday nights, they made a picture, and it was *this* image he wished to project to all who'd come to watch the flickering shadows on the beaded screen. Ralph thought of every possible way to establish their alliance in the community. He even got Sheila to meet him outside the church door before Sunday services began, so that they could walk down the aisle during the organ prelude, making people wonder if a going-down-the-aisle of another sort weren't a dream they both shared. He'd insist on a front pew so that nobody'd miss seeing them together. It was almost as if banns had been read. During Lent, with midweek services in addition to those on Sunday morning, Ralph and Sheila could appear even more often.

One Sunday after church, something stiffish in the manner of Ralph's mother annoyed Maureen, who must have gushed too fulsomely over "the young folks." Maureen couldn't imagine why Ralph's people weren't elated by these romantic developments, since it meant his future in agriculture was assured. "Unless . . . they're wondering if Sheila's all right now, will keep on okay."

"And what she might pass on to her children," I added.

"Our family line's just as good as theirs!"

"She's got a history, that's what I mean."

"Oh, I wish they'd hurry up and marry—and be done with it!"

"You know Sheila—she won't talk about it."

"I hope they don't put off the wedding so long I won't be around to see it happen."

"Oh, there you go!"

"Since it's too late for me . . . to ever live in California, at least I'd like to—"

"Maybe I'll quit farming, if they *do* get together. Turn the land over to them. We'll go soak up a lot of sunshine, eat all the oranges we want."

"You'll make the trip, but not me." As she spoke I had the feeling she saw accurately into the future: a presaging that scarcely mattered to her, however, since she'd share none of those leisure days with me in the promised land out West.

Easter arrived, weddings flourished, but Ralph offered no diamond—or Sheila refused to accept one—we didn't know which. Furthermore, he didn't seem to move closer to her on our hard parlor couch. Then, the second week in April, he was called up in the draft.

"What the hell am I going to do?" he said to me, shaken by the news.

I thought: that's the end of him for Sheila. "Maybe it won't be so bad. I did *my* service once, you know."

"Do you think, if you filed some kind of affidavit saying you needed me as hired man, I could . . ."

The meeching tone annoyed me. I hadn't expected to discover a cowardly streak in him; but now he really looked scared. "No farm deferments this war, so I hear." With mounting crop surpluses and plenty of older men available for labor, farming was no longer a vital war industry short on manpower.

"Then there's Sheila."

"What about Sheila?"

"You know."

"No, I don't. Can't figure out *what's* going on between you two."

"This—this letter here might do the trick, finally. I got only two weeks."

"That's up to you." Remembering the basketball coach who sought her pity because he might not advance his career if she wouldn't join the team, I knew if Ralph suggested she marry him to save him from going to Korea, she'd spit in his face.

Every time a man showed himself to be as weak as women were supposed to be, she scorned the display. Such namby-pambies wiped out the entire male sex as far as she was concerned. Deferment because of marriage was unlikely in any case.

But Ralph wasn't a fool. He knew better than to fling himself, teary-eyed, upon her mercy. He kept his manner tight, his courage buttoned up—and let her imagine what he was going through. If he left Kaleburg for an Army hitch I knew he'd forget Sheila, once he found himself in the knockabout soldier world—bar girls, booze, and all the rest. A snapshot of Sheila kept in his wallet or propped over his bunk would never keep him in line. After straying once or twice or three times with the camp followers around any Army base, he'd look back upon six-foot Sheila and her stern, tough attitude toward him and thank the Lord he'd been delivered from her nuptial embrace. Two years in the Army and he'd be so changed the thought of marrying Sheila would seem bizarre. In the service they'd teach him a trade and he'd be qualified for some city job upon discharge. He'd realize there were no prospects for a future back in Kaleburg. And so, this letter from Uncle Sam not only suggested the possibility of death by gunfire in Korea but a chance for a wholly different life, provided he survived. I knew, because World War I service had changed my life so profoundly. America's wars have always done this to our young.

I knew the draft board men wouldn't listen to any pleading from me; pressure like that would make them furious. Furthermore, Ralph in asking my aid was coming to the wrong person, for I was ambivalent about his best interests and how they conflicted with mine. In some ways I secretly enjoyed the prospect of living here the rest of my days with Sheila. One of these months I'd be a widower—lonely, beyond the age to do something different, find a fresh companion. Then a good daughter's devotion, her cooking, housecleaning, and care would mean more and more—justified by the notion that perhaps Sheila wasn't suited to a conventional married life with babies, wifely tasks, and submission to a husband. She'd already demonstrated a capacity to run things and could do a man's job in farm management. Why should she forget this independence?

And yet, if I gave her the right nudge, pushed her a little into Ralph's arms, I might be helping her toward a female wholesomeness she needed and would appreciate later, particularly with the birth of children. I could make that small, crucial difference, if I just knew what would be best. But all by herself —given the crisis of his imminent leave-taking for the battlefield—perhaps she'd agree to the marriage, submit to his serious lovemaking and eradicate all memories of that horrible prom night. They still had time to marry quickly and spend a few days together in a Black Hills honeymoon lodge, where Ralph could put to good use all he knew about making love to women. On his furlough from basic training they'd have another nuptial session. Then, during the months he'd be away, she could get used to the idea of being his wife; she'd know where her future lay and could prepare herself psychologically for it. And I'd have a good stretch of time to figure out what I might do next, whether we *should* pick up and go to California, when Ralph and Sheila took over the farm.

Plenty of brooding—but no action. I couldn't bring myself to do anything, say a word. I made no move to intervene in the draft board's decision. I offered Ralph no advice, for it was none of my business—any of it—and I'd no right to interfere. I could adjust to any development, accommodate myself no matter what the roll of the dice.

Once I understood why I remained aloof, I concluded I'd learned something after all from the mess I'd been embroiled in, the past decade, and from which I'd only lately become free. I would never again maneuver about with other people's lives or set limits for myself with them, fix boundaries. The gates were all open, and I knew it wasn't my business to try to shut this one or that. I'd no longer that kind of control over anybody (never over myself).

And so, inexorably, the day for Ralph's departure for Fort Leonard Wood arrived; he was to report for basic training. Maureen, alarmed at the prospect of losing her prospective son-in-law, blurted out to Sheila that something ought to be done *now*. "Better not let this chance slip through your fingers."

"Shut up, Mom, I'm not listening."

Ralph strode up the walk for a final farewell. Yesterday he'd sold the last of his pigs, and I'd vowed to give him a chance to start in again when he returned. "I'm a veteran myself. It's the least I can do. The country owes its soldiers every break possible."

He glanced at me cynically, said slowly, "Yeah, if I don't get my ass blown off."

"You might stay right in Japan, or travel around. Why, when I was shipped east to Camp Mills, I saw New York and Long Island, mostly. If I'd—" I stopped because Ralph looked bored, impatient. I'd talked too often already about New York City, Camp Mills, and Denver.

Today I was determined to keep the goodbyes cheerful and spoke of his first furlough coming up in only six weeks. "See you then, Ralph."

He was distracted by Maureen at the foot of the stairs, calling up, voice breathy, agitated.

"Sheila's a bit upset today," I said quickly. "I don't think she wants to come down now."

"Hardly slept all night, I know for a fact!" Maureen shook her head, half smiling in pity over this romantic tragedy. She hobbled to her chair next to the radiator, and I helped ease her down into it. "Ralph . . . it must be your bedroom eyes that does this to girls."

He turned scarlet.

"You let us know your address right away," I said, "so we can write. Tell us how you are." I didn't want him to imagine Sheila'd gone off the deep end over him—or believe Maureen's nonsense. She'd made her decision and would abide by it; take the painful consequences. By having kept up her resistance to him, despite the soldier-going-off-to-war pressure, I figured her mind was made up. There'd be no going back on the decision, even if Ralph returned to Kaleburg after his Army stint and tried to court her again. Once a position had been taken, after such agonized consideration, there could be no second time round. Or so—in my foolish wisdom—I thought.

To everyone's astonishment, Ralph popped up next week, home from Fort Leonard Wood, rejected on the physical. Too much albumin in his urine. "What does *that* mean?" I asked him. Diabetes, or some other lifelong illness? Yet he looked so healthy! We stood talking at the gate, next to his father's car. Maureen was asleep and hadn't been awakened by the dog's barking; Sheila was hauling silage for the steers.

Ralph assured me he felt perfectly okay.

"But you better hear what your own doctor has to say."

"I already have."

"He took tests?"

"First thing, and he couldn't find a thing wrong. Checked out A-okay."

"Maybe they got your piss mixed up with somebody else's—something lucky might've happened."

"We'll never know—the truth on that," he said, grinning, "and I don't care, long's I'm all right."

"Didn't the doctor give you *any* clue—why the lab report went against you?"

"Should get more sleep, watch my diet. More liquids, maybe —but not beer. Fruit juices, milk. 'And a little less worrying,' he says."

"Called up to fight in Korea, and you're not supposed to *worry?*"

" 'Take it easy now and then,' he says. 'Have some fun. Get yourself a girl. You'll be fine once you get yourself a girl friend.' "

" 'I already got one,' I says to him."

" 'Then you don't need a prescription!' He tells me that, and by God, his secretary hands me a bill for the office call—five dollars! That's a pretty stiff fee for commonplace advice."

"Oh, I suppose the advice was free. It was your piss cost money."

He turned, physically jerked—and I saw Sheila looking at him from the open barn door. Just standing there quietly like some mourner who's just received terrible news, all the way

from the distant war front to this peaceful farmyard. She neither moved nor smiled; just stood there as if her world had
stopped. I expected him to climb into the car and speed off, but
he did no such thing. He smiled, master of his fate and hers,
too, and walked slowly across the yard. He knew things were
going right for him, and now was the time to press—
everywhere. His tall, rangy body blocked out hers completely
when he reached the door. I don't know if he kissed her—or
said anything—but they went inside together, disappearing in
the darkness of the stalls.

Ralph's parents threw a celebration party that weekend and
invited us over. We played cards and drank a lot of soft drinks
and coffee. Although Maureen tired before eleven o'clock, I
was surprised she lasted that long. Euphoria over Sheila and
Ralph's pairing lifted her up, provided a special energy. Sheila
had said nothing to either of us about a settlement, but she'd
not put up her hair in curlers in a long time, nor had she
bothered recently with wearing dresses. All evening she had a
dazed expression, as if she couldn't conceive fully what was
happening—or why.

Initially, I was surprised Ralph's folks included us in the fes-
tivities, along with their many relatives, but I took it as a sign
that they, too, accepted the coming marriage. Ralph's connection with our family had brought them special luck. Although
they hadn't approved of this alliance with Sheila, if God were
to show such a strong hand in shaping their destiny this way,
they'd better put an agreeable face on events to come. Of
course, they felt superstitious about what a close call it'd been
for Ralph. The minister said a special prayer in his Sunday
service, at their request. Their gratitude was such that all past
prejudice must now be wiped away, for in this way they'd show
themselves worthy of the good fortune Ralph enjoyed. They accepted all the hidden, fateful meanings—just as Sheila accepted
Ralph—and their willingness to open up and let things flow,
however and wherever it might, perfectly matched Sheila's own
capitulation to the series of events. Little wonder Sheila's former resistance crumbled under the onslaught of these new developments. She was wholly unprepared for such aces, such an

overreaching of her small, tight game. It was trumps all the way, and Ralph played them well. Sheila showed us her Keepsake diamond solitaire when the night was over, slowly lifting it toward the kitchen ceiling light as if the stone's bluefire glitter could ignite her own hopes with similar flashes.

"When's the wedding? When'll it be?" asked Maureen.

"Maybe they haven't decided yet," I said quickly—too quickly—as if I still reserved for Sheila a margin of time in which she might change her mind. "They waited this long— what's the hurry?"

"Will you be a June bride?"

"We don't—don't know for sure."

"It'll take time to have the dresses made, plan the wedding showers. With all the presents *we've* given over the years, it's good we'll be getting some in return."

"Maureen, that's not important."

"We're not having any bridesmaids. Or any showers."

"What? You're having a church wedding, aren't you?" Her voice almost a sob. Just as for funerals, all weddings were to take place in church.

"No—I mean, not in *our* church."

"Why not, child?"

"A justice of the peace—will it be?" I asked calmly.

"Ralph's folks got married back east—at the Little Brown Church in the Vale. We thought we'd go there."

"Where *is* it, anyhow?" asked Maureen.

"Somewhere near Mason City," I said. "You remember that song written about it?"

"The Little Brown Church, the Little Brown Jug—I don't know any songs."

"No, no, those are two different pieces, Maureen."

"Sheila, you think . . . for yourself. Don't be too quick to agree, everything Ralph's mother wants." She slumped deeper into her chair near the radiator. "I'll find the strength to put on a good wedding for you. My only daughter. I mean, if you're wondering—if *that's* why you thought you had to elope."

"I just don't want to go through a big wedding. Have people gawk at me."

"And afterwards—where'll you live? Like to come here? . . . They can stay with us, can't they, August?"

"Plenty of room upstairs."

"We want to be by ourselves."

"Of course," I said quickly. "Anybody can understand that."

It occurred to me, I could provide them with a handsome wedding present: a place to live. Wolbers had spoken to me several times about buying back E.J.'s old farm. "We're not in the business of farm management, or shouldn't be. Takes too much time—and it's too easy for renters to cheat us. I look over the grain-sales receipts and wonder, what else? What slipped by I never had a chance to study?"

By now I'd accumulated a sizable down payment in my savings account. I could negotiate a long-term mortgage, which Sheila and Ralph would assume if I died. That way they'd have a farm of their own to manage, right now. Not have the possibly abrasive situation of son-in-law on my payroll, working for me (which, aside from his pig operation, appeared to be his only means of livelihood).

No buildings existed on E.J.'s old property, but just as well! We'd construct a modern one-story ranch house with wide-view western windows facing spectacular prairie sunsets. Instead of high, fat barns of olden times, we'd build ground-hugging shelters and sheds for the animals; properly planned utility spaces for the machinery. Oh, I'd happily plunge into debt for the chance of helping Sheila and Ralph start right. What else was I living for? I'd have to speak to them about all this in a gentle, not pressing fashion. Broach the subject as if it were the most natural thing in the world. Similar discussions had transpired on other farms around here, as each generation prepared for its passing.

Ralph would have too much tact to suggest he was now *due* to come into his own time on the land. But eventually I'd fade out and he'd be there in the forefront. Now we'd work out a simple verbal agreement in the usual fashion, sharing crop expenses and splitting the profits on a share-rent basis. I'd pay the mortgage and taxes, plus all building costs (as a wedding present). In a far corner of his mind he might think of some future year when the children born of his union with Sheila would make a similar claim upon *him*. However much Ralph and Sheila might greedily crave actual deed ownership of a particular chunk of land, they'd have to earn their right to it, just as I'd done—and it was important that when they finally arrived at full possession they view ownership with a necessary detachment. The land would be indifferent to these newcomers and unheedful of ownership; Ralph in time must become shaped by its contours, not the other way around. I felt that such a terrestrial bind upon us both was good; it gave me a curious sense of peace and rightness. I knew I was coming to terms with my own eventual death—that it was possible to do so. It was good indeed to be a farmer.

Fortunately, the bank had held up issuing a lease on the old Walczak property, even this late in the season, because the farmer renting it was angling for better terms, refusing to sign. Wolbers chuckled at the thought of how surprised that guy would be when he learned he wouldn't be getting a crack at that land at all. "He's already done his plowing—all but planted his corn, thinking we'd give in to his terms."

I accomplished most of the arrangements with Wolbers in a single day, taking the deed down to the county courthouse myself to have it registered. What pleasure I took in concluding the deal without telling a soul! When Maureen learned what I'd done, she said, "Wonderful! They'll always be nearby. It's so much better, they'll have their own place. Parents and children don't mix, as the years go on." If there was one thing she'd learned from nursing her father, it was that; but only now could she say it out loud.

Sheila took the news coolly, at first not comprehending I meant the Walczak farm to be *theirs*. Then a slow smile. Had I spoken to Ralph yet? she wondered. Pleased I hadn't. "Then *I* will, before you say anything."

I sensed a maneuver in the offing. She'd never understood why I favored Ralph over her when it came to farm management, and now she certainly intended Ralph to realize I was doing this because of *her*. At the outset of their marriage, she'd keep her leverage. Perhaps it wasn't necessary for her to make this point, for surely his interest in marrying her had partly stemmed from the farm she sat on. As any peasant knows, love and property are usually so intermingled they can't be separated strand by strand, even in one's mind. If you try to push too hard, you don't necessarily squeeze out the right answers.

I felt drawn to inspect the old Walczak place in private, with a sense that this land mysteriously intermingled with my destiny in ways I'd half known from the very beginning, when I first became involved in E.J.'s personal troubles. My excitement over what I'd accomplished by buying it again for Ralph and Sheila seemed far greater than theirs could ever be. They were only marrying each other and sharing husbandry, but I had forged the very shape of the future in precisely an appropriate fashion. I could tell no one of this supreme satisfaction. But I was full of it. I kept driving over to those bare acres, as if just by pacing out the boundaries I might learn still further revelations; not from the land, of course, but from what the idea of it did to me.

I drove into the old yard and parked where the box elder had been, and where insistent shoots still sprang up no matter how often they were hacked down. The soil was a darker color where the house, barns, and feedlots had stood, with here and there a yellowish streak, where the deep underclay had been churned to the surface in the remaking of these two acres into a tillable piece.

I wondered where Ralph should build the ranch house and knew we ought to talk about it soon, since the wedding was set for June 20. Even in prefab construction, with no basement, the basic facilities had to be planned: water, electricity, sewage. So far Ralph and I had only discussed the crops to be planted, what grains should go where. He was out in a field now with his Massey-Harris. I listened to the moaning tractor as it strained up a slight hill in the hollow.

I hoped they'd want the house right where the old one had been, only with a proper grove for shelter. Instead of allowing random trees to sprout along the road, they should plant fast-growing poplars for a windbreak, hardwoods behind them, plus whatever fruit trees they desired. It seemed important that the new house supplant the old; their lives should finally cover and flourish over the dead events of the past decade. I wanted to arrange their lives in the patterns of soil. All of this rich earth was an intricate mixture of decomposed plant life and other elements accumulated through time, not simply a fixed thing. The notion of land was partially imaginary, however—as farmers in the Imperial Valley proved, when they grew enormous vegetables in no proper soil at all: just sand, water, and chemical fertilizers.

I looked at my callused hands, scarred and chafed by labor, the insides crosshatched in a way some people found occult. They bore testimony to my years as a farmer, just as the weathered face of any person you meet tells a particular tale about that individual, if one is able to read the message. I studied my hands closely. I'd cupped water in them from the pasture spring to drink on hot days; covered my face with them in anguish and in moments of grief; put them between the legs of women in lust and had smelled the fecundity of the earth. What these hands hadn't done! Grasped and pulled, clenched and caught, and whatever they'd held on to seemed real—yet the tighter the hold, the more quickly everything disappeared. I understood why Maureen threw herself into religion and why the Bible Belt was the rural midsection of America, because such a heavenly extension of one's life became essential when daily existence was so bestially combined with earth, air, and the whims of the weather—when one's hands were always touching the things of this earth. I'd hankered after "something other" than the dominion of incessant work, which my occupation imposed upon me, but I'd never clapped hands in a glory rhythm, thereby releasing angels to save me. I'd always desired to see everything through to the end with my own unblinking eyes, with my own two hands. And here I was on the very spot that mattered.

Ralph drove toward me, gliding through the narrow fence opening with great skill, roaring up to within five feet of where I stood. He snapped off the ignition and silence hit us like a tidal wave.

"Fields drying out?"

"It's just right."

"I got to thinking. What kind of house do you and Sheila have in mind? And where'll you put it?"

"We're not having a house. Too expensive."

"I know . . . but don't you understand? I plan to stake you to that." In an obscure way, now that he was about to marry my daughter, he seemed to have something on me. There on the tractor seat he was higher than me; he loomed over my life. I couldn't stop talking, as if the words would somehow ease matters between us. "Maureen and I—we figured all along we'd have the cost of building the house. I thought Sheila told you. These new ranch models aren't so steep in price, though I'm not keen on the cement-slab foundation. It'll be cold in winter on your feet . . . and for little children especially, you know? I wouldn't really recommend it. On a farm a person needs a basement, and that's all there's to it! For storing canned stuff, potatoes—you know! Maybe in town it works all right, having a house sit flat on the ground—they don't have to think about tornadoes much, or where to go for shelter. But out here in the country, that style of house isn't suited. These contractors— they'll push anything that'll save *them* money."

"But . . . I'm sayin', we're not goin' to live here."

"You're not?"

"Nah. We talked it over."

"But . . . where'll you—where'll it be, then? With your folks?"

"God, no."

"Sheila's not said a thing."

"The way we look at it, there's no sense living in the country when you can find quarters in town, close to the stores and all."

"But Sheila *loves* it out here."

"These days, each of us with a car, it's better to live in town and I'll drive out to work the land. That way Sheila's near other women down the street. There's no waiting around for the mail carrier—just go to your own box at the post office. School's right there, everything—why not? We're renting an apartment over the Gambles' store. They're doing over those old rooms up there, and we think it's gonna be pretty nice. Of course, when we can afford it, we'll build."

I'd never heard him say so much in one spiel. He was having done with me. I was put on notice not to interfere in his life any longer. From here on it'd be pretty formal and businesslike. He wouldn't tolerate any other relationship, wouldn't submit to the role of beat-down son-in-law. This move to town served as the signal—and I caught the message.

The noon siren from Kaleburg blew and we paused while the sound died, each looking in different directions. "Come on home and let's have dinner," I said.

"Thanks, but I've got to change a sprocket. If I hurry, I can finish that piece by sundown. I hear it's rain tomorrow." He spurted out of the yard in road gear, twenty-five miles an hour.

I was left standing in eloquent prairie silence, a mantle of sunshine on my shoulders, distant barking dogs, an occasional trill of meadowlarks, and motor noise from my neighbors' tractors—on a piece of land that had lost its special qualities of place for everybody except me. Now I was about to turn from it, too.

My grandfather had emigrated from Germany to avoid conscription and escape the 1848 political upheavals, but also to free himself from the locked-in continuity of the family, where the preceding generation so definitely molded, shaped, and sat upon the one coming up: a situation in which no individual had a chance to make of his life what he wanted, what might be different.

We'd never done it that way in this country, and Sheila and Ralph were showing me that simple fact, all over again. Although she felt a tenacious connection to our land and loved living in the country, she was free enough to want a new set of circumstances for her life. She chose to become part of modern times.

When the buildings here had been removed, the foundations hauled away, and the whole plot made tillable, I'd thought the virgin land in full cultivation would call attention to itself, that people would be reminded of the pioneers and how the tough prairie grass had been cut through, the sod finally broken by straining teams of oxen. No doubt the corn *did* grow higher on these two acres, but there were limits to the wonder; if I didn't notice, nobody would. And now that this soil had become scarcely any different from any other, particularly with commercial fertilizers responsible for the size and quality of a crop, what had happened here would soon be gone from human memory. It was going from mine, even, because I knew what this land had done for me—and now, also, what it could never do.